Anne Glynn

The Runaway Mail-Order Bride

BLACKPOOL
PRESS

The Runaway Mail-Order Bride

Blackpool Press

Copyright © by Anne Glynn
Naughty Cowboy Edition 2021

Cover illustration by 1 Rat Studio Graphics

ISBN: 978-0-692-02346-4

Printed in the United States of America

10 9 8 7 6 5 4 3 2

This is for L.M.,
who is greatly missed

Chapter One

From the outside, the lawyer's two-story building was grand, with three full porches and a large metal swing. The outer walls were decorated with a delicate gingerbread trim, and imported stained glass windows were visible on every facing.

The interior of the structure was less impressive. While there were a few expensive flourishes to be found, such as the crystal chandelier hanging in the entry, the front waiting area was strictly utilitarian. Its windowless white walls lacked any ornamentation except for an unremarkable painting of a rowboat floating on a body of water.

The waiting area fed into a corridor that ended at a dark brown door. On the door's mahogany face, a brass plaque announced its occupant's name in a swirl of curls and flourishes. It read, *Rupert Capehart, Esquire.*

I shouldn't have come here, Lisa thought.

Three wooden chairs had been positioned around a reddish-brown table. Propped on the round table was a black picture frame, enclosing an ivory-colored sheet of paper. On the sheet of paper, block lettering requested all visitors to PLEASE WAIT.

I don't want to WAIT, she thought. *I want to LEAVE.*

But what else could she did? She'd been summoned and not showing might have caused a stir within the community. She didn't need people talking about her.

The chair closest to the office door was filled by a stout woman in a lime dress. When she looked at the newcomer, Lisa's heart sank. Nodding politely, she prayed the woman wouldn't start a conversation with her.

"I'm Felicia Arnold," the woman said. Her day dress had a purple ribbon at its waist. Defeated by the solid form beneath it, the ribbon had come undone and its strands now lay limply along her sides. "Come closer, dear. Don't be shy."

She had the look of a woman who wouldn't let the subject drop if Lisa tried to ignore her. Trying to hide the annoyance she felt, Lisa moved forward, taking the seat closest to the stranger.

"Don't even think about calling me Mrs. Arnold," the woman told her. "Call me Felicia."

"I'm Lisa."

"Lisa… Hanlon? Ted's niece? From St. Anders?"

"That's me."

"I've seen you at New Hope Assembly. Once or twice, anyway. You always disappeared before we could be introduced."

"It wasn't intentional," Lisa lied.

Felicia's round face grew solemn. "I was sorry to hear about your uncle. If there had been a funeral, half the town would have come to the ranch."

"Uncle didn't want a service." Lisa tried to smile but the effort felt forced. "He never liked crowds."

"Men have no sense, do they? A funeral's not for the dead. It's to help the living accept what's happened. It's to help us move on."

"I suppose so."

"Let me give you a bit of advice."

Don't, Lisa wanted to tell her. *I've had all I can stand. I don't know if I can bear another mournful well-wisher, offering a trite pearl of wisdom. I've heard enough for this week, this month.*

Please not again.

Felicia said, "Never marry a man named Ethem."

"Pardon?"

"Without exception, men named Ethem are wastrels. They drink too much, they earn too little, and they take credit when no credit has been earned. Good riddance is what I say."

Strangely, Lisa's spirits seem to lift at this exchange. "I don't believe I've ever met a man named Ethem."

"Then the Lord has blessed you, child. I've only known the one. He was useless. Marrying any man is a mistake, though. I've studied the lot. There are only bad mistakes and worse ones."

"I'll bear that in mind."

Felicia glanced at the other woman's left hand, free of rings or adornment. "You're unmarried, but of age. Any woman of age has experienced her share of man trouble."

Lisa didn't reply.

"My Ethem has gone away again." Despite her stated disgust with her partner, Felicia didn't sound entirely happy with this. "Off to Colorado, he told me, hunting gold or silver when there's likely none to be found. In Loganville, of all places! Leaving me and our business behind."

"Is that why you're here?"

"I'm here because I allowed Rupert Capehart to whisper into my ear."

"The man we're both her to see. The lawyer."

"The very one. That's what lawyers do best, you know. They talk a dark story and their words burrow into your head. Suddenly, a person becomes worried about what-might-be. What terrible awfulness might happen."

"What terrible awfulness did he suggest?"

"It was all very vague, but I listened because Capehart reminded me of something that couldn't be denied. My husband's not to be trusted."

"Because he's named Ethem," Lisa said.

"Because he's a ne'er-do-well. Capehart told me I need to draw up papers to protect myself and the ownership of my store. There's no doubt he'll be charging me for every word his girl jots down."

For the first time, Lisa wondered if this visit might cost her. *I can't afford it*, she reminded herself, clutching at her handbag.

"The more I think about it, the less I believe I need Capehart's services." Felicia leaned forward from her chair, her ample form squeezing up through the curled side arms. "When Ethem left this time, I warned him not to return. The moment he stepped aboard the stage, the shop became mine and mine alone. I'm the one who keeps it running, anyway."

Placing her hands on her hips, she glared at the room around her as if daring anyone to say differently.

"Yes," Lisa agreed.

8

The office door opened behind them. The room inside was streaked with color, the sun's rays pushing through the stained-glass window at its back wall. Lisa caught a glimpse of heavy curtains and cream-colored wallpaper behind the blonde-haired woman who came out to greet them.

"Mrs. Arnold?" she requested.

"I've changed my mind. Why should I pay a lawyer to keep what's already mine?" Felicia pointed a finger at Lisa. "She's next."

Grasping the purple bands at her side, Felicia tied the ribbon across her waist. Determinedly and defiantly, she left the house.

Lisa rose to meet her uncle's solicitor.

*****

"I didn't know Ted well, not like some of the folks around here," Rupert Capehart, Esquire, told her. "I'd seen him around, as one will, at the church social or the like. Sheriff Bishop said he was a good man. A righteous man."

"He liked Sheriff Bishop."

"Bishop's not like most. A lot of men who wear a badge, they've got a bit of bend in them. Not him. He's a stickler for the law." Capehart appeared mildly disappointed at this. "Not a day passes, I don't meet someone who speaks warmly of Ted Hanlon. I don't know why it was, but we'd never any dealings together. Not until seventeen days ago."

Waiting for him to continue, Lisa folded her hands across her lap.

9

"Some of these old-timers, they prefer to do everything themselves. They don't understand the law. When a man has legal matters, he's best served by going to a barrister."

At that, Wyatt Ridge's only lawyer beamed at her. Short in stature and thin in build, he appeared almost insignificant behind his impressively-large mahogany desk.

Lisa remained in the room's only other piece of furniture, a hard chair that matched the set in the anteroom. At her feet, there was a porcelain cuspidor, decorated with flowers but stained with brown lines of tobacco.

The place smelled of old cigars and a thick sense of self-satisfaction. She couldn't wait to return to the ranch.

The dark-haired man reached out, as if to pat her hand. Seeing something in her face to dissuade him, he rested his fingers on the desktop. "Were you and your uncle close?"

"Not at first. More so, of late."

"How long had you known him?"

"Three months."

"Three months?" His professional demeanor slipped a little as Capehart allowed himself a curious stare at his visitor. "You must have made quite an impression."

A questioning tone lingered behind his statement. "If that's the case, I'm pleased."

"Ted said he was proud of you. Proud of his niece. He told me you were the strongest woman he knew."

Feeling like a terrible fraud, burdened by sadness, Lisa said, "I'm here because you asked to see me."

"On Ted's behalf, yes, I did. My girl has copied the pages he left for you. Corrected the misspellings, as one must do, but otherwise, everything is word for word. I've kept the original in case Jeffries from the bank needs to see it." Opening the desk's uppermost left drawer, Capehart withdrew a brown envelope. He offered it to her. "I guess you were all of the family Ted had left."

"He was my only family, too."

Rising to his feet, Capehart extended his arm. Lisa shook his hand, her fingers taken inside the solicitor's grasp. His grip was dry but hot, as if he'd recently held his hand over a candle's flame.

"Thank you." She released his hand as quickly as she could. Tucking the envelope under her arm, she left.

Chapter Two

It had taken her almost two hours to get into town and a little longer to return to the Broken H. Lisa waited until she was home to break the seal on the brown envelope.

Two large pages were folded inside, with a smaller half-sheet tucked between them. Removing the papers, she smoothed them against the kitchen table in front of her.

Ted Hanlon had made his last, long ride into the Ridge to draw up his will. It read:

In the name of God amen. I, Theodore Augustus Hanlon of Wyatt Ridge, being of sound mind, do ordain and declare this to be my last will and testament. No other wills or testaments by me were heretofore made.

It is my Desire that my just debts be paid as speedily as can be done.

The half-sheet listed the sums that were outstanding. When her uncle died, he'd owed $2.05 to Kevin Tennant, the town's blacksmith, and another $3.50 to Arnold's Dry Goods.

Item: To my dearly beloved niece, Louisa Jolene Hanlon, I give and bequeath my full and worldly goods. This is to include all of my belongings, my home and my land. My markers are placed North of Daggett Road and leading full and unobstructed to the dry beds of the Angel River, bounded Easterly and Southerly as described in the tract, making all together 160 acres.

"Oh, Uncle Ted," Lisa said out loud, feeling tears well up in her eyes. Barely knowing her, this good-hearted man had left everything he'd owned to her.

The ranch wasn't much but it had been his treasure. He'd been proud of his worn and weathered house, his nearly barren land. Just as he'd been proud of his weak and foolish niece.

If he'd known the truth about her, he wouldn't have given her as much as the half-cent at the bottom of his coffee can.

Tunk! Tunk! Tunk!

The noise sounded sharply, startling her. Dabbing at her eyes, Lisa scraped the chair's legs over the floor. She peered through the opening that led from the kitchen into the front room.

Tunk! Tunk! Tunk!

The front door rattled with each repetition of the sound. Someone was on the front step, knocking loudly and insistently.

Lisa bit gently against her lower lip, a nervous habit left over from childhood. She almost called out to ask the visitor's name, but fear kept her silent.

The nearest neighbors had left the month before, their land returned to the bank, leaving Lisa in the middle of nowhere and surrounded by nothing. Now that Ted was gone, no one had reason to call. No one in Wyatt Ridge knew much of anything about Lisa Hanlon.

I shouldn't have gone into town. Someone must have noticed me.

Since her arrival here, she'd made an effort to avoid the citizens of the Ridge. Her uncle had insisted she attend the town's church services, but she'd always stayed for as little time as possible. She always slipped away before anyone could approach her.

I can't afford any friends, she thought.

Her reaction to strangers contrasted sharply with her uncle's behavior. When she'd first tapped on Ted's door, he couldn't have appeared more delighted. He'd welcomed her into his house and into his heart.

He told me that's the way it is in the West, she reflected. *People open their arms to those who stop by.*

It wasn't the way she'd been raised in St. Anders. In that metropolis, an unfamiliar face was cause for suspicion. Lisa still carried those feelings from her childhood, but that wasn't why she felt frightened now.

There was a butcher knife hanging from a peg above the Dutch oven. She took it in hand, comforted by its size and weight. She tucked it behind her back.

If Rupert Capehart has come to call, won't he be surprised?

She knew it was unlikely the barrister would venture this far from his comfortable office. If he'd wanted to see her again, he'd have sent a messenger to fetch her.

One of his men might be on the step now, waiting to collect her. Or there could be someone else.

Crossing the main room, she reached for the handle of the front door. A tow-headed boy was walking from the house as the door swung open.

"Yes?" Lisa asked, loudly enough to catch his attention.

Her voice caused him to stop abruptly. Turning, he grinned, relieved to discover that someone was home.

"Can I help you?" Lisa asked.

Returning to the entry, the boy dug inside his shirt to find a small clipboard. "Louisa Hanlon?"

"I'm Lisa Hanlon."

This change in name confused him. For a moment, it appeared the clipboard would disappear inside his shirt again.

"People call me Lisa," she said. "My legal name is Louisa Hanlon. Do you have something for me?"

"A telegram. To the attention of the recipient only." The boy wiped at his shirt's upper pocket, cleaning the dust from the round badge pinned there. The badge read, GREAT HILLS TELEGRAPH COMPANY.

"You're a bit young to be working for the telegraph company."

"I'm thirteen years old. Fourteen, next September." He held out the clipboard, indicating where Lisa should sign. Proudly, he offered her a yellow envelope.

"Who sent this?"

"Not my name on it, is there? Full-rate telegram with delivery isn't cheap. Three dollars to the penny for this message." He licked thirstily at his lips. "I have the reply form ready, you want to respond."

"Too dear a price for me, I'm afraid." Distracted by the envelope in her hand, she rubbed her thumb over its surface. It felt thin and smooth. "Would you care for a cup of lemon grass tea?"

Waiting for his response, she brought the knife from behind her back. Using its sharp tip, she sliced through the top of the paper.

The messenger's green eyes widened at the sight of the blade. Stumbling down the wooden step, he hurried for his speckled horse. By the time Lisa noticed his reaction, he was mounted atop his steed and galloping for the main road.

A light laugh bubbled up inside of her, her first in days.

She slid the telegraph from its sleeve. FOUND YOU, it read.

Involuntarily, her hand started to tremble. The telegram slipped from her fingers. Fluttering, it drifted out of the house before landing, facedown, on the outer landing.

She slammed the door shut behind it.

Chapter Three

Lisa let the rocking chair carry her back and forth. Usually, the motion helped to calm her but, tonight, its magic wasn't working.

The same thought pressed upon her, time and again: *What do I do now?*

Behind the front window's yellow cotton curtains, the sky had faded to black. Sitting inside the farmhouse's main room, Lisa welcomed the darkness. Rather than light a lantern, she let it surround her.

Rain drummed against the roof of the farmhouse. Its staccato beat picked up force and volume but she barely heard it.

FOUND YOU.

She should have known that Donald would be able to track her. That's one of the things he did for a living. He hunted people down and made certain they paid for their crimes.

That wasn't all he did. There were times when he ignored the niceties of the law and took matters into his own hands. It wasn't legal, of course, especially on those occasions when he lost his temper. Prizing results over behavior, no matter how foul, his employers had learned to look the other way when such things happened.

It's not as if I have to stay here, she thought. *If I abandoned my inheritance, would anyone notice? When they care?*

I should take the carriage and leave.

The buggy was a small two-seater, but it had proven dependable for weekly runs into town. Her uncle had used it for years, but it wasn't built to go long distances. If she was lucky, it might carry her as far as Kingsbury before it broke down.

"Then what do I do?" she asked herself.

If Donald had found her in Wyatt Ridge, he'd have even less difficulty locating her once she reached a fair-sized city. The stagecoach that ran through Kingsbury would provide other options, but she couldn't afford the fare. Not when the ticket sellers demanded sixteen cents a mile; not when she had less than ten dollars to her name.

FOUND YOU. It felt like a curse.

Why had Donald sent her the telegram in the first place? If he hadn't warned her, he could have caught her unawares.

That's Donald's way, she realized. *You've seen what he's done in the past. He loves to stir the anthill, just to watch what happens next.*

If he can send me scurrying about in a blind panic, he'll be all the happier. He's only playing this game for one reason.

It's not enough to frighten me. He wants more.

Donald had a black heart, the darkest she'd ever known. If she ran again, he'd be close behind her. When he caught her, he'd remind her of how angry it made him when people tried to escape his clutches for a second time.

He'd feel she deserved an even stronger punishment for her misdeeds. He so enjoyed punishing people.

She remembered him taunting Abbie May Foster, a dressmaker whose services he'd used and someone whose work he claimed to admire. He'd scared Abbie May into leaving the state.

All because he thought she'd laughed at him. No one laughed at Donald. Not twice, anyway.

Thunder boomed overhead, its noise so loud it almost sounded as if Heaven itself had split. Some nights, Lisa would lay in bed, listening to the thunder as it rolled across the sky. On the best nights, its roar echoed in the canyons and hills surrounding her. It was magical.

It had been different in Massachusetts. There, those rumbling noises had been a distant beast, so contained that people ignored the sound. In Wyatt Ridge, it growled hungrily outside the front door.

It was the sky's most powerful music. It amazed her. She'd hoped it always would.

As it did now, the storm's presence distracting her enough to quiet the fury in her brain. She listened to the rain, pounding against the roof.

A new thought intruded: *The rain!* Unless she replaced the bucket in the second bedroom, the floor there would be soaked.

Opening the iron mouth of the wood stove, Lisa used its fire to provide the light she needed to guide her into the second room. Even before she'd entered the bedroom, she heard the sound of water splashing onto the floor. Half-hidden in the dark, the bucket that lived there was already full. It had never filled this quickly before.

Blindly, she looked toward the ceiling. This was either a storm for the ages or the hole in the roof had grown larger.

Bending for the bucket's handle, she straightened when she saw a light flicker from outside, masked behind the room's gingham curtains. It was a curious sort of light, flickering rather than steady. Not driven by the moon or the stars, but by something that shouldn't be there.

Fear clutched at her. *Fire!*

In this part of the country, there was no greater danger. Out here, there were no volunteer firemen to call for help, no citizens' brigade to fight the flames. With thunder came lightning, and lightning was nothing less than God's personal matchstick. No matter the strength of a downpour, his jagged bolts could set anything ablaze.

Spreading the curtains apart, Lisa looked for the source of the light. To her relief, the fields remained in darkness. The property's closest outbuilding, her uncle's barn, was still intact.

While she was looking at the structure, the light reappeared. It glowed with a peculiarly white and artificial light. A lantern's light.

Someone was in the barn.

Leaving the bucket where it sat, she ignored the water splashing around her feet as she returned to the front room. She reached for the Braxton rifle mounted upon the wall.

Until the telegram had arrived, she'd been content to leave the long gun in its position of honor, sitting across from the wood stove. Now she wanted the weapon with her.

It won't be Donald that's out there, she told herself. *The telegram came from Tate City. It was sent this morning. Unless he's learned to fly, Donald can't possibly be here for days.*

She only wished she could be certain of that. Gripping the rifle at its carry point, she cradled the rifle.

"Come on, Braxton," she told the carbine softly. "Let's collect our umbrella, then go check on our visitor."

Chapter Four

The umbrella was unlike any she'd owned before. Specially-made, it had a thick shaft and a heavy crook. Held overhead, it felt weightier still with the rain beating upon its reinforced canvas covering.

Moving through the storm, Lisa could feel the ground softening beneath her feet. Picking her way forward, she traveled atop a carpet of matted wild grass. If she veered onto bare land, her boots would sink into the mud.

Ahead of her, the barn's twin doors weren't completely closed. Through the sliver of an opening, she could see a lantern's light glowing softly. The lamp's owner had thrown a piece of cloth over its glass, seeking to cloak its glare.

Briefly, a shadow flickered against the building's side wall. Whether it was male or female, she couldn't tell.

Has to be a man, she thought. *Only a man would be foolish enough to travel in weather like this.*

No one should have been out there at all. If the trespasser was a lost rider, seeking shelter from the onslaught, he would have come to the ranch house. In this part of California, no one turned away from an open hand or refused to feed a hungry mouth.

Lisa doubted the intruder was a thief, either. The barn contained a few bales of hay, a horse, and Ted's double buggy carriage. Hay went for two cents a pound, the last time she'd checked; Pearl, her uncle's twenty-year-old nag, wouldn't fetch much at market, even if she didn't carry the Broken H brand; and, while the carriage was worth a few dollars, Ted had carved the Hanlon name onto its side panel. Seeing it, a would-be buyer would fetch the sheriff.

There was nothing here worth stealing. A single flash of lightning would have revealed that to anyone.

FOUND YOU. The telegram's two-word warning returned to her, as fresh as when she'd first read it.

What if Donald didn't send the message? Lisa thought with horror.

He'd picked the recipient and chosen the words, absolutely, but that didn't mean he'd gone to the telegraph office himself. He might well have had an accomplice do the chore for him days after Donald, himself, had ridden west.

If so, he could have timed his arrival in Wyatt Ridge for the afternoon that the telegram was delivered. He could have been hiding in the barn, watching as the messenger boy delivered the message.

Or… he could have sent someone after her. He'd used such men before.

Overhead, thunder bellowed again. Almost instantaneously, lightning flashed across the sky, casting a blinding whiteness over the area. Lisa increased the speed of her steps, the world growing dark again as she reached the open slit between the two doors.

A stranger was inside, shirtless. His gun belt had been removed and looped over a wooden beam. When a horse whinnied in alarm, he moved, smoothly and calmly,

23

away from the doorway. Shifting position to get a better look, Lisa could see him working to settle the brown and white mustang he'd brought with him.

The man's shoulders were wide and his stomach was flat. When he stroked the neck of his horse, she saw the strength in his arms. His black hair was cut short, accenting his strong face and powerful jaw. His expression softened when he murmured to his horse, but there was nothing soft about him.

His leather belt was hand-tooled and carried twin holsters that were cut to allow for a fast draw. In each holster, there was a matching pistol. The guns were polished silver and carried ivory grips.

A valuable rig like this would excite comment in the saloon or on the streets. Sooner or later, it would elicit the attention of Sheriff Bishop or stir a challenge from a would-be gun hand. Only a dangerous man dared carry such gear.

Donald carried weaponry like that. So did the men he hired on occasion.

"You came for me," she whispered to her foe, her words disappearing in the swirling wind.

She'd imagined that Donald would leave her fretting for days about his impending arrival. She'd also believed, when the time came, he'd prefer to confront her on his own.

She'd been wrong. But was this hired gun going to force her to return to Tate City – or was he here to do something even worse? Would Donald allow it?

He might. Oh, yes.

I can't let him act first, she thought. *I have to do something.*

With the gunman in the outbuilding, the carriage and horse were lost to her. She couldn't run away, not in this kind of weather. The only shelter available to her was her uncle's house.

There was nowhere to hide and no help to be found. She was on her own.

Watching the broad-shouldered man, Lisa was caught off-guard when a burst of wind caught the umbrella and pulled it from her hands. Slipping past the opening, she ran after it. It only took seconds to capture the handle again but, in that short time, her blouse and skirt became soaked. The fabric pressed against her, chilling her. Her hands and feet, already cold, somehow grew colder.

She retreated below the building's overhang, grateful to have escaped the shower, however temporarily. Checking the rifle, she reassured herself that its hammer was resting fully against the rim of its .44 caliber cartridge.

If it came to it, could she shoot a person? Another human being?

Lisa pressed her ear against the side of the barn. A steady drumming greeted her, the sound of nature's torrent hiding all other noises. If she wanted to know what was happening, she'd have to look inside.

One of the two front doors was open. Fully open, with enough room for a man to exit – or a woman to enter. Was this stranger going to take advantage of the night's storm to come after her?

Not if I get you first, Lisa declared. Mentally offering a short and heartfelt prayer, she stepped into the barn. At the same time, she pressed the Braxton's stock against her shoulder while leveling the rifle's barrel. Her finger curled around the trigger.

The horses and buggy were still there. The intruder had disappeared.

The room in front of her appeared to offer no hiding areas. The two-seater carriage was to the right of her, its seat unoccupied. The scattered bales of hay provided no cover and the horses stood apart from one another, giving her a full view of their bodies and the spaces around them. The brown stallion noted her appearance with mild alarm while Pearl, Ted's speckled mare, barely bothered to glance in her direction.

Lisa lifted her eyes to the empty attic space above her head. Too late, she thought of the door that was open behind her.

He could have hidden behind it….

She started to turn as the rifle was yanked from her hands. The action happened so quickly that she didn't have time to pull the gun's trigger.

Lisa gasped.

Holding her weapon, the man stood face-to-face with her. He was wearing a shirt again, neatly buttoned and tucked into his trousers. His piercing blue eyes bored into her before she broke the gaze.

Stepping back, she gripped the shaft of her umbrella with both hands. She pointed its sharp tip in his direction. "You get back. Right now."

The gunman grinned, letting his gaze sweep over her. Lisa was suddenly and intensely aware of her outfit, wet and clinging to her body. In some areas of her body, the clothing was nearly transparent.

The stranger said, "Bad night to be outdoors."

Chapter Five

On a different night, in a different setting, Pearce would have enjoyed making the acquaintance of this appealing stranger. She appeared to be exactly his kind of girl: bold, full of spirit, and revealing more of herself to a man's eyes than any proper woman would rightly consider.

Apparently, she was also ready to shoot him on sight. This was something new. In his past experiences, it had usually taken a few weeks before the women he'd met had wanted him dead.

"What are you doing?" he asked. "Alone out here, on a night like this? You're more than a little foolish, girl."

"I'm twenty-five years old. I'm hardly a girl!"

"You're right about that." Again, he allowed himself the pleasure of viewing her. She was dark-haired, with hazel eyes and a pale complexion. Her frame was nicely proportioned. Noting her attire, he realized his visitor had dressed modestly, but the weather had overcome her good intentions.

For the first time in his life, Pearce felt grateful for an unexpected downpour.

The woman's face colored under his gaze. Seemingly aware of the blush reddening her cheeks, she frowned. Her jaw tightening, she went from discomfited to angry in just a few seconds.

Having embarrassed and angered his share of the female population, Pearce had met with this type of reaction before. He said, "Aren't you a firecracker."

The firecracker didn't respond.

He was used to the silent treatment, too, but he still considered it a shame. He rather liked her voice.

If he was being honest, it was more than just her voice he enjoyed. There was a quality about this woman that stirred him.

Something he hadn't felt in a long, long time. Maybe something he'd never felt before.

It's been a long day, that's all, he told himself. *Whatever you think you're feeling, it's only because you're bone-weary. Get a good night's sleep and you'll be yourself again.*

He knew he wouldn't get any rest while this woman remained in the barn, glaring at him. He wanted to ask her where she came from and why she was traveling so late at night. He was curious to know why she hadn't sought shelter when the weather started to turn.

From the look in her eyes, he doubted she'd answer anything he asked.

Repositioning her hold on the unusually stout umbrella, she lifted it even higher. Whoever had made the device had intended for it to last a lifetime; obviously, it was too heavy for her to hold in that position for long.

Finally, Pearce knew what to say: "Aren't you tired of holding that thing?"

She let his comment pass without response. Instead, she lifted the umbrella's metal tip, aiming it in direction from his chest to his neck.

"Don't know what you're doing with such an ugly storm buster, anyway," he said. "That's a man's tool. A proper lady carries a parasol."

"I never claimed to be a lady."

Well, good. She was speaking again. He'd been right about the sound of her voice. Its feminine lilt contrasted rather interestingly with her attitude. "What's your name?"

The question appeared to catch her off-guard. "You claim not to know? You'll excuse me if I don't believe you."

"If I knew your name, I wouldn't be asking you, girl."

His second use of the word '*girl*' slipped past without thinking. Once again, she chose to take offense at something he'd said.

"I won't give my name to the likes of you," she snipped. "Pretend you haven't heard it before, if you like. We both know better."

"Do we?" Suddenly, this conversation felt like a bit much. Pearce was tired, he was wet, and this person, no matter how fetching, was trying his patience. "Just tell me your name, damn it."

"To verify who I am?" A spark flashed in her eyes. "What will you do if I don't?"

"Don't tempt me. I'm holding a gun."

"I doubt you know how to use it," she said. "It's not some silver-plated showpiece, left in a holster to impress the gullible. That rifle's a real weapon, a man's gun."

"It's wet, too. It's not a good idea to take a firearm into the rain." He studied the rifle. "Think it still fires?"

"Give it to me and I'll find out."

He couldn't help but smile: *This one doesn't let up. Where has she been all my life?*

The thought arrived unbidden, irritating him. He'd had more than his share of relationships in the past and he was done with that kind of thing. He knew what worked for him: short, temporary flings, nothing more.

He said, "This isn't the gun for a lady. Cocked or not, the Braxton tends to discharge unexpectedly. Its cartridge is about the size of an adult's finger. If it hits you in the leg, in the arm, you'll lose the limb. More than one man has learned that lesson the hard way."

"If the rifle's so dangerous, why don't you set it aside?"

"I might have cause to use it."

"You aren't going to shoot me."

"A woman as aggravating as you? It would be a pleasure."

"If you wanted to, you'd have done so. You've had ample opportunity."

At that moment, lightning lit the sky again as the sound of thunder raced behind it. For a second, the sky was so bright that it appeared as if daylight had arrived early.

Almost instantaneously, Pearce heard the mustang whinny in fright.

"The barn's been hit!" the irritating woman cried. She was turned from Pearce, her arm pointed upward. "It's burning!"

He whirled around, seeking the flames. The walls were unchanged. A glance at the horses reassured him that the animals were uninjured.

Facing the woman, he saw only the black canvas of her umbrella as it flew open at his face. His arm caught part of the blow before he stumbled backward. Losing his balance, he drove the carbine's wooden stock into the ground as he fell.

The Braxton fired, its discharge so loud it sounded as if another burst of thunder had erupted beside his ear. Almost instantly, pieces of the ceiling sprinkled around him. Pearce pulled himself into a sitting position as rain poured in from the sky.

The woman remained in place, struggling with the post of her umbrella. There was no reason to be engaging in such tomfoolery – just as she'd had no reason to strike him – but he was tired of trying to make sense of her actions.

I'm done with this, he thought sourly, struggling to his feet. Lurching forward, he curled his large hand around the umbrella's cover. He felt its internal ribs bend under the power of his grip.

"Give me that!" he commanded. With a strong tug, he yanked it away.

The woman's eyes widened, seemingly shocked that he'd recovered so quickly.

He threw the umbrella aside. "I've had all of this I'm going to take. I don't know who you are, but you need to get one thing straight. I'm in charge here. For once in your life, you'll do as you're told."

Her tongue peeked out briefly, wetting her dry lips as if she was considering the words he'd said. Before he could act, she whirled around and ran out of the building. Within seconds, she'd vanished from sight, swallowed by the night.

Pearce stepped closer to the barn's opening. Outside, the storm was raging. "You damned fool! I wasn't –"

Wasn't what? He didn't know himself. There was something about this woman that left him feeling oddly off-balance.

This uncertainty made no sense. When it came to the weaker sex, he was always in control of himself. Women liked it when the man was in control.

Didn't they?

"Go, then!" he shouted into the field, knowing his words would be lost in nature's fury. "Run!"

Return to your carriage, to your horse, to… to wherever it is you came from, he thought. *Find shelter and leave me alone. Whoever you are.*

He had no idea why she thought he'd know her name. Women got the craziest notions sometimes. But, even for a woman, the one was a pest. Foolhardy. Foolish enough to travel alone and careless enough to do so at night.

If she'd asked properly, he'd have shared the barn with her. Although, if she'd displayed any type of manners, he'd have told her to go to the main house for the night. In weather this sour, old Theodore Hanlon wouldn't have turned her away. He'd have set her up proper.

What was she doing in the middle of nowhere, anyway?

Was it all bad luck? In this part of the country, when the weather turned savage, no one was safe. Sink holes grew out of a rabbit's burrows. In a heartbeat, a gulley washer could transform a dry ditch into a death trap.

Once the stars were covered by cloud cover, once the rain started to fall, she'd probably gotten lost from whatever trail she was following. With the downpour building, she might not have seen the flickering light in Ted's ranch house window. It was entirely possible she hadn't even seen the ranch house itself.

If the woman's horse had been spooked or injured, if she'd had to abandon her buggy and had arrived here on foot, this outbuilding might have seemed like her only sanctuary. In this open stretch of scrub grass, she might not have thought she'd find another place to go.

I've been in such situations myself, Pearce reminded himself. *The very first time I met Ted, for that matter.*

He walked over to the open door. Outside, the wind howled.

Now that you've found her, his mind queried, *are you really going to let her go?*

"Found her?" he asked out loud. "She doesn't mean a thing to me."

The rain pounded against the ground, furious at the world.

Chapter Six

She stood somewhere in the middle of the fields, the sky punishing her for having abandoned the shelter of the barn. Clothed, she'd never been this wet at any time in her entire life.

For some mad reason, she couldn't help thinking of the man she'd left behind.

"You'll do as you're told," he'd said. Lisa remembered Donald using similar words, not so long ago.

On our wedding day.

In the barn, even while frightened, she'd found herself attracted to the stranger. Physically, he was so striking that his appearance had taken her off-guard. His black hair, blue eyes and powerful body were etched in her memory.

She remembered his manner as well. There was a cocky self-confidence in how he carried himself. There was nothing soft or uncertain about him. Some women liked that type of man. She'd have been among their number several months ago, before she'd experienced some harsh life lessons.

He was also a dangerous man, wearing a gunman's pistols with too easy a familiarity. He now held her uncle's rifle, as well.

A shiver went through her as the rain turned colder. Using her hands to shield her eyes from the downpour, she scanned the horizon. When she'd sprinted from the barn, she'd run without direction in an attempt to evade her pursuer. Winded and lost, she only stopped when the building had disappeared in the distance.

The ranch house was lost inside the veil of the storm burst, as well. She should have expected as much. Before leaving the front room, she'd damped the wood stove's fire to hide its light from the visitor's eyes.

Her strategy had worked too well. Black house against black sky, the structure was invisible at this distance.

Lisa knew she couldn't stay out here all night. She started walking.

I don't even know if I'm moving in the right direction, she thought. *Born without a functioning internal compass, it's no wonder I'm lost. I'm a city girl.*

Lightning flashed; one strike followed by another. In those brief seconds, the landscape opened itself to her. The ranch house was to her left, much farther away than she'd imagined. A sea of mud stretched ahead of her.

Correcting her course, she continued ahead doggedly. On her third step, the surface of the ground opened up beneath her. Her legs sank into the earth, stopping sharply when her right foot struck something hard and jagged. A jolt of pain went through her ankle, pitching her forward.

Lisa splayed her fingers against the ground. Muck splashed onto her blouse as she felt the sludge ooze over her hands. Without a handhold, she couldn't pull her lower body out of the mire.

"Try… harder," she commanded to herself. Using all of her strength, she lifted her torso a few inches higher before the sludge tugged at her again. Her hands sank into the surface even as she struggled against it.

Her arms shook under the strain. When the lightning flashed again, she didn't bother looking for the ranch house. Her face was focused on the treacherous ground beneath her.

"There you are," a voice said from above her.

It was the stranger, wearing a wide-brimmed hat on his head. He squatted beside her. "My name is Pearce, Pearce Folsom. Pleased to make your acquaintance."

Lisa's arms strained as she tried to escape from her hole.

The man said, "If you wouldn't mind, I'd appreciate it if you did me a kindness. Tell me your name."

"Why do you keep asking?"

"I have an inquisitive mind."

Donald must have wired this man, this Pearce, to come to the ranch, giving him nothing but my name and location. He knows I'm almost certainly the person he seeks.

But he isn't sure.

Lisa refused to give him his answer. She pushed against the treacherous ground, but it refused to release its hold.

"I'll let the earth swallow you," Pearce said. "I swear I will."

Lisa's struggle ended when her muscles gave out. Mud splashed around her as she slumped forward. She started to sink.

"Damn it."

A big arm curled around her. She felt herself being lifted upward, pulled from the ooze that wanted to keep her.

"These holes have taken down horses," Pearce told her. "That's why right-thinking people don't venture into a thunderstorm."

He brought her higher, his chest pressed to hers, and she studied his face. As handsome as he was, he couldn't hide the strain of his day.

She thought she saw something else, too: a concern for her well-being.

His head dipped forward, as if he might try to kiss her. Catching himself, he abruptly lowered her to the ground.

"Owww!" Lisa's right leg collapsed the moment she placed weight upon it. The intruder caught her before she could fall, bringing her into his arms again.

"I've – I've hurt my leg," she told him.

"I noticed that."

"I can't stand on it."

"Serves you right, I'd say." He placed his hat on her head, its brim offering a small protection from the rain. The headpiece smelled of wet leather and dusty trails.

Lisa reached for the brim, intending to pull the hat from her hair.

He caught her arm. "I'm trying to be nice."

She left the hat in place.

Pearce picked her up again, gripping her outside shoulder with one hand while his other arm swept below her legs to provide a support. Carrying her, he started forward.

"Where are you going?"

"I can't leave you to drown in this rain, can I? You're going to the house."

He knows about the ranch house? In this storm?

His knowledge of her home struck her as slightly sinister. Had he been watching her from afar? Spying on her?

This wasn't the time or place for those questions. She said, "I don't want to go there."

The rain forced thick strands of hair to droop over his forehead. He looked at her questioningly.

"Take me to the barn."

"But –"

"The barn. Please, Pearce."

Her use of his name seemed to please him. He turned, carrying her easily as he trudged in a different direction. He avoided the mire, his boots moving over carpets of wet grass.

In a short time, the opening to the barn appeared in front of them. Pearce carried her inside.

Removing the hat from her head and transferring it to a post, he said, "For all the trouble you've caused me, I ought to let you drop." Instead, he lowered her softly to the nearest full bale of hay. "Raise your skirt."

"I will not!"

Closing his eyes briefly, the tall man shook his head. "Do you somehow suspect I went into this weather to *seduce* you? You should see yourself."

Lisa considered her appearance. Her clothing was filthy. She was spattered with streaks of mud from head to toe. Her lower body appeared to have been painted in brown and black. "Oh."

"Lift your skirt and take off your shoe. I have to see if you've hurt yourself."

She reached for the side laces of her boot, loosening them. Even with its ties undone, the shoe refused to release her. It felt as if her foot had puffed to twice its usual size.

"Let me." Gently, Pearce opened the footwear's leather mouth. He eased her from its hold before peeling off the inside stocking.

The ankle had swollen. The arch of her foot was red and angry, as well.

"You're not going to like this," Pearce said. Before she could react to his words, he griped her right heel. His thumbs prodded over the top of her foot, the pressure of his grip stabbing at her like hot pokers.

Lisa cried out. When he did the same thing along the length of her ankle, the pain redoubled.

"Nothing broken." Pearce appeared surprised by the tears glistening in the corner of her eyes. For a moment, she thought he might wipe them away.

Lisa said, "You might have warned me."

"I've learned, when it comes to the unpleasant things, most people take the news badly. It's best to do what needs to be done and move on."

"Is that what you were doing?" Lisa asked. "Whatever needed to be done?"

"I hurt you, but, come the morning, that ankle will be the better for it. Trust me."

That's the last thing Lisa would do.

"Apply a wrap, keep off the limb, and you can ride in a day or two," Pearce said.

"Ride?" She felt her heart drop into her stomach. "On a horse? Perhaps as I go to Tate City?"

He frowned at her, either displeased by the statement or by the defiance behind her words. "It's not going to be any joy, making that trip. Tate City is a good many miles from here."

"I expect you're right." She felt like a fool, imagining he'd been concerned about her. She saw now that his only concern was how quickly he could return her to Donald and collect his pay check. "Can I have my umbrella?"

It remained where he'd flung it, at the base of the carriage. The Braxton rifle stood behind it, leaning against the frame of the wheeled platform.

"Thinking to hit me again?" he asked.

"The umbrella's pole is quite stout. I can use it to support myself when I stand."

Pearce studied her, apparently unconvinced.

"I can barely walk," Lisa said. "I won't be using it to escape, if that's what you're thinking."

"Escape?"

"If you bring the umbrella to me, I'll tell you why I asked to return to the barn instead of the house."

Her promise stirred him into action. Having collected the umbrella, he kept it in his hands. "I return this to you, you'll need to give me something of value in exchange."

"I haven't any money."

"I want to know your name."

"All right."

Pearce carried the umbrella to her.

Taking it, she said, "Look how badly you've bent its arms. I doubt it will ever again function properly."

"Fulfill your promise."

"My name is Lisa Hanlon. Louisa Jolene Hanlon, if you want to be entirely correct." She pulled at the umbrella's post.

"Hanlon?"

"Did you think I would use a different last name? Never." She paused in her efforts. "Do you hear me? *Never*."

The heat of her pronouncement left him speechless. He stood beside her, watching as she twisted the base of the umbrella. "You're not going to be able to fix it."

"Obviously."

Pearce shook his head. "Why didn't you want to be taken to the house?"

The shaft clicked as it started to separate. "Finally."

"Does the handle come off? For what purpose?"

Lisa gestured for him to come closer. She said, "I asked to come to the barn because I wanted to retrieve this umbrella."

"Why?"

"I need some answers." She removed the handle's crook, pleased to discover that the hidden derringer remained dry and intact. Cocking its trigger, she pressed the gun's barrel to Pearce's throat. "You're going to provide them for me."

Chapter Seven

Standing this close to him, Lisa could see that Pearce hadn't shaved for the last few days. His eyes were sunken into his face, as if he'd needed sleep for a while but had refused to give in to his body's demand.

He said, "Aren't you full of surprises." Despite the gun pressed alongside his Adam's apple, his voice remained unaffected. "Double shot Colt derringer, is it? Spits a bullet about the size of a pea."

"Two bullets, each somewhat bigger than any pea."

"I expect you've used the gun before."

"Several times."

"I don't believe you."

Lisa wished she was a better liar. She barely knew the weapon at all.

Months ago, a few hours after purchasing the trick umbrella, she'd carried it into a private wooded area. Releasing the pistol from its hold, she'd stood in front of a sizeable tree trunk before firing the surprisingly-loud gun.

With the first shot, she'd somehow missed the trunk in its entirety. The second time, she'd sent splinters of bark flying into the air, an indication that the derringer's bullet had only grazed the left side of the big elm.

"I'll feel better if you sit down. Over here, on this bale of hay."

"As you wish."

Lisa kept the pistol trained on Pearce as he lowered himself to her side.

"Funny, isn't it, how the handle locked up inside that umbrella," he said. "The Colt didn't want to come out, no matter how you struggled with it. Almost as if it had been left inside its holder for a little too long."

The long sleeves of his wet shirt were molded to his arms. When he moved his right hand moved slightly, his biceps tightened.

It wasn't a casual movement. Pearce was planning something.

"Might cause a person to wonder if the thing still works," he said.

"If your right hand moves as much as another inch, we'll both find out."

Her comment seemed to amuse him. Letting both of his arms relax along the sides of his body, he waited for her next move.

"Why are you here?" she asked.

"Why don't you tell me what you think, Louisa Jolene Hanlon?"

His use of her name was irritating. But that was the point, wasn't it? To get under her skin.

"You didn't come here to get out of the rain. And you don't strike me as a man who gets lost to often. This ranch was your destination."

"Seems like sound reasoning," he said. "Let me tell you what I think. Even if that toy still functions, you won't pull its trigger. You're not that kind."

"Don't bet your life on it."

An eyebrow lifted. "You say you're a Hanlon. I didn't know old Ted had any relatives."

He said her uncle's first name with such warmth and feeling that Lisa wondered if she'd made a mistake.

Pearce knew about the ranch house, she remembered, *even though it's nearly impossible to see from the trail. He found the barn, too, in the middle of the night and in the midst of a storm.*

Slowly, she lowered the derringer. "You've met him."

"Last time I visited, he didn't say word one about you," Pearce said.

"When was that?"

"Too long ago. Almost two years now."

"I arrived in April."

"Such a clever fox, Ted. He knows how to keep his secrets, doesn't he?"

Ted hadn't said a word to Lisa about his failing health. He hadn't shared anything about his visit to his lawyer, either.

"You're right about that," Lisa admitted.

"When I was here, he loved to scan the Gazette, looking at the personals. I thought he was just following the advertisements. I never believed he'd take things any further." The sound of friendly affection bled from Pearce's voice. "Ted – and you."

The last word held in the air, touched by a forlorn melancholy.

"Yes," Lisa said, not knowing what else to say. A strange feeling lingered in the air between them, but she was lost to its source.

If Pearce knew her uncle, he surely had heard that Ted had died. He had to have known.

Didn't he?

"Ah." He sighed the word. "Ah, well." Making up his mind, he presented a stiff, unnatural smile. "So, you're a mail-order bride?"

The question sent a shock through her body. "How did you know?"

"No other explanation for it. How else would a prairie dog like Ted have found someone like you?"

What is that supposed to mean? she wondered. Then it came to her: *Pearce* doesn't *know about my uncle's death. Despite the age difference, he thinks Ted – he thinks Ted and I….*

Outside, the storm was starting to lighten. Its drumming force was now light enough that Lisa could lower her voice and still be understood. Gathering her wits, she said, "I think you're confused."

"You don't have to pretend, not with me. I know some people stick their nose up when they hear the words, 'mail-order bride'. I have no truck with such folks. Whatever the two of you have told the locals, I'll go along."

"Well… thank you."

He moved closer to her. "Don't I get to kiss the bride?"

He leaned over to kiss her cheek. Taken back by the boldness of his action, Lisa turned her head to protest. When she did, his lips brushed against hers. He pressed against her.

As their mouths touched, she felt a rush of heat burn through her body, unlike anything she'd experienced before. Need and desire took her suddenly.

This wasn't anything like the kisses she'd received from men in the past. Nothing like what she'd experienced

45

when she'd been courted. This was much richer and arousing than any of the intimate moments she'd shared with Donald.

The derringer started to slip from her hand, catching her attention as its grip rubbed across her fingers.

What's wrong with me? she thought. *I don't know this man!*

Breaking off the kiss, Lisa saw Pearce's eyes open in surprise. She slapped him, a hard, stinging blow. "Shame on you!"

Rubbing a hand over the reddened cheek, he moved away from her. "I didn't intend for this to happen."

"What did you think you were doing?"

"I hadn't expected for things to become so – intimate." He refused to meet her eyes.

"You should have stopped." Her cheeks burned a bright red, heated by shame.

"Part of me didn't…." Awkwardly, he cleared his throat. "You needn't look so vexed. I promise you that it won't happen again."

Hearing those words, Lisa felt a pang of regret. She buried the feeling, refusing to acknowledge it.

Pearce's behavior had been inappropriate. More than inappropriate, her dearly-departed mother Judy would have insisted.

Once their lips had touched, he'd kissed her passionately – not in error, not by mistake – and she'd never forget how it felt.

If Pearce was this brazen when he thought she was married, what might happen if he learned the truth of her situation?

I mustn't let him know, she realized.

She couldn't allow this brash stranger to discover that she was living by herself in this patch of nowhere. Considering how she'd responded to his embrace, she didn't trust herself in that situation, either.

"You haven't said why you're here," Lisa told him.

"Repaying a debt." On her questioning expression, he added, "Ted hasn't mentioned a word about any monies owed to him, has he? Not even to his new bride."

"We don't discuss money."

"That's his way, keeping his cards close to his chest. I expect half the people in the Ridge are indebted to him in one way or another."

"A generous man," Lisa agreed. He had given her a place to stay when she'd needed one. When he'd realized his end was near, he'd even arranged for her to have his home.

It's like you said, Pearce, he kept his secrets. He kept what he knew of mine, too.

Pearce said, "I expect your husband will come looking for you soon."

Hearing those words, Lisa felt as if she couldn't breathe.

"I'd never have sent my woman outside in this storm," Pearce said. "Ted has slowed down a lot, but I'd have thought he'd feel the same way."

"He was… asleep when I saw the light in the barn. I didn't want to wake him."

"If this thunder didn't do the job, nothing will." Pearce looked through the opening in the barn door. "Those clouds are about done spitting on the world. Funny thing about weather out here; it appears in a heartbeat and vanishes just as quickly. Why don't we go to the main house?"

"The house?"

"If your husband wakes up, I'd like to say hello. Maybe get a glass of Ted's sweet tea."

Lisa bit at her lower lip worriedly. If Pearce went into the ranch house, he'd learn the truth about her uncle.

To her dismay, she couldn't think of a single reason to stop him from leaving this enclosure and crossing the field with her. Worse, she needed him to carry her over the sodden ground.

Lisa struggled upright, using the umbrella as her prop. Her uninjured leg kept her upright as she tested the damaged limb.

Her ankle ached in protest.

Walking toward his horse, Pearce didn't notice. "I have something to bring with me."

A pair of worn leather bags rode on the hips of the mustang, one on either side of the saddle's cantle. When he reached for the nearest bag's flap, a puzzled expression crossed his face.

"What is it?"

"Tie's been broken." He opened the side pocket and peered inside. Not satisfied with what he was seeing, he swept his hand inside the sleeve. His hand came out empty.

"It's gone," Pearce said. "Not just Ted's money. My entire bankroll."

Chapter Eight

"Perhaps it's in the other bag?"

He gave her a sour look. "I know where I keep my things."

"You simply haven't learned to secure them," Lisa snipped in return.

Reluctantly, Pearce checked the second bag. When that proved fruitless, he scanned the floor of the barn. Focused on his task, he didn't notice when the heel of one boot stepped into the puddle on the ground.

His foot slipped out from under him. The loss of support nearly caused him to fall; instead, almost as if he'd practiced the move, he shifted his weight to his remaining limb. Steady again, he sought the source of the spill. The hole in the ceiling displayed an inky patch of night sky, reminding him of his accident with the rifle.

An idea flowered in Lisa's mind. "How much money do you owe, um – my husband?"

"Still getting used to the idea of being married, Mrs. Hanlon?"

"How much money, Mr. Folsom?"

"Ted never gave me a total. By my reckoning, fifty dollars, probably more. Twenty-five for the horse he gave me, another twenty-five for the saddle and a few other items."

"How much are you including for the roof?"

"Say again?"

"The opening above your head, the one you created through your careless handling of my rifle. It needs repair."

"I'll not take the blame for it."

"You'd leave it for Ted to fix? He'd never be able to balance on that steep incline. We'll have to hire someone."

"Not my concern."

"The damage wouldn't have happened if you hadn't been here."

"It isn't my fault," he protested. "You're the one who choose to come out here, carrying that blunderbuss. It was an accident."

"Accidents carry a price." Lisa let her voice grow small. "I was only trying to protect our property. There was an intruder in the barn."

"Ted would have done things differently. You should have woken him."

"I thought about it." She searched for a convincing lie. "He can barely walk when the ground is dry, much less on a night like this. Still, you might be right."

His stern manner softened. "Not that much harm was done. Some wooden planks were splintered, a few shingles were lost. What transpired could have been much worse."

"It needs repair. I'll have to find someone who knows such things, someone with skills."

"To patch a hole? It requires no training for that type of task. I've done it myself, more than once."

"You have?" Lisa let herself sound dutifully impressed.

"Many times," Pearce said. "Ted must have done such patching himself; he has all of the needed supplies in the corner over there. There's even a ladder to be seen."

"You're making light of it. It won't be an easy job."

"It will, for almost anyone. Something like this would take a day's time at most."

"I doubt I have the strength to handle that long ladder," Lisa confessed, "and I'm fearful of heights. Do you think I could fix this myself before the next monsoon comes?"

"You?"

"I'm a city girl, but I'm certain I can learn. You said it's easy."

"Not if you've never been on a roof like this. I'll add another few dollars for a repairman."

"You've lost your money."

"I meant, once I'm flush again. Upon my return."

"What are we to do until then?" Lisa asked.

"You... I...." The lines creasing Pearce's forehead deepened. "Let's go into the house. Ted probably knows someone who can do the work. I'm certain we can come to an understanding."

"Am I not reasonable?"

"You're a woman," he said, as if this explained everything. "These types of decisions are best left to men."

He appeared unaware of it but his tone had shifted from weary to patronizing.

Pearce Folsom needs to learn some manners, Lisa thought. "I'd appreciate your help in bringing me to our front porch, but you'll not speak with Ted this night."

Or any other, she added to herself.

"But –"

"He hasn't been well. He was asleep when I left and you won't disturb him this evening. Nor will I invite a man to spend the night in our home without his permission."

Heavily, Pearce said, "Permission which can't be given at this time because Ted needs his rest."

"If it were up to me, I'd allow you to use the second bedroom. It's much more comfortable than an old barn with a hole in its roof. However, such decisions are best left to a man."

He studied her face.

"I'm only a woman," Lisa said. "You understand."

Pearce sighed. "I do now."

*****

It felt as if it had taken forever, but, at last, her hair was clean. It was too wet for sleep at the moment, but it was finally free of the mud and windborne bits of debris that had found shelter there.

On the wood-burning oven, the kettle was heating. Adding the hot fluid to the buckets of water she'd pumped from the well, Lisa could soon start the task of cleaning the rest of her body.

Confronting Pearce, her emotions high, she'd had no idea she was quite this filthy. Even as a child, she couldn't remember ever being quite so disheveled.

You should see yourself, he'd told her, and he'd been right. She was a mess.

Vanity has never been your curse, Lisa Hanlon, she thought, *yet you made Pearce leave you outside the front door while he returned to bed down beside the horses. You feared he might otherwise be unable to resist your charms.*

The corners of her mouth lifted. As quickly as it had come, the smile faded. "If I was such a fright, why did Pearce kiss me?"

She understood that their kiss had happened by mistake. He'd moved as she'd turned, and their lips had touched. Once that had happened, however, he'd kissed her passionately. It had started innocently enough, but it hadn't finished that way.

Perhaps that's the kind of man he is, she reflected. *An impulsive bounder.*

But, no. If such behavior was simply his manner, he wouldn't have been embarrassed afterwards. He was ashamed to have held his friend's woman so boldly.

He'd done it, anyway. Almost as if he couldn't help himself.

"Vanity rears its head once again," she chastised herself.

She was letting a moment's foolishness affect what had happened between them. Just by looking at him, she could tell Pearce was no stranger to the fairer sex. He might not be a complete rapscallion, but it was clear that he wasn't a gentleman.

It was obvious. Anyone could tell just from… simply from….

His kiss. She'd never experienced anything like it.

"It meant nothing to him," she told herself. "It needs mean no more to me. I've met his kind before."

The kettle puffed, blowing its soft whistle. Looping a wrap around the handle, Lisa carried the pot into the kitchen. Inside the tin tub on the floor, the pump's cold water waited to be warmed.

She removed the stopper from the kettle's spout and poured out its contents. The hot water fell, steam rising as it splashed into the container below.

Uncle Ted had preached to her about the healing properties of a cold bath, but Lisa remained unconvinced. Even less so at this time, now that her father's brother had been buried along with his beliefs. If the hour wasn't so late, she'd have returned the kettle to the stove and boiled a second pot to join the first.

Slowly, she removed her bloomers. Letting her soiled chemise join the first garment on the floor, she stepped into the tub. No longer cold, but still far from warm, the water rose over her feet. It felt soothing against her swollen ankle.

She dipped a cloth into the fluid before wiping at the dirt on her face. A stream of brown muck was squeezed from the cloth before she dipped it into the water again.

Once more, her thoughts returned to the visitor. *If Pearce is a scoundrel, would Uncle Ted have invited him into his home? Would he have given a horse to a rake?*

Ted had been generous with his time and funds, as she well knew, but he didn't give either carelessly. His help was directed to those persons he judged of good character.

Not that his judgement was without flaw. He'd made a mistake when he told the lawyer that Lisa was a strong woman. Had he made another when he'd shared his belongings with Pearce?

Out here, a horse can be more valuable than gold, she thought. *Where did Ted find that mustang, anyway?*

The stranger's animal didn't look anything like the sorrel mare that pulled her carriage. The brown-colored horse more closely resembled the feral animals ranging the hills and flat lands outside of the ranch.

Was there a time in the not too distant past when her uncle was capable of taming such a creature? If he'd managed that feat, would he have given the beast up?

Her face clean, Lisa drew the cloth over her neck. "You could have sent the man away," she reminded herself. "If you'd insisted, he'd have left."

Why, then, had she kept her silence, watching him as he'd returned to the barn?

It was his kiss.

She shook her head, irritated at herself. No, that brief encounter couldn't have anything to do with it. She wasn't a schoolgirl, any longer.

Besides, she was done with romance. Done with men.

"Done with Pearce, too," she told the dirty water lapping at her ankles.

Her experience with Donald had left its mark. The opposite sex was trouble. Given the opportunity, she was ready to embrace spinsterhood for the rest of her days.

She had to accept the darker reason why she wanted Pearce to remain nearby. She thought, *I can't be alone when Donald arrives.*

Presented with an audience, Donald pretended to be who he wasn't. He shook hands and slapped backs, presenting himself as everyone's best new friend. It was only when the audience drifted out of sight that he smiled his shark's smile.

Only in the shadows that he felt free to do as he wished.

Donald would arrive in Wyatt Ridge shortly. There would be a badge on his chest, likely granting him a few favors from the town's officials, but he carried no legal authority in this part of the country. In this place, he couldn't indulge his appetites and expect that others would pretend indifference to his actions.

If he'd done his research, he knew Ted Hanlon was dead. When he rode up to the ranch, he'd expect to find her there alone. He wouldn't be prepared for Pearce Folsom.

Whatever else he might be, Ted's friend wasn't a man who frightened easily. When her derringer was at his throat, he didn't flinch. His voice didn't quaver and his hand didn't tremble.

He wasn't afraid of danger. She suspected he wouldn't be intimidated by the gleam of a silver badge, either.

If she could convince Pearce to remain at the ranch, his presence alone might buy her some time. Time enough, perhaps, to convince Donald to leave her in California. If her pleading didn't work – and she doubted it would – a few extra days might give her the time she needed to build her courage.

Because, if all her other options failed, she had one last, desperate plan:

Kill Donald.

Chapter Nine

Overhead, the sun glowed in white fury, its ferocious rays beating upon him until Pearce couldn't stand it any longer. Balancing against the pitch of the roof, he peeled off his long-sleeved cotton shirt. He draped it, sweat-stained and unwanted, over the barn's unmoving weathervane.

He left the plainsman's hat on his head, shielding his face. He had no doubt he looked a fool, wearing a topper while bare-chested, but who would see him? The prairie dogs, sleeping in their barrows below? The lone hawk, circling overhead?

Lisa?

"If the sight of a half-naked man offends her, she can keep her feelings to herself," Pearce told the world below him. "It's her damned fault I'm up here."

Resting his knees against the hot roof, he gripped the hammer and slammed a nail into the shingle in front of him. The job was proceeding more slowly than he liked. He'd already lost the morning to an unexpected task, replacing two of the barn's support beams. The first timber had been damaged the night before, torn by the rifle's errant bullet; the second had been weakened by mold and the sharp teeth of some unknown creature.

It was as if Nature herself was conspiring against him. Five hours were lost before he'd finally climbed onto the roof itself.

Walking along the gambrel slope, Pearce discovered a number of shingles needing replacement. The shakes were top quality, grain cut from red cedar, but nothing lasted forever. Summer storms, the blistering heat, and time had all taken their toll.

He'd be lucky to finish patching the roof before the sun went down. It wasn't like Ted to ignore such basic repairs.

How long had his friend been sick, anyway?

Pearce sent another nail into the shingle. His family wouldn't believe it if they could see him now, toiling on another man's rooftop because he owed a fifty-dollar debt. They might not even recognize him, bronzed from the sun, with his arms, chest and shoulders having grown larger from hard labor.

"Prince Pearce," his much older brothers had called him. A late-in-life baby born with a silver spoon in his mouth – and a silver fork in each hand – his early life had been lived in glorious splendor. His father was a shadowy presence in his life, too busy with his business to spend much time with the last of his children; and his mother was always pleasantly distant, but sweetly indulgent.

In short, his parents had demanded less of him than they'd demanded of his siblings. As he grew older, he'd accepted their generosity as his due.

Given a task to do, he'd slip away, comfortable in the knowledge that someone else would pick up his chore. The mansion was filled with servants and that's what servants were paid for, after all.

Racing toward adulthood, he'd preferred to spend his time with a deck of cards or a pair of dice until he discovered the sweet joy of the opposite sex. A woman of easy morals became one of the few distractions that could pull him away from the joys of gambling.

Such women were infinitely more interesting than anything his family – or the family business – could provide. Or so he firmly believed, once upon a time.

From the oblong-shaped stack at his side, Pearce lifted a second shingle. Like the first sheet of building material, it appeared red and vibrant when placed beside its aged brethren. Fresh and new always stood in bright contrast to old and weathered. Once the roof was finished, Ted would be able to see its patchwork appearance from his front porch.

His friend wouldn't like it. He was a man who welcomed harmony in the world around him. He preferred it when things blended in, functioning efficiently without calling attention to themselves.

"It is what it is," Pearce muttered. "There's nothing to be done about it."

He rocked back on his heels, suddenly struck by the words he'd said. He told himself, "Now I'm sounding like my father."

*****

Two weeks following his 19th birthday, Pearce had been summoned to his father's study. Randall Folsom sat behind his elegant yew wood desk, looking like a ghost enfleshed.

He tipped his head in the direction of the chair across from him. Pearce lowered himself gingerly to its cushion. It was still early in the day, at least thirty minutes before the lunch hour, and his head was throbbing softly.

"Barton tells me you failed to come to work yesterday," his father said. His eyes were a soft blue in color, pleasant but not striking. The hair on his head was silver, his beard was turning gray, and his skin seemed to be turning a paler shade of white by the day.

Father's looking old, Pearce thought. *He knows his days are numbered. He needs someone to run his empire.*

Well, why is he speaking to me? He has two other sons. Jackson can do it. He's the eldest and disgustingly eager to please.

Or Nicholas. He lives to study balance sheets. Yes, there's your winning choice, father dear. Get Nicholas to take over. He never learned to enjoy his life, anyway.

Pearce was surprised to have a hangover. Although he remembered little of the night before, he couldn't forget his first glass of absinthe. Sweetened with sugar and diluted with generous splashes of water, the green liquid had tasted pleasant but not potent.

It hid its power well. He was eager to try it again.

"Barton tells me you declined to make an appearance last week as well."

"I've got no use for his chatter," Pearce managed to say. "He's not a Folsom. He works for us."

"Barton works for me," his father corrected him. "I sent you to work in the warehouse. Had you done as I'd asked, he'd have been your supervisor."

"I walked through the warehouse. The men working there stink of dirt and sweat."

"If you'd succeeded at your job, you'd have been moved into shipping and fulfilment. In two years, maybe three, I'd have moved you into management. Such were my hopes."

Pearce couldn't imagine a more tedious, terrible fate. Waiting for the lecture to finish, he felt a curious itching sensation in the inner canals of both ears. He couldn't scratch inside his ears, not with his father staring at him so intently, so he focused on trying to ignore the feeling.

Is it the absinthe? he wondered. He'd heard that the drink could cause hallucinations. Was that what was happening here? Was he only imagining that his ears itched?

"Do you know what Folsom Mercantile and Supply offers to our community?" asked Randall Folsom. "Not just to Granville itself, but to our state and the states around us?"

Pearce did know, of course. He might have lacked ambition but he wasn't ignorant. Aware of the power of the family name, he'd invoked it a hundred times. He used it as a bit of additional leverage whenever he wanted a loan, a gift or a kiss.

His last name was a blessing.

"We sell people their pickaxes and shovels," he said. Seeing the anger flare in the old man's eyes, Pearce added, "I'm not saying that's all."

It was simply all he remembered at that moment. Unable to resist the urge any longer, he let his index finger explore inside his ear.

Randall Folsom said, "We supply the equipment needed by farmers and by bankers. By soldiers and by physicians. We provide the tools that allow the hard-working people of this nation to do their jobs. Not that you know the meaning of hard work."

Pearce couldn't argue with his judgment.

"For the first few years, we struggled to keep our doors open. You came along later, but your brothers remember. There was a time when our company almost went bankrupt." Disappointment pulled at the corners of his father's mouth. "I've told you our history before. It means nothing to you. It is what it is. There's nothing to be done about it."

At last. Pearce rose from his chair, eager to leave. His father lifted a hand, slowing his escape.

"I've told Barton to expect you for first shift tomorrow morning," he said. "You'll be on time, do you hear? If you decide you can't be bothered to do as I've asked, you'll leave this house. You'll be on your own."

"Mother will never allow it."

"It was your mother who asked me to speak with you."

This revelation slowed Pearce's escape but it didn't stop him. He walked toward the door.

His father continued, "We get our biggest shipments in on Thursdays so dress appropriately. It won't be easy, the first few weeks, but you may find you like it. There's satisfaction in a job well-done."

Pearce opened the door to the outside corridor. His brother, Nicholas, peered at him from the end of the hall before quickly withdrawing from sight.

"You made the commitment, not me," he told his father.

"As long as you live under my roof, you'll honor my wishes."

"I have money of my own."

"I expect you do. The last few years, cash is all you've wanted on your birthdays."

"Not just gifts, given to me. I have more than those few dollars, much more. I've taken my presents and tripled their value, playing cards and throwing dice."

"You're proud of this?"

"When I sit at a table in the saloon, the other gamblers open their wallets for me. From the day of my birth until this very moment, Lady Luck has favored me."

"You've been blessed, I'll grant you," his father said. "You and everyone else in this family. It's a sin to take good fortune for granted."

"Let Jackson lift the boxes in your store. Let Nicholas keep your ledgers. I don't care to do so. Such toil is beneath me."

"It isn't," his father said. "Honest labor is beneath no good man."

"Then I must not be that good," Pearce smirked. "Tell Mother she needn't worry. I'll be gone by morning."

Chapter Ten

How long did the money last?

Almost two years, if memory served. Longer than either of his parents would have imagined, he believed, but not before he'd lost much of his enthusiasm for gambling. He remembered when his wallet had gone flat, his luck and his erstwhile companions seeming to vanish at the same time. Soon after, dodging a kitchen knife as he scrambled through an open window, he'd learned that not all easy women were willing to be lightly dismissed.

Better educated by experience than he'd ever been in school, Pearce found himself broke and homeless. By then, he'd drifted far from his hometown. Too proud to return to the family estate, he'd had to roll up his sleeves and learn how to make a living.

"Hard work's no stranger to me these days," he advised a nail before hammering it down. Over time, his hands had become callused and his arms had grown strong. His brothers might laugh to see him on this rooftop, setting shingles under the noonday sun, but it was far from the first time he'd done such a thing.

There were occasions when he found a certain pleasure in such chores. It was satisfying to fix what was broken. Given the opportunity, he could see himself building a life as a tradesman.

Loading boxes in Father's warehouse would have been easier than most of the tasks I've done, he thought. *If I was offered the job now, I'd not be so quick to dismiss it.*

Some of what had happened to him was due to his own actions, but not all of it. Aggravated by his boastful words those many years ago, Lady Luck had turned her back on him. That's all there was to it.

He couldn't rely on chance to show him the way. If he wanted his life to change around, it was up to him to do it.

Pearce was trying to be a better person. Attempting to follow in the footsteps of his brother, Jackson, he'd tried to live his life in a discrete and cautious manner. He'd failed rather spectacularly, abandoning the quiet life when he left Abilene in a hurry, a saloon in flames behind him.

Following that failure, struggling to be as responsible as his brother, Nicholas, he'd been saving his money and living in Tombstone as parsimoniously as possible. He had big plans. Those plans had changed abruptly when a saloon girl had taken a liking to him and a gun hand had beaten her for her display of interest.

Not as quick with a pistol as he'd thought, the gun hand had bled out in the middle of an Arizona street. Advised that the man's gang was riding toward Tombstone, Pearce decided to return to Wyatt Ridge.

One of his few remaining friends lived there, Ted Hanlon, and Pearce finally had the cash to pay him for past favors. He knew the old man would act as if he'd done nothing special, pretend as if he hadn't practically saved Pearce's life, but he'd have taken the money. With his home and outbuildings in some disrepair, Ted clearly needed the funds.

Riding into California, Pearce had considered asking if he could stay on the land for a month or so, working as a handyman and helping with repairs around the place. He even had a few ideas on how to bring the ranch back to life, if Ted was interested in making the effort.

That plan was long gone.

The roll of cash had vanished and Ted no longer lived alone. Once Pearce finished patching the barn, he'd speak with his friend briefly, then take his leave.

Repairing a roof is easy, he thought. *Telling Ted I've kissed his wife....*

He was ashamed of himself. Not because of what had happened; as wonderful as the kiss had felt, the action wasn't intentional. That should have been the end of it, though. Wanting to hold Lisa in his arms again while knowing she belonged to a man he liked and admired, an honorable man – this felt like a betrayal of trust.

He wished he could quit thinking about her.

We've only just met, he thought. *How can you already be haunting me?*

The night before, exhausted, he'd fallen into a fitful sleep. His dreams had been filled with memories of their first, brief encounter. Her warm and yielding body, held in his arms. The taste of her lips, sweet and slightly salty. Her bravery during the storm, struggling against the mud's hold, but refusing his help if it meant offering her name.

He'd never met anyone like her. Confronted by an armed stranger, she'd refused to back away. Filled with blind courage, she'd actually pulled a gun on him.

Ted was the luckiest man in the world.

In all of his years, with all of his experience, Pearce had never desired a woman more. His feelings didn't matter. He couldn't let them matter.

He'd never again allow himself to touch Ted's wife.

Lifting the hammer, he paused before sending it against its target. "What the hell is the matter with me?" he asked himself, the tool frozen in his hand.

It was a kiss, one single kiss. She's probably forgotten it by now. I should, too.

When he saw Ted, he'd say hello, then inquire about his health. He wouldn't mention anything about the previous night. If Ted brought up what happened in the barn, he'd give it to him straight.

It was a brush of the lips, not worth remembering.

That last statement was a boldfaced lie. But that's what he'd say.

Pearce slammed the hammer down, burying the nail beneath its head. On his previous visit, the ranch had a few areas in need of attention, but nothing as significant as what he'd seen today. Since then, conditions had gotten strikingly worse.

Climbing to his feet, Pearce shaded his eyes to view the property. Directly behind the barn was the corral… or those pieces that remained of it, anyway. Several of its timbers had fallen, either from rot or hard weather, and only the outline of an empty animal pen remained.

A pair of storage sheds were of decent construction and still usable, but, standing off by itself, the chicken coop needed to be completely replaced. Turning toward the main house, Pearce saw the center of its roof had sagged inward, an obvious sign of structural damage.

"What happened here, Ted?" he asked his absent friend.

It had been decades since the Broken H was new, but deterioration on this scale indicated many months of neglect. How wick was Ted, anyway?

Or how much in love? Until yesterday, Pearce would have argued that no woman could have captured a man in so strong a fashion. Not any longer.

A glint of light caught his eye. Following its white gleam, he saw a starburst wink at him from the property's far left border. Something metal and small was on the ground.

Whatever it was, it couldn't have been there very long. If it had lain there long enough to grow rusted, it wouldn't have been bright enough to catch the sun's rays and throw them back at him.

A silver coin maybe? Or a gold piece?

His saddlebag had held a few of each when he followed the trail onto the Broken H. But if this was a coin from his bankroll, what was it doing so far from the path he'd followed?

Climbing higher, Pearce straddled the rooftop of the barn. Knowing where to look, he found the reflection again. Whatever the object was, it rested a good distance from the trail leading onto the property.

Still think that's your Half Eagle caught in the scrub? It's a good three hundred yards from the path you were traveling.

Considering the force of the storm, he supposed it could have been thrown there. He'd check for it later. If he was lucky, he might find a little more of his lost fortune scattered about the area.

But you're not lucky anymore, are you?

No, he was not.

For the moment, his job was to patch this roof. After he was done, he'd look in on Ted, pretend to ignore Ted's wife, and tell them both that he'd sleep in the barn and ride out at daybreak.

It was better that way.

Chapter Eleven

"Sweet tea?" Lisa called from the bottom of the ladder.

High above her, a wide-brimmed hat appeared over the edge of the roofline. The headpiece rose higher when Pearce stood upright. He was bare-chested, his trousers cinched tight against his flat stomach.

His upper body was brown from the sun and his stomach was as rippled as the washboard Lisa used for her clothes. Once she realized she was staring, she averted her gaze.

"How's your ankle?" he asked.

"Much better."

"I'd welcome a drink." Wherever he'd left his shirt, he'd found it by the time he came down the ladder's rungs. Loosely buttoned, with its sleeves rolled up, it did little to hide the width of his shoulders or the power in his arms.

Again, Lisa found herself struck by the strength in his face and the beauty of his body. She wasn't interested in such superficial matters – *Absolutely not!* – especially since she'd decided to avoid romantic relationships for the rest of her days.

It was better when she was alone. Safer. But, even when she was open to being courted, Pearce wasn't the type of man she'd have invited to her door.

He's appealing in an unsophisticated sort of way, she admitted to herself. *Physical attraction is hardly enough.*

Oh, some women would welcome such a brute in their bed chambers, I'm certain. I always sought a deeper, more cerebral connection.

Pearce Folsom was a touch too brash, a little too full of himself, to win her favor. It was obvious that he'd never learned how to act around a lady.

Stepping from the bottom rung, he turned and faced her. Seeing her up close, he involuntarily took a step backwards.

"Is something the matter?"

"You look – um, nice." The words came out in a strangled sentence, as if he didn't want to pay her a compliment but somehow couldn't prevent himself.

"Thank you." Lisa had spent her morning getting ready. She'd done her hair as nicely as she could manage with a sponge, a bar of soap, and a pitcher of tepid well water. After she'd wrapped her ankle, she'd selected her favorite flowered dress for the day.

You'll catch more flies with honey than with vinegar, Poor Richard's Almanac had promised her, and she intended to test its theory. Needing the gunman to stay at the ranch, she felt it was in her best interest to appear attractive for him.

Men are more willing to help a pretty woman, she thought. *Everyone knows it; we've all seen it a hundred times before. It's been this way since the dawn of time.*

As long as Pearce believed that Ted was in the house, no matter how feeble, he'd behave himself. He wouldn't want to disappoint his friend. When the cowboy lifted his glass from the serving tray, Lisa took another opportunity to observe her visitor.

He hasn't made any such effort to be presentable for me, she thought, feeling unreasonably disappointed. *That's fine. I don't care.*

Pearce is strong – she remembered the power in his arms and legs as he carried her across the wet field and to the house – *and he certainly has a presence about himself. He won't be easily intimidated.*

He won't hesitate to stand up to Donald Skroch.

There was a knot in the base of her stomach, reminding her that her scheme wasn't fair to the man in front of her. She forced herself to ignore the feeling, hoping she'd think of a better plan in the near future.

Pearce took a swallow of the sweet tea. His eyes widened when the liquid filled his mouth. Manfully, he retained the fluid, forcing it down in a desperate swallow.

He managed to say, "This isn't Ted's mix."

"It's my recipe." Preparing a pitcher of sweet tea for the first time, Lisa had tested the end result. She'd thought the mix tasted cloying and thick, as if a layer of molasses was smothering her taste buds, but she'd always hated Ted's concoction, too. "Too much syrup?"

Pearce lifted the glass to his lips, testing a second, much smaller, sip of the tea. Quickly, he returned the glass to the serving tray.

"Appreciated." The falsehood hung in the air as his lips pressed together.

Behind his closed mouth, Lisa could see the movement of his tongue, trying to wipe his teeth clean. Unable to stop herself, she asked, "Aren't you going to finish your drink?"

Refusing to meet her eyes, Pearce turned away to study the barn's roofline. "I'll have everything patched and secure in a bit. I'll see Ted before I decide what to do next."

"What do you mean?"

"If he's doing okay, I'll ride out in the morning. Maybe head up north. You don't need me around here."

Yes, I do! An invisible hand clutched at her chest as Lisa fought off a wave of panic. *You can't go!*

Something in her expression caught his attention. "Something the matter?"

"It's – I forgot – I thought I heard Ted call."

"If you need something, let me know. I'd best return to work." Then, as if he was worried that she might forget it, he added, "Take the pitcher when you go."

"How much longer will you be working?"

"Four hours, maybe five."

"Just in time for supper."

Pearce opened his mouth as if he was going to protest.

"After a hard day, a man needs to eat," Lisa said. "I'm making…." She tried to think of an enticing meal. "Do you like chicken and dumplings?"

It was one of Ted's favorite dishes and he'd always insisted on preparing it in the past. Lisa knew the larder held most of the ingredients for it and the chicken coop held the rest. She even remembered seeing Ted's recipe for it.

It was only a one pot meal. How difficult could it be?

"Is Ted preparing it?" Pearce asked.

"It's his recipe."

"You're making my mouth water. It's been a while since I've had a home-cooked meal. Will Ted be joining us?"

"I expect so."

"Good."

What I truly expect, Lisa reflected, *is to find another excuse why Ted isn't available to be seen. Then I'll need to create a new reason to keep you at the ranch.*

This next fabrication, whatever it might be, was beyond her at the moment. It wouldn't have to be too clever. Not for a man like Pearce Folsom.

"Until then." He tipped his hat toward her. Giving a last, baleful glare at the pitcher of sweet tea, he climbed the ladder.

Lisa watched him leave, enjoying the view with an interest that wouldn't have been seemly if anyone else had seen her. On Ted's patch of nothing, the only one who might notice would be a circling hawk or one of the wild horses that roamed the distant range.

But it isn't my uncle's property any longer, she reminded herself. *It's mine now. One hundred and sixty acres of dirt and scrub brush.*

Once Pearce was out of sight, she started toward the chicken coop. After a few, short steps, she changed her mind.

"My best Sunday outfit isn't going to be exposed to the mire of that coop," she decided. "No, thank you."

Once she'd changed into something more suitable, she could venture out again. She dreaded having to select the hen that would serve as the basis of the evening meal.

74

Until this day, she'd never killed one of the birds. Ted had always managed the task. She'd never plucked the feathers from a bird, either.

The memory of her own thought teased her: *How difficult can it be?*

Chapter Twelve

Her calico dress, purchased new and once worn so gaily, had grown faded. The tail of its skirt showed wear from its skirmishes against the ground.

If she still lived in St. Anders, she'd have replaced it by now. But she was a long way from her birth city, and many dollars short of being able to replace a still-serviceable outfit.

Knotting the ties of her bonnet, she stepped from the front porch and started walking toward the chicken coop. She moved briskly, hoping her exertion would dispel the chill in the air. Within a few minutes, she was nearing her destination.

Even before she saw the small coop, she could tell something had gone wrong. In the past, the chickens had greeted her with a flurry of sound, anticipating their next meal. Today, there wasn't any rustling of feathers, no excited clucks of anticipation. There was only the sound of her footsteps as she neared the structure.

The chickens had vanished. Their home, a long rectangle built from reclaimed bits and drabs of wood, had collapsed. Its side supports had broken, causing its front wall to pitch outward as its ceiling caved in.

Tugging the roof aside, she found the only remaining occupant of the pen. The master of the coop, King Richard was pinned against the pen's last standing wall. The rooster's head was twisted awkwardly, its shrill voice forever silenced.

"Poor King Richard," Lisa said sadly. "Whatever shall I do with you?"

The mean-tempered fowl stared at her lifelessly. Just the day before, she'd seen him strut inside the enclosure, moving with the confidence of a bird enjoying his life. Servicing a trio of hens, feeding on dribbles of feed and bugs in the dirt, King Richard cherished his life as the ruler of his domain.

His life had ended. There were only a few scattered feathers to provide any evidence of the harem that had once shared space with him.

Did the storm's fury cause this? Lisa wondered. *Or did the coyotes sneak in when the coop fell apart, taking advantage of the weather's brutality?*

In the end, the result was the same. Her chickens were lost, scattered by the rain's onslaught or carried away in the jaws of any number of predators. All that remained was the body of King Richard. The oldest, stringiest, least-appealing rooster to ever walk the face of the earth.

If she still intended to prepare chicken and dumplings, she was going to have to make an enjoyable meal from his remains.

It's impossible, she thought. No one, no matter their cooking skills, could manage such a miracle.

Lisa lifted the bird from its bed. When she did, the straw bed beneath him shifted. A glimpse of white peeked out at her.

Hope returned at the sight of this surprise, the sensation so strong that she nearly dropped the coop's only tenant. She breathed one soft word to the dead rooster: "Salvation."

*****

Expecting his knock, Lisa still jumped at the sound of it. A gentleman would have tapped at the door gently, politely, entreating for the homeowner to allow entry.

Pearce pounded at the door, demanding it be opened. He didn't have any sense of propriety.

She should have expected as much.

Lisa smoothed her flowered dress into place. She touched at her hair, reassuring herself that it remained nicely coiffed, and stood to light the lantern.

Dusk had already arrived and the room was growing dim. Since she'd gone to considerable trouble to make herself presentable, she wanted Pearce to be able to appreciate those efforts.

Placing her hand on the doorknob, she took a deep breath. *Be honey, not vinegar,* she told herself. *You need this particular fly to buzz about the Broken H for another week or so.*

Forcing a smile upon her face, she opened the door.

Pearce waited on the step, still wearing the same clothing he'd worn that afternoon. She couldn't tell if he'd as much as washed his face for the visit.

"This is how you come to supper?" The words slipped out before she could think.

"It's how I come to this one."

Sweet as honey, she reminded herself, *and as pleasant as a lovely spring morning.* "Please come inside, Mr. Folsom."

78

"Call me, Pearce," he told her, his voice sounding oddly removed.

"Pearce, then."

He removed his hat as he entered the room. "The parlor stove's new."

"It was the first in the county." Lisa's uncle had been extraordinarily proud of the purchase. He'd owned both a stove and a wood-burning oven. It was rare for such a modest home to have two sources of light and heat. "The barber and his wife came all the way out here, just to see it."

"Still not much in the way of feminine touches. Flowers or quilts or such."

"Should there be?"

"I presumed, once a man was married, there would be changes."

"There will be," Lisa said. "Decorate in haste, regret at leisure, my mother used to say. I'll make my mark when the mood suits."

"Where's Ted?" The statement came out flat and uninvolved.

"Come into the kitchen and I'll tell all."

His eyes studied her coolly. "I wonder if you will."

A curious man, this Pearce Folsom, and difficult to read. Lisa left the front area with her lantern in hand, confident that he'd follow in her steps.

The cast iron frying pan was heating on the oven when she entered the room. Draping an apron over her dress, Lisa collected the eggs she'd found. There were only three of them, matching the number of hens that had vanished, but she was grateful to have anything to cook.

When Pearce entered the kitchen, she was cracking the first egg against the side of her mixing bowl. "I hope you like omelets."

"Eggs?"

"Nothing so satisfying as a simple country omelet." This night, it certainly seemed so to Lisa. It was one the few recipes she knew by heart.

When all of the shells had been cracked and the eggs were in the bowl, she added three teaspoons of cold water. Stirring the mixture, she sprinkled in a bit of salt and pepper.

If she'd had some basil, that would have gone into the bowl as well. Since she didn't, Pearce was going to have to make do.

"The child instead of the mother," he said. "Eggs, not chicken."

"That is so."

Pearce's stomach growled loudly. When Lisa turned toward him, he dipped his head. "Pardon."

For a few seconds, his stony gaze weakened and she saw a look of hunger on his face. *When did you last eat?* Lisa wondered.

She felt ashamed. As his hostess, she should have offered him something stouter than a glass of sweet tea for lunch. Since he hadn't asked for a meal, she'd assumed that he'd carried hardtack or some such in his remaining saddlebag.

It appeared more likely that he hadn't eaten all day and, possibly, not since the day before. She hadn't had much to eat recently, either, but she hadn't been hammering on a roof top for hours, either.

"Sit at the table like a proper guest," she said. Waiting until he'd done as she asked, she put a tablespoon of sweet butter into the frying pan. "I'd like to have served chicken and dumplings, but I no longer have a hen house. Don't tell Ted, he loved that ornery rooster of his."

Pearce rested his hat on the seat of an unoccupied chair. "Where's Ted?"

"Asleep. We had an early supper. You'll be dining on your own this evening."

The butter melted almost instantly. When it shimmered from its own heat, she poured in the eggs.

The smell of the simmering meal filled the kitchen. Pearce's eyes closed and his nostrils flared slightly, taking in the aroma.

Just as the one side of the omelet was finished, Lisa turned it quickly, heating its opposite face. When it was done, she folded the eggs over and slid the golden concoction onto a plate.

Pearce picked up his utensils. "Odd."

"What's that?" Lisa lifted the tea kettle, pouring warm water into the frying pan. A stiff brush followed, helping her remove the remaining residue.

"You've put two plates on this table. Two pairs of knives and forks. Almost as if you'd expected the two of us to share these fixings."

"A silly mistake. I'm so used to setting a table for two."

Pearce sliced through the omelet. Balancing the half-portion along the length of his knife, he slid the meal onto the dish across from him.

"Sit," he said. "Eat."

"I'm not –"

"If you don't eat, neither do I. We'll both go hungry."

Lisa dried the frying pan before taking her seat. "Shall we say grace?"

"Doesn't seem fitting." His fork cut through the edge of the omelet.

A very curious man, indeed.

Lisa brought a bit of egg to her mouth. "You finished with the barn over an hour ago."

Chewing his food, Pearce didn't respond to her unasked question.

Her first bite of egg tasted delicious, reminding her of how hungry she'd been. She realized she'd eaten almost nothing since receiving Donald's telegram.

"I saw you put away your supplies," she continued. "Then you mounted your horse and rode out."

He took another bite, filling his mouth.

Sweet, golden honey, she reminded herself. *No matter how irritating the fly, no matter how much you want to kick his shins under the table, you mustn't let your aggravation show.*

You need this pest. She fluttered her eyes at him. *You can swat him later.*

They finished their meal in silence. Pushing his dirty plate aside, Pearce told her, "I'd like to speak with Ted."

"Tomorrow morning, perhaps."

"I won't be here in the morning." Standing abruptly, he took the lantern and left the room.

Lisa hurried after him. Using the light to guide him, Pearce had already reached the master bedroom door. She reached him just as he threw the door open.

Blackness greeted them. Pearce pushed his arm forward, forcing the lantern's flickering flame to provide a view into the chamber.

Inside the darkness, a few vague shapes were revealed to them. A wooden dresser was flush against the wall and a hat stand was in the corner. On the bed, a body faced away from them, a comforter pulled over its shoulders.

Lisa had used an extra pillow and a spare blanket to shape a form on the mattress. *Just in case,* she remembered thinking at the time.

To her relief, this last-minute ploy created a believable illusion. If she hadn't known better, she'd have believed her uncle was asleep in the bed.

"I told you, Ted's not been well," she whispered harshly. "Don't you dare wake my husband."

Pearce nodded.

His fingers opened, allowing her to take the lantern from his hand. She started for the main room, expecting him to follow.

Within a few steps, she realized she'd been mistaken. She turned around, panic gripping her.

The floorboard creaked beneath her feet as she returned to the bedroom. She raised the lantern to see Pearce's figure standing inside the murk of the bedroom.

"Please," she said softly.

He yanked at the bed's cover. The extra pillow and coiled blanket spilled to the ground. From inside the gloom, he said, "Don't pretend to be surprised at this. You're not."

Desperately, Lisa tried to think of how to respond.

"This afternoon, I found Ted Hanlon's grave," Pearce said, his voice growing hard. "His final resting place. Who are you, really? What did you do to my friend?"

Chapter Thirteen

Pearce reached into his right pants pocket, pulling out a watch chain. Its silver links reflected the lantern's white flame. "Recognize this?"

A pocket watch dangled from the end of the chain. Its face was locked behind a white metal case.

"It belongs to Ted."

"He never left the house without this watch. Told me once it was more precious than gold to him. So why did I find it face down in the dirt, only a few feet from a newly-turned grave?"

Lisa knew that the grave wasn't new but, even after the recent downpour, the soil would have appeared fresh compared to the land around it. The man across from her wasn't in any mood to debate the fineries of the situation.

Keeping the lantern, she walked away from him.

He followed her to the front room. "He wasn't just some old farmer. He was a pioneer, did you know that? The first person to settle in Wyatt Ridge; he named it after one of his relatives. The families that followed him here would have been lost if he hadn't been here to teach them how to use the land. They'd have starved."

With her lie revealed, Lisa didn't know how to tell Pearce the truth. Wondering what to say and how to say it, she placed the lantern on a hook in the wall.

Before she could retreat to her rocker, Pearce blocked her path. "Thirty-six years later, the town he built can't bother to remember him. At the end of his days, what does he get? Thrown in a pit, a little dirt sprinkled on top. Given less respect than I'd give a dog."

Lisa slapped him. Pearce jerked back, his right hand dropping instinctively to the ivory grip of one of his pistols.

"You think Ted Hanlon deserved a grand funeral, do you?" she said.

"As grand as any." Pearce said the words defiantly, his cheek reddened by her blow.

"Spread out in a fine coffin, perhaps, its mahogany lid propped open? We could have placed the box in the back of Hurley Wallace's campaign wagon for everyone to see. Give the townspeople a chance to pass by, offer their due regards."

"Nothing like that, no. But something should have been done."

"Mayor Wallace wanted a banner hung across Main Street. 'RIP, Ted Hanlon.' He'd hired a photographer for the event," Lisa said. "He wanted to be shown standing beside the corpse, smiling like he was my uncle's last, best friend."

"I can't believe Hurley Wallace won the election. He's as crooked as a dog's hind legs." His indignation spent, he added, "Ted couldn't stand him."

Beneath his words, Lisa could hear his sense of loss at the death of his friend. His face was still pink where she'd struck him.

This is the second time I've slapped him, she realized.

Feeling as if she should apologize for her actions, but not knowing exactly what to say, she decided to talk about Ted, instead. "When I met him, he knew his time was coming to an end. He was at peace with it. He told me what he wanted: no funeral, no tombstone, no coffin. No crowds. Ted liked it when things were quiet. He asked to be wrapped in a bed sheet and put to rest near his oak trees."

"He loves – loved – those Blue Oak. I feared he'd try to use the acorns in one of his meals."

"Uncle asked that his grave be marked by a simple cross, one he'd nailed together himself from two pieces of wood he found on this land. There was no eulogy, to Reverend Leydecker's dismay."

"No one said words over him?"

"I did," Lisa told him. "After he'd been buried, when it was just the two of us. And what was said belongs to him and me alone."

The words ended in a quaver, her voice failing her.

"His watch?"

"It was the only thing he still had from his brother. It's going back to the top drawer of his dresser."

I never should have removed it, Lisa thought. Three days earlier, she'd made the mistake of carrying the timepiece to Ted's graveside. Just holding his favorite possession had made her feel closer to him. "I don't know why I brought it with me, the last time I went to see him. I won't do it again."

Pearce looked at her doubtfully.

"Are you going to pretend you don't know about losing things?" she challenged.

"You still claim to be your uncle's mail-order bride?"

"You made some assumptions," Lisa reminded him. "I only called him my husband after you said I was his wife."

"That's not how I remember it."

"Then you remember it wrong."

"Ted never mentioned having a niece."

"He never mentioned you, either," she countered.

"Humph." Slowly, Pearce curled the pocket watch's chain around his fist. "You say I made an assumption about your relationship. I say you let the assumption stand. You lied to me. A person lies to me once, I have no good reason to believe them a second time."

From the deepening frown on his face, Lisa assumed he was coming to an unhappy conclusion about her story. "Open the watch face."

"What?"

"Ted's watch. Release its latch. I want you to see what's inside. What he considered more precious than gold."

"Whatever it is, he never had cause to show it to me." Pearce's thumb pulled against the side latch without effect. "You leave a Dollar Watch in the rain, the elements will ruin it."

Lisa held out her hand. Reluctantly, Pearce slid the chain over his fingers before giving her the timepiece.

"This is no such thing, and you know it." Lisa manipulated the latch carefully. "Old isn't the same as cheap."

Finally, its face lifted. Inside the watch cover, there was a small, circular photograph.

Lisa said, "It's Ted in his younger days."

Pearce accepted the clock again, studying the picture inside. "I've never seen this."

"He's practically a boy," Lisa said. "He looks happy, doesn't he?"

"Who's the man standing there? The one in the vest?"

"My father, Wyatt. His brother."

"Peas in a pod. And the woman beside him?"

"My mother, Judy."

"Beautiful woman," he said spontaneously. "She looks a lot like you."

"She's gone, now. Father, too. Uncle Ted was the only relative I had left."

"Is that why you came here?"

"You have no good reason to believe me," Lisa reminded him, feeling sad herself, "no matter my response."

Lifting the watch until its photograph was at eye level, Pearce considered the woman in front of him. Satisfied, he pushed the watch face closed.

He said, "What was it like, the first time you knocked on Ted's door?"

"When I first arrived here, I heard someone coughing inside," Lisa said. "When Ted saw me, he called me by name, even though we'd never met. It was almost as if he'd been expecting my visit."

"I suppose you were all the relatives he had left, too."

"He didn't ask how long I'd come for. It could have been for the single day or the next ten years. He let me know I was welcome to stay."

Pearce took her hand into his open palm. His skin felt rough to the touch, made hard by the work he'd done in the past.

Returning the watch to her, he curled her fingers over it. "How long ago was that?"

"A little over three months. I didn't intend to remain, but I tarried. I felt welcome here. I felt… safe."

It was strange how quickly she'd adapted to her new living arrangement. She'd never lived on a ranch before, but the Broken H had felt like home.

Lisa said, "Ted tried to hide that he was sick, but he couldn't control that cough. The first time he brought up blood, I realized I needed to stay."

She seated herself in the rocker. She pushed against its seat lightly, and it carried back and forth.

Ignoring the bench seat positioned across from the wood stove, Pearce lifted a ladder-backed chair from the opposite corner of the room. Placing it so that he faced her, he sat on the chair's woven corn shuck seat. "Did you think about taking him into town? Letting him see a doctor?"

"Uncle didn't want people to know he was sick. A man's pride, I imagine. Doc McCauley came out here instead, bringing his heavy metals and lancets. Nothing he used did any good: the injections, the purging, the bloodletting. All the treatments did was to make his patient feel worse."

Gently, Pearce asked, "Did Ted go hard?"

"He smiled at me before he closed his eyes. He never opened them again. McCauley was here, too, standing over the bed when he passed. The doctor's cure-alls weren't good for much, but he stayed long enough to help dig the plot. For a man wearing a suit and tie, he seemed fairly experienced at digging graves."

Following that grim statement, they sat together in silence.

Chapter Fourteen

Outside of the front window, the sky was dark. Most evenings, moonlight pressed against the curtains, begging entrance while starlight filled the sky. For Lisa, a woman raised in the east, it was a glorious sight.

Cloud cover insured that she wouldn't see any stars this night. Without the lantern's light, they would have been surrounded by blackness.

Lisa sensed that Pearce was trying to frame his goodbye. Before he could speak, she said, "I expect you'll be going."

Pearce nodded his head. The motion came slowly, as if he was so weary that he could barely make the effort.

"It's for the best," she lied. "A proper lady doesn't share her living quarters with a single man. Not without a chaperone. People would talk."

"Who would? There's no one around for miles. No one even knows I'm here!"

"As long as you understand the delicacy of our situation. As soon as you've paid the debt you owe me, you'll have to leave."

He straightened in the chair. "What?"

"I'm not expecting a cash payment."

"Generous of you," he said, staring at her.

"You can work off what's owed. There's more than enough to be done. The house is deteriorating; just a week ago, a hole the size of my fist appeared over the second bedroom. The outbuildings are worse, if anything, and the land is untended. The wildlife is taking over. Have you heard the coyotes howl? When the sun falls, I'm certain they skulk about outside my bedroom window."

Pinching his fingers at the bridge of his nose, Pearce shook his head.

Lisa said, "During the day, the wild horses strip the fields of their vegetation. Unless something is done, there will be nothing to protect the land during the next flash flood."

"Remind me of this debt," Pearce said.

"Fifty dollars, didn't you say? What was owed to my uncle is now owed to me. I'm his heir."

"His heir! By nature of your birth?"

"As written in Ted Hanlon's last will and testament," Lisa said. "As you can easily verify by speaking with Rupert Capehart, Wyatt Ridge's foremost attorney-at-law."

"Capehart. He works out of the red-brick house at the end of Main Street, doesn't he? The one with the octagonal bay?"

"You question my veracity?"

Lantern light flickered over Pearce's face.

Lisa said, "In St. Anders, a common laborer is paid nine dollars a day. Wyatt Ridge is a good distance from Massachusetts, however, and the wages here are somewhat less substantial. Six dollars a day is about right."

"Does it?"

"I think anyone would agree."

"Even by Burdick County stands, twelve hours for a half-dozen cartwheels feels a bit shy."

"You'll also receive room and board," Lisa reminded him.

Leaning forward, Pearce placed his elbows against the top of his legs. Curling his hands together, he rested his chin on his closed fists.

Lisa felt her stomach tighten anxiously.

He said, "Let me order the situation as I understand it. If you don't mind."

"Facts are facts."

"I said the same thing to my father once. He told me, in any argument, there's your facts, there's my facts, and there's the truth. His 'facts' would have set me to work in a warehouse, moving boxes; my 'facts' sent me on the road." A whiff of regret lingered over the last statement. "I want to get to the truth."

"Go ahead."

"When I was in dire straits, Ted Hanlon stepped up to help me," Pearce said. "I was a stranger, but he offered me a place to rest and recuperate. Provided me with a horse and saddle. Gave me a pistol so old, I was surprised it didn't have a flintlock."

"He gave you a gun?"

"One man doing another man a favor, that's what it was. He never mentioned a word about repayment. He could have demanded my signature on an IOU, and I'd have signed it. He did not."

"What happened to your own horse?" Lisa asked. She couldn't believe the question hadn't come to her before. "How did you come so far from town without a steed to carry you?"

"That's not the point of this discussion."

"Why would you come to the Broken H, needing a gun? Why would he give you one?"

"It was a long time ago."

"You said he didn't know you."

Pearce raised his index finger, requesting her silence. Lisa gave it to him.

"I came here because I felt it was time I paid him back," Pearce said. "Ted was getting older, he'd stopped raising cattle, and he was never a man of means. Riding out here, I decided I was going to insist he take the money I was offering. He'd refuse at first and we'd argue some. If it was necessary, I'd remind him of the time he'd saved my life."

About to interrupt, Lisa fell quiet. Each time Pearce spoke at length, some new and bizarre fact came to light.

Ted saved your life? My uncle?

She remembered her father's brother as a quiet man with a loud cough. Small in height, with thinning, gray hair, he didn't have any of the physical attributes of the heroes she'd found in literature.

He wasn't anything like Seth Jones, for example, the protagonist in the Beadle's Dime Novel she'd found in Ted's dresser. Seth Jones was strong and powerful. In the novel, he was brave to the point of foolhardiness.

Ted wasn't anything like him.

Maybe it's time I revised my concept of a hero, Lisa thought.

"That's what I expected to happen," Pearce said, "but things turned out differently. When I arrived at the ranch, it was in the middle of a storm. I set up in the barn, hoping to see my friend in the morning. I had no idea that

Ted had died. While I readied my bedroll, his niece snuck up on me. Posing as Ted's wife, she tried to shoot me."

"That isn't the way things went."

He waved her words away. "Today, that same niece tells me she owns the Broken H. She also tells me that she's Ted's heir."

"I do. I am!"

"And, minutes ago, she tells me I'm indebted to her for money I was never asked to repay."

Lisa couldn't disagree with Pearce's recounting of events. She sounded like a terrible person.

A weight settled upon her shoulders, joining the growing knot in her stomach.

"Am I understanding things correctly?" he asked.

The lantern's light allowed fingers of gloom to stretch over him as he waited for her response. His shirt was wrinkled and his pants showed dirt and wear. Flattened by the hat he'd been wearing, his hair pressed against his head.

The Lord help her, he still appeared so much stronger and capable than she felt. So able to be the hero she needed.

But Seth Jones isn't real, she thought, *and it isn't right to ask Pearce Folsom to fill his shoes.*

This isn't his fight.

"The lamp is starting to fade," Lisa said. "There's more kerosene in the other room, but I'll fetch it in the morning. For now, we need to get some sleep."

"I asked you a question."

"You're exactly right, Mr. Folsom. You may have been beholden to my uncle, but you owe me nothing."

Her sudden capitulation surprised him. Prepared to argue a case he'd already won, Pearce didn't know how to respond.

"I don't want you going –" Her voice broke briefly "– not when it's this late. The trails aren't safe even when the moon is shining."

Despite her words, she felt like pleading with him, begging him to stay, offering him anything he wanted – yes, *anything* – if only he would keep her safe from Donald.

She wouldn't let herself do it. It might have been her pride asserting itself at last or, perhaps, she was just too ashamed to admit the truth of her situation to anyone.

Rising from her chair, she said, "In the morning, I'll pack you something for your travels. Ted still has a supply of smoked and seasoned beef strips in the larder. There's hardtack in the pantry, as well."

Pearce stood beside her. "What about the deterioration you spoke of? Your need for a laborer?"

"If you're applying for the job, you know my terms."

"Work all day, get paid a dollar and a quarter less than the meanest job in the Ridge, and be fed half of whatever eggs can be found for my troubles?" He said the words lightly.

His eyes met hers and Lisa felt a jolt of excitement run through her body. As if he'd felt the same sensation, Pearce moved closer to her. She could feel the heat of his body and she knew he desired her, too.

Do you truly want him? Or do you only want him for what he can do for you?

Both, she admitted to herself, feeling the sting of this bitter truth. *But why would he want you?*

Pearce had the confidence of a man who knew how to pleasure women. Lisa suspected he would be good in bed, a skilled and talented lover.

He would be her first, but she wouldn't even be his twentieth. In the morning, he would ride away from the ranch and never return.

She would never forget him. After a few days, he'd struggle to remember her name.

My life is a shambles, she decided. *This man would only make things worse.*

Turning from him, she lifted the lantern from its nail. "I'm going to bed. You can find your way to the barn, can't you, cowboy?"

The horsemen in this area viewed the term 'cowboy' as a disparaging term. From the hurt in Pearce's face, he did, too.

"Don't forget your hat," she said flatly.

He strode away. A minute later, the front door slammed shut.

Lisa carried the dying lantern into her bedroom.

Chapter Fifteen

Pearce pushed a stiff curry brush over Gambit's back and sides.

"I'm ready to ride the trail again," he told the horse. "What do you say, boy?"

Resting a blanket high on the horse's back, he eased it lower, smoothing the hair beneath it.

"We'll be in Wyatt Ridge by mid-day." He placed the saddle on top of the blanket. "Once we're in town, first thing I'm going to do is get rid of these saddlebags. Can't leave them here or that woman would find them. Then she'd dun me two dollars for storage."

He lightly tightened the saddle, lacing the latigo strap in place. "I knew better when I bought them but I wanted to squeeze my dollar, didn't I? Trying to save us a little has cost me most of what we had."

Gambit's large brown eyes studied him solemnly. Pearce welcomed the warmth of his gaze.

When a horse looked at someone, they weren't judgmental. Unlike some people.

"You're ready to go, too, aren't you?" Pearce asked.

He knew better. To his surprise, Gambit had quickly taken to sharing a stall with the barn's other four-legged companion. His horse welcomed this new and more comfortable life.

Pearce was far from certain that he wanted to leave, either, even if Lisa Hanlon was the most exasperating woman he'd ever met. One minute, she was demanding he work at the ranch to repay his debt; the next, she was packing him food for when he left. In a very short span of time, she'd kissed him, slapped him, enticed him and rejected him.

She'd shown great tenderness and depth of feeling in regards to her uncle. It was apparent that those same rich feelings would never extend to Pearce himself.

Best to saddle up and leave, he told himself. *Lisa's made it clear, she sees you as nothing but hired help.*

In her eyes, you're only another sod-buster. Good for heavy lifting and minor chores. Fit to sleep in a barn but not in the main house.

Nothing but a cowboy.

The stallion lowered his head when his master stroked his muzzle. When Gambit opened his mouth, Pearce slipped its bit into place before sliding the bridle's crown over his ears.

He fastened the buckles on the bridle. After adjusting the bit's placement, he checked the ties on the saddle again. In the stillness of the barn, he caught the smell of dried hay. Somewhere inside of that odor was the aroma of dust and dried sweat.

"I smell like a bull in heat," he told Gambit. "No wonder she thinks I'm a cowboy."

Given the opportunity to express an opposing viewpoint, Gambit didn't respond.

"I guess those saddlebags can be chucked later. The *absolutely* first thing I need to do is scrape some of this dirt from my body. You remember Yellow Rock Pond?"

Yellow Rock Pond was close enough that he could reach it in an hour yet far enough off-path that he could strip down and wash himself without being seen. The water would be cold, but Pearce could handle it. Handle it more easily, anyway, than the lingering scent of travel that held to him now.

Gambit snorted softly.

The sound meant nothing but Pearce responded to it, anyway. "The pond is free, that's why. The Wyatt Ridge bathhouse won't be. I need to be presentable. People are hesitant to hire you if you're not presentable."

He remembered the last time he needed some ready cash. Charlie Nelson, a speckled toad of a man, had offered him twenty-five dollars if he could somehow ride a wild bronco that Charlie, himself, couldn't even catch.

Pearce had done it – nearly breaking his neck in the process – only to discover that his employer was a little over twenty-three dollars short of meeting his promised obligation. To settle his debt, Charlie had offered him a fancy gun belt, and two silver-plated, ivory handled pistols.

A gunman's gear, and more than a worthwhile trade. Even in hard times, the guns and their belt were worth at least seventy dollars.

It was too sweet a deal, especially since Charlie was the person presenting it. Pearce took the offer, anyway, selling his own gun and belt in order to wear his newest prize. Twice the fool, he took the cash he'd received from the sale and went to the closest saloon.

After all, he believed Lady Luck had finally remembered his name again. After a couple of hours at the gaming tables, he was certain of it.

He was up by two hundred dollars when a hand fell on his shoulder. "My brother says you cheated him."

Pearce looked up to see Ted Nelson standing over him. George's older, just as ugly, brother. Known throughout the territory as the Prescott Kid.

The Kid wore a chain around his neck. Four spent cartridges dangled from the center of the necklace, each shell representing a man killed by Ted Nelson's hand.

The other players pushed away from the table. One of them, Arnold Gatchell, got up and walked away, leaving his stake for whoever wanted it. He didn't want to be caught in the crossfire when blood was spilled.

Pearce said, "You got it wrong, Kid."

"You sayin' my brother's a liar?"

"I'm not a cheat."

"Make your choice, Folsom. Unbuckle the gun belt and leave what you stole on top of that table – or meet me out on the street."

Collecting his winnings, Pearce wondered if he'd have a chance in something like this. He knew how to use a gun and he'd hunted for food, certainly. This wasn't close to the same thing.

He wasn't a gunman. He'd been in fights a couple of dozen times, but only with his fists. He'd never pulled a pistol on another human being.

Ted Nelson smirked at him, confident of the other man's response. The Kid was a bully and a blowhard. At least one of the cartridges he carried had been "earned" after he'd shot a man in the back of his head.

Pearce's pride wouldn't allow him to back down from either one of the Nelson brothers. He wasn't a man who would be knowingly swindled, either.

"Since I didn't steal anything," he rose from his chair, "I guess we'll settle this outside."

The Kid's twisted smile faltered. His pale, freckled face appeared to grow even paler and Pearce felt a flutter of hope that he might survive this encounter.

Even if he didn't quite believe it himself, the Kid thought his opponent had a chance.

"Your funeral," Ted Nelson said. Five minutes later, he'd proven himself wrong again.

I got lucky, Pearce thought. *The last bit of luck I've had in a long time. I should have sold the damned guns.*

After what happened, I can barely stand to wear them, anyway.

Finding no honor in killing another human being, Pearce had left Tucson in a hurry. He didn't want the reputation that beating the Kid would bring. He could only hope there hadn't been a warrant issued for his arrest.

Pearce was in California now and Wyatt Ridge would serve as his base for the next few months. He'd take a room at one of the boarding houses. Since he'd worked iron, he could probably find occasional employment with Kevin Tennant, the town's master blacksmith. If there wasn't any metal work to be had, he'd see if anyone was in need of a day laborer.

Pearce smiled, recalling his last conversation with Lisa. She'd offered him six dollars a day for the same type of work. It was a poor salary for any man of age.

So why was he standing in the center of her barn, strangely tempted by her offer?

He walked through the building's open doorway to stare at the ranch house.

"You won't find any kind of worker for that kind of money," he told the unseen Lisa. "Nobody worth a plugged nickel, that's for certain. A woman like you, out here all alone, you have to be careful who you hire."

If I stayed, I could set things right, he reflected. *Finish fixing the barn, do a few repairs on the house. Replace the fencing – there's no way to save it – and rebuild that chicken coop.*

As a way to remember Ted, to honor him.

A fleeting thought introduced itself: *Maybe for Lisa, too?*

For her? Hell, no!

Lisa was the kind of beautiful woman that had always drawn his attention. Hazel-eyed, ivory-skinned, and with the types of curves that a man couldn't ignore.

As pretty as she was, there was something off about her manner. She was too guarded, with a smile that never lingered for long. When she walked, her back was always held a bit too rigidly, as if she didn't dare relax.

Lisa was hiding a secret, something she wouldn't or couldn't share with a stranger. She was wrapping her miseries around herself until they threatened to suffocate her. Until the time came that she confronted the darkness troubling her, she wouldn't be capable of a relationship.

"Not that I'm one to speak," he muttered to himself. His longest relationship had ended in less than six months and he'd been delighted when it had sputtered away.

"Let her live her life," he decided, saying the words out loud. "I'll live mine. Kiss your girlfriend goodbye, Gambit. Let's get out of here."

Chapter Sixteen

The morning sun was alone in a cloudless sky, glaring at the world beneath it. Knotting the tie beneath her chin, Lisa shifted the bonnet on her head. The soft head covering would protect her eyes while she searched for her lost chickens.

You'll not find those silly birds, she told herself discouragingly. *If they remained anywhere close to the hutch, you'd have heard them yesterday.*

Acknowledging the truth of this thought but refusing to abandon her project, she pulled a white cotton wrap over her shoulders. Despite the watching sun, the day was cold. Lifting her stout walking stick, Lisa marched through the unwelcoming field in front of her.

She'd slept poorly the night before, her mind in a whirl over the events of the evening. She knew she'd driven away her one, thin hope of remaining a free woman. Not only that, she'd insulted him to boot.

She'd felt so guilty over her cold rejection of Pearce that she'd risen at daybreak and packed him some supplies for his coming journey. He would almost certainly go away mad, but he wouldn't go away hungry.

Tying the foodstuffs into a bundle, she found her worries still weighing on her. Deciding she needed to do something, no matter how pointless, she dressed to go in search of the vanished chickens. The chore would get her out of the house and, more importantly, it might distract her from her thoughts.

"If I'm miserly with my funds, I should be able to stock the larder," she told herself, her walking stick thumping to the ground, "but I can't go to town while my visitor remains in the barn. I'll give him his sleep. Once he leaves, I can retrieve my carriage."

She felt a pang at the thought of Pearce leaving.

You gave him no choice, an inner voice intruded. *Do you want him to stay?*

I don't, she protested mentally. *I only wanted him with me because Donald is coming.*

That's the only reason.

The end of the stick *thunked* against the earth. Two days before, the storm had turned the surface into sludge, sticky and dangerous. Now, the same covering was brown, hard and cracked.

It's not as if I enjoyed his company. It is NOT.

He's barely civilized.

Ahead of her, she saw the bird hutch. Even at this distance, it appeared to be irredeemably broken. The parts that remained were beyond her efforts at repair, certainly.

She supposed Pearce would have been able to fix it in an afternoon's work.

It wasn't all bad that he came here, she reluctantly admitted. *He helped out a little. From his work on the barn's roof, it appears he has some basic skills.*

He's appealing enough, in a rough, rather unpolished way. If I was the type of woman who liked that sort of man.

Was she, then, that type of woman? She'd never thought so before. She couldn't deny it with quite as much vigor now.

It's foolish not to acknowledge the natural attraction that can occur between opposite sexes, Lisa thought. *There was a certain spark when we kissed.*

Once I got to know the cowboy, really know him, the attraction would undoubtedly fade. Pearce is a drifter, moving from place to place. He's likely a gunslinger as well. Just look at the pistols he carries.

Men such as that don't care about the finer things in life. Offer him a book and he'll use it as kindling. Given a fountain pen, he'll likely stare at it with incomprehension. I doubt he can sign his own name.

What kind of name is 'Pearce', anyway?

Lisa stopped beside the chicken coop. As twisted and ruined as the day before, its front wall remained where she'd left it, toppled atop the empty straw beds. The broken, silent King Richard lay not far from her feet.

The straw still had value, as animal bedding or as mulch, but the structure itself was destined for the parlor stove or the kitchen's oven. All four sides were cracked and splintered, revealing wickedly sharp edges wherever she looked. She'd have to wear gloves when the time came to discard it.

Looking for some vague something to guide her chicken hunt, Lisa pushed at the straw with her walking stick. Using her foot, she gently pushed the rooster aside.

Behind her, there came a growling noise. Grasping the stick with both hands, she turned to face whatever had joined her.

In front of her, a coyote blocked her escape. Larger than most of its kind, its head was pushed forward aggressively with its weight shifted to its front legs. Agitated, it snapped at the air around it, as if to drive away some unseen tormentor.

"Go away," Lisa said in a commanding voice. She shook the stick at the animal.

Growling again, the animal huffed twice, blowing short, shallow bursts of air without apparent thought behind the action. Its eyes were unfocused. Thick yellowed mucus dripped from its muzzle.

Rabies, she thought.

Her uncle had warned her that some of the local animals carried the disease. She thought of the Braxton rifle, returned to its mount inside the house. If she'd had it in her hands, she'd have used it without hesitation.

Keeping her eyes on the beast in front of her, she shifted her pole into her left hand. Bending her knees and moving slowly, she used her free hand to reach for the dead King Richard. Lifting it by the neck, she tossed the bird's body toward the coyote.

"Take it," she said. "Go!"

The rooster fell to the dirt, a loose feather released on impact and sent into the air. The coyote huffed again, not looking at the meal that lay beside it.

Backing away, Lisa stumbled over the broken supports of the hutch. When she fell, the walking stick flew from her hand.

Weaving drunkenly, the diseased canine snapped at the air around it. Its bloodshot eyes focused on the woman on the ground.

Lisa cried out.

*****

Pearce turned his head, hearing something. The noise was faint, almost buried beneath the sound of the wind.

A woman was screaming.

Lisa was screaming!

*****

Gambit's hoofs pounded against the earth.

Pearce stood in his stirrups, his body leaning forward as he made a *click*ing noise behind the horse's ear. His knees pressed into the steed, urging it to go faster, *faster*.

Faster than ever before.

Guided by the sound of a second cry, he was at the chicken coop in less than a minute. Lisa lay in the henhouse's ruins, her frightened eyes locked on the animal in front of her. Foam dripped from the bottom of the creature's muzzle. Ignoring the dead bird at its feet, the coyote snapped at some invisible foe.

Reining in his horse, Pearce swung down from the saddle. He trusted Gambit to remain nearby; horses weren't afraid of coyotes and only the maddest of wild dogs would dare risk the certain death that came beneath a mustang's hoofs.

An angry wound festered on the coyote's upper thigh; the bite too large for a bat, but too small for a fox. Pearce recognized the mark.

A skunk caught you, he thought. *Nothing to be done about it.*

He reached for the pistol at his side. His hand slapped against his side before he remembered that his gun belt was still in the barn, looped over a wooden beam. He'd left the building so quickly, he'd given no thought to his own protection.

Lisa scooted across the dirt, trying to distance herself from the advancing coyote.

"Hey!" Pearce cried to the animal. He swept his hand over the ground.

The creature didn't react to his call. Cocking his arm, Pearce threw a rock at the beast. It struck the coyote in the side of its body, its matted fur flaring upon impact.

The animal paused briefly, holding one leg in the air as it considered this unexpected sensation. Lowering its foot, it took another step forward.

Another step toward Lisa.

"Over here, damn you!" Pearce fired a second rock at the coyote. By luck, the sharp-edged square of stone caught the canine in the ear. The coyote gave a high-pitched squeal as a tiny flower of red appeared where the missile had landed.

Shaking its head in pain, it stumbled around to face its new enemy. Its fevered eyes fastened on the cowhand.

Over the years, working in a variety of jobs, Pearce had learned a few things about animals. He could tell that this one was dying. In another few days, in a week at the utmost, it would have been carrion feed.

For the moment, for today, it was driven by madness. Its insanity was giving it strength.

Lisa clutched at the coop's broken front wall. Straining, she pulled herself to her feet.

"Get out of here!" Pearce shouted at her. "Take the horse and go!"

In front of him, the coyote hunched its body for a new attack. Snarling, it leapt at its tormentor.

Keeping his arms in front of him, Pearce caught the animal's shoulders as it took him to the ground. Before the canine could bite him, he wrapped his hands around the coyote's muzzle, forcing its teeth together.

The coyote's claws cut lines in the earth as it pushed itself forward. Shaking its head, it tried to free itself.

Pearce coughed as the animal's fetid breath washed over him. Tightening his hold, he knew there was nothing more important than keeping the monster's wicked teeth away from him.

Lisa rose up behind the animal. Lifting a jagged wooden board over her head, she slammed it down as hard as she could. Pearce's arms shook under the force of the impact as a sharp splinter of wood penetrated the coyote's skull.

Instantly, the predator's eyes glazed. Its body went limp.

Pearce threw the beast away from him. Standing, he pulled Lisa to his body.

"Are you all right?" he asked, not caring that his voice was thick with emotion. "Were you bitten?"

She shook her head. "I'm fine, Pearce. Fine."

Smiling weakly, her eyes rolled back in her head. She fainted into his arms.

Chapter Seventeen

Surrounded by a colorless void, the dream left Lisa feeling as if she were floating. It was a peaceful sensation, her body drifting in the air. Gradually, it dawned on her that she was dropping, slowly and safely, onto the unseen surface beneath her. Resting onto something soft, she realized she had landed.

Where am I? Blanketed in blackness, she realized her eyes were closed. *How silly of me.*

Opening her eyes, she discovered she was sitting on a bench seat, its cushions smelling of horsehair. Sharing the long seat with her was a young woman. The woman was slender and small-breasted, physically notable for the thick red hair that was straining to escape its green, cotton bonnet. Her oval face was friendly.

Across from them was a brown-haired, middle-aged man in a white shirt and brown pants. Clutching the edge of a bowler hat, he made no acknowledgment of Lisa's existence. He was watching the room's only other inhabitant.

This fourth occupant had his eyes closed. His head was shaved and his nose was crooked, as if it had been broken at some distant time. Dressed expensively, the man was in his early thirties. He wore a holster with a single sidearm.

There was something ominous about this stranger. Asleep, his body appeared coiled and ready to strike.

The room lurched. One of the compartment's leather side curtains lifted at the movement, offering a glimpse at the passing landscape outside.

"We're in a stagecoach," Lisa said, surprised.

The younger woman looked at her questioningly.

"Where are we going?" Lisa asked.

When the sleeping stranger opened his eyes, they were as gray as granite. In a deep, lightly-accented voice, he said, "Tate City."

At that moment, Lisa remembered everything. *Of course! How could I have forgotten?*

Days ago, she'd boarded the Cook Brothers stage at the St. Anders depot. There were eight people in the coach originally, but stops in Fort Smith and El Marco had thinned their numbers. As passengers departed, new riders had joined them, but in lesser numbers. Their total now divided by half, the travelers were continuing on to Texas.

For some reason, Lisa couldn't recall the names of any of the other people with her. Had any of them introduced themselves?

The only name I need to remember is Donald's, she reassured herself. *Donald Skroch, the man I'm going to marry.*

A disquieting sensation tugged at her, as if her memory was trying to remind her of something unpleasant. Whatever it was, the feeling disappeared as quickly as it had come.

She clutched her handbag. The rest of her belongings rode in the stage's leather boot, alongside packets of mail and various goods and valuables. Of all her worldly possessions, there was one parcel she valued most: Donald's letters.

My darling, he'd written just days before she'd started her trip, *I sit in solitude, wrapped in misery because you are not yet beside me. Oh, what a glorious life we shall live together.*

Seventeen days on a dusty trail was a small price to pay for the future that lay ahead of her.

The girl beside her offered her hand. "Claudette Cambis."

"Louisa Hanlon," she replied, her own voice sounding strange to her. Again, some fractured piece of memory pulled at her before fading away.

"Mail-order brides," the gray-eyed man grumbled, his voice sounding as if he'd spent time on the Emerald Isles. "The both of you."

"Proudly so, sir," Claudette responded. "Who might you be?"

"He's Quincy Fix," squeaked the white-shirted man beside him. "Gun for hire. He's the one who killed Joseph Olen. He killed Cole Tunstall!"

"Cole Tunstall," Lisa repeated. "The famous bandit?"

"Is this true?" Claudette asked the gray-eyed man.

"It's true that my name is Quincy Fix," he said. "That's about the end of it. Someone has spent too much time absorbed in penny dreadfuls. You embarrass yourself, Mr. Tice."

"Penny dreadfuls?"

"Stories about the West," Mr. Tice explained in a high-pitched voice. "Factual tales about gunmen. About heroes. About… about villains."

"Pages filled with high stories and nonsense," Fix said. "Reading. I've no truck with it. It's something best left for children and women."

The other man pressed himself into the far corner of the booth. "I like my books."

"I expect you do."

"And mail-order brides?" Claudette said. "Will you have nothing to do with us, either?"

"You are correct, miss."

"Why?"

His gray eyes seemed to grow colder. "I've had experience with your kind."

Lisa said, "Our kind?"

"Women willing to marry a man they've never actually met," he clarified. "There are only two types of females who would ever do such a thing. Desperate, lonely old women and women who want money. Since neither of you are old...."

Lisa couldn't understand his disdain. This gun hand didn't know her. He didn't know anything about her or the life she had led. "Don't you believe in love, Mr. Fix?"

"The reason you're on this coach has nothing to do with love."

"What of the men marrying us?"

"They know what they're getting."

She closed her eyes. The journey ahead of them was still several days longer and she hated the thought that Fix would be sitting across from her, staring at her in disapproval. He'd ruin this happy time.

Donald is an officer of the law, she thought. *A good man and a respected man. Do you think he had to "settle" for a mail-order spouse?*

He did not.

I've read his letters. I've seen his photo. He could have had his pick of the single women in his town. He didn't want them.

He wanted me.

Not that I'll share any of this with you. Nor would you believe me, if I did.

I just wish you weren't here. I wish you were gone.

When Lisa opened her eyes again, he was.

*****

"Donald?"

He smiled at his name. Lisa was in Tate City, her bonnet not completely shielding her from the glowing sun that filled the topaz-colored sky. A carriage rolled past her, the rider tipping his hat as his horse trotted by.

She remembered feeling uneasy when she'd arrived here, just two days earlier. In many ways, Tate City felt too new to have any permanence. Burdened by the hopes and desires of a thousand new immigrants, its history was yet to be written.

There were people everywhere she looked. This afternoon, the downtown area was alive with construction. Sidewalks were being built, brown wooden frames were being lifted into place, and everyone was in a hurry to fill the empty spaces around her.

They were creating new buildings to hold new businesses. New businesses to be staffed by people daring enough to venture into a new frontier. People filled with dreams.

Foolhardy people, a voice whispered in her ear. *People acting too rashly.*

Lisa didn't know where this new thought had originated, but she didn't like it.

I wasn't rash, she protested. *I didn't do anything until Donald and I had corresponded at length. I made a bold decision, not an impulsive one.*

I know exactly what I'm doing.

She curled her hand around the arm of her fiancé. Walking together on Main Street's wooden sidewalk, she couldn't help but notice the admiring glances that came their way.

Well, why not? She was wearing a new, flowered day dress and Donald was resplendent in his ebony double-breasted coat and dark vest. Wide-shouldered, almost stocky, he exuded a power that caused other men to step off of the wooden sidewalk as they went by.

In person, his face was a bit more square-shaped than was evident in his photograph. The tintype had also failed to reveal that Donald's hair was less golden than faintly yellow and already thinning. Before he reached forty years of age, he would be bald-headed.

This was the smallest of disappointments and one easily overcome. Hair didn't make a man better or more special. It just made him… hairier.

She giggled.

Instantly, Donald's proud smile faded. "What is it?"

"Pardon?"

"You made a rude sound. What was it?"

Absurdly, Lisa felt frightened. In their short time together, Donald had never acted like this.

"Were you laughing?" he demanded to know. "Tell me!"

Chapter Eighteen

A burly man strode past them, his boots causing the sidewalk to creak. The man stared down the length of the walkway, as if the two of them had suddenly grown invisible.

"I didn't mean anything by it," Lisa said.

"I didn't like it," Donald told her. "A lady never laughs in public. That's what Mother always said."

"Your mother?"

His frown remained, an angry slash twisting his face and accenting the tight muscles in his jaw. Slowly, the downturned lips relaxed.

"Sorry," he said, sounding contrite. "Sorry, my darling."

"You sounded so harsh," she said softly.

"I don't know what came over me. Wedding nerves, I guess. It won't happen again." He took both of her hands in his. "I promise."

"Thank you."

Donald's face brightened. Stopping at a doorway, he turned its knob and gestured for Lisa to enter. "Speaking of our nuptials…."

Mystified, Lisa stepped through the opening. Inside the modest store, a cutting table and multiple bolts of cloth revealed why she was here.

"It's a dressmaker's shop. My wedding gown!"

Curtains rustled along the wall. A small, raven-haired woman appeared from the back room. "Sheriff."

"Abbie May, this is Louisa Hanlon, the woman I've been telling you about. The one I've told everyone about!"

Lisa dipped her head modestly, warmed by the enthusiasm in his voice.

"Abbie May is an aces-high modiste. You'll see. When you're laced into your gown, people are going to swear it came from Durmand of France."

Abbie May went through the curtains again. When she returned, she carried a dress. The color of freshly-fallen snow, its train draped over her outstretched arm.

"I wanted white," Donald said. "Do you like it?"

"Very much." Lisa had never seen a more beautiful dress. If Donald had asked her, she might have suggested something more practical, an outfit she could have worn again at church or in a social setting. To use a dress only once was so extravagant!

But they'd never discussed their wedding. He'd insisted on taking care of all of the details.

"Guess how much it cost," Donald said.

Would a lady venture such a guess? Lisa wondered. *Would a gentleman ask?*

"It's exquisite." She let her fingers play over the lace. "I haven't any idea."

"Eighteen hundred dollars."

The sum staggered her. A sheriff made a few hundred dollars annually. Supplementing his income with various court duties, he could increase his wages to two or even three thousand dollars a year, but rarely more than that.

Lisa said, "You can't afford it. *We* can't afford it."

"I expect we can," he told her. "The day you answered my advertisement, I started setting money aside for the event. Besides, Abbie May knows my situation. She's not going to charge me what she might charge Hank Johnson."

Abbie May viewed Donald with surprise. Her green eyes studied him warily.

He said, "You haven't met Hank, Lisa, but you will. Good man. He came across a slick a few weeks ago and started carving her up. Put a knife in a butcher's hand, what do you expect?"

"What's a slick?" Lisa asked.

"Four legs of beef without a brand on it," he explained. "When I found out about it, Hank grew a little nervous. I told him, some fool forgets to mark his heifer, it could belong to anybody. Relieved his mind, right then and there. We do that in this part of the country. Neighbor helps neighbor. One hand washes the other."

The dressmaker carefully slid the dress from Lisa's hand. She said, "I need to hang this up."

When the curtains closed behind her, Lisa asked, "That's all it was, a neighbor helping a neighbor? Did Hank Johnson offer you anything in return, Donald?"

"What's that supposed to mean?"

"I know how such things work in St. Anders. I'd like to know if things work the same way here."

"I expect they do."

They stood in silence until Abbie May rejoined them. Donald said, "My bride-to-be is wondering if Hank maybe did me a favor in exchange for my silence. Isn't that right, Lisa?"

His cool voice sent a chill down her spine.

His face remained pleasant, with no hint of his earlier anger. He said, "If we want steak at our wedding, my sweetheart, we're going to have to pay for it. Hank doesn't owe me anything for another man's carelessness. He knows as much."

Relief washed over Lisa.

"I didn't ask him for a favor, just as I won't ask Abbie May for one, either. Even though Abbie May owes me much more than Hank ever did. Don't you, Abbie May?"

Beneath the tan on her face, the dressmaker appeared to pale. "Clarence left town."

"Didn't have to, did he? Nobody proved he did anything wrong. If he was the one broke into the telegraph office, he'd have left some kind of clue, wouldn't he? The morning I went to investigate, I'd have found some evidence."

"He got on the stage Saturday before last. I don't know where he went."

"Clarence is an odd stick, he don't fit in the rest of the world. Likes his fancy words, don't he, almost as much as he loves you, Abbie May. He always circles back to you. Just like a horsefly dancing around a cow turd." Donald rested his big palm over the seamstress' smaller hand. "Don't you worry, he'll be back."

"Fifteen hundred," Abbie May said. "I could go fifteen hundred dollars for the gown."

"What about the party dress? The green one you made for dancing, the one without the bustle?"

"No one else has a dress like that. We already agreed on a price. Don't you remember?"

On her words, Donald's entire face turned to stone. His earlier warmth disappeared along with his smile.

Abbie May's face fell, exposing her sad vulnerability. "Thirty-two dollars."

"You see, Lisa, that's what I was talking about. Neighbor helping neighbor." Donald returned his hand to his pocket. "You girls get acquainted. I want that wedding dress to fit like a second skin, Abbie May. Just like it would in Paris."

His lips brushed across Lisa's cheek. His boots striking the floor with authority, he left the shop.

Abbie May looked at her customer. She said, "I hope you know what you're doing."

For the first time, Lisa wondered if she did. *This isn't the man I fell in love with. Donald is harder, coarser… crueler… than I imagined from his letters.*

I could leave. I still have enough money. But what would I return to? My job is gone. The room I let is almost certainly occupied by someone else. There's nothing for me in St. Anders.

I can't stand the idea of starting over. Can't stand knowing what others would think when they saw me again.

Can't stand the idea of being a spinster for the rest of my life.

Speaking very softly, Abbie May said, "There are worse things than being alone." *Yes. She's right. Yes!* Lisa hurried to the store's front door. Throwing it open, she stepped outside – and into her room at the Usher Street boarding house.

Chapter Nineteen

Donald had told her, "Sally Stuckey's place isn't the only boarding house in Tate City, but it's the best. She kept a room empty, waiting for your arrival."

The wooden bedstead nearly filled the space. The frame was large and remarkably stout. The mattress it held was thicker than any Lisa had seen before. At the cost of sixteen dollars a week, she'd been provided with a four-drawer bureau, a single but solid chair, and a washstand with its own bowl and pitcher. The pitcher appeared to be new.

Most importantly, the room had its own full window, not just a tiny transom space. When she drew the curtain from the glass, she could see the church at the end of the street.

Looking there now, she studied the crowd that was forming. Dozens of people were milling outside of the building's large double doors. They were dressed in their nicest outfits, their Sunday clothes. Most of them were walking inside but a few circled around a man in a frock coat and a dark silver vest.

Like horseflies dancing around a cow turd.

She forced the rude thought from her mind. Although she couldn't see anyone's face distinctly from this distance, she knew the man in the silver vest was Donald. He was shaking hands, his head nodding as the other members of the community offered their congratulations.

From here, she couldn't tell if he was smiling or not. He might have been frowning, wondering why his bride-to-be hadn't yet entered the changing room.

A rhyme from her childhood came to her:

> *You'll marry on Monday for health,*
> *You'll marry on Tuesday for wealth,*
> *Wednesday is the best day of all,*
> *Thursday for crosses,*
> *Friday for losses,*
> *and*
> *Saturday for no luck at all.*

Today was Saturday.

Even before she'd left the stagecoach, Donald had scheduled the hour and day of their ceremony. Would he have changed the date, had she asked? She doubted it. It would have inconvenienced Reverend Warner and, besides, he'd already told everyone who mattered.

Everyone except for her. She'd been the last to know.

Opening the bureau's third drawer, she removed the letters her fiancé had sent her. Sinking onto the bed's mattress, she released the ribbon tying the notes together. Picking an envelope at random, she unfolded the paper inside and read its message.

My darling...

The letter itself spoke of nothing grand or important but a sense of joy infused its words. When Donald put his thoughts to paper, he dropped his pretense of being a blustery, self-important pillar of local society. In private, an oil lamp providing the light to guide his pen, he allowed himself to be seen for who he was at heart.

His handwritten words revealed him to be a gentle man, concerned for his community and eagerly desiring to build a family. A lonely but loving man, seeking his soul mate.

From outside, the church bells rang. Once, twice.

It was two o'clock. The wedding was to start at two-thirty.

This is the Donald I know, Lisa thought, the letter in hand. *This is the man I shall wed. Not the public figure, strutting to impress the city politicians, but the sweet soul who shared so many of his inner secrets to me.*

Is he embarrassed to have revealed so much? Perhaps so. He's lived behind a façade for so long, he must wonder how to escape it.

I shall show him.

Tears filled her vision and she dropped the paper to dab at the corners of her eyes. Removing the expensive wedding gown from its hook on the wall, she laid it beside the collection of letters. In a reflective mood, she slowly unbuttoned her outer garment.

She was stepping into the wedding dress when her landlady entered the bed chambers. Carrying a clutch of orange blossoms in one hand, Mrs. Stuckey said, "I worried I was running late. I'm pleased you're still here."

"Time slipped away from me, I'm afraid. There's no time to change at the church now. Can you help?"

The middle-aged woman tightened the laces on the dress. "You'll be a sight, walking from here to the church. It will excite some conversation."

"A touch of excitement never hurts."

A worried tone entered the older woman's voice. "The sheriff doesn't appreciate it when tongues wag about him or his."

"You've known him for a while, haven't you, Mrs. Stuckey? You know he's a good man."

Instead of answering, she picked up Lisa's fallen letter. Her eyes scanned over the words. "This is sweet."

Lisa stepped into her embroidered shoes. "It's a private message, not to be shared."

"Don't worry, my dear, Clarence won't mind. He isn't one for secrets. He hasn't had an unshared thought since he was a boy. Pour him a glass of whiskey, he'll write you a poem. Offer him a bottle of Old Overholt, he'll pen a novel."

"Clarence? The dressmaker's husband?"

"I recognize the writing. I've used Clarence myself, for letters of sympathy and such. You want to watch your valuables when he's around, but he can find the words for any occasion."

Turning the letter over, the landlady saw the note at its bottom: *Forever yours, Donald Skroch*. She dropped the page, her face turning pale.

Lisa said, "Donald didn't write this, did he? He didn't write any of the messages he mailed to me."

"I shouldn't have spoken. It wasn't my place."

"I've been such a fool." Lisa buried her face in her hands. Fighting the panicked sensation building inside of her, she said, "Such a stupid, *stupid* fool."

"You mustn't blame yourself."

"Who else is responsible? Whatever shall I do? Where shall I go?"

"It's your wedding day," the other woman reminded her. "Despite your doubts, you go to the church."

"I go to the church? What does that mean?" When she didn't get an answer, she said, "Mrs. Stuckey?"

A bird chirped from outside, causing her to look in its direction. When she turned back, Lisa found herself standing outside of the church's side door.

I'm dreaming. But why did it feel so real?

Donald was in front of her, dressed for their wedding. The pearl buttons on his silver vest matched his pearl-colored gloves. He looked angry.

She was wearing her wedding gown. It had been laced so tightly, Lisa could barely breathe.

"Where in Hades have you been?" Donald asked. "I want you inside."

"I can't. I won't. I'm so sorry, this is a mistake."

Using the fingers of his left hand, Donald removed the right glove. "You decide this today, you stupid bitch?"

He hit her in the stomach and Lisa fell to the ground. Afraid he'd strike her again, she covered her face with her arms.

The side door opened and someone stepped outside. Donald paid no attention to the newcomer.

"Stand up," he told Lisa.

"It was a mistake!" she cried.

When Donald raised his hand, Pearce caught the other man's wrist. "You're not to touch her."

The cowboy was dressed in the same dusty clothing he'd worn at the Broken H. Taller than the sheriff but not as solidly-built, he stepped in front of his adversary.

Donald fought to pull his hand free but couldn't break his vise-like grip. "She's mine."

"She doesn't want to be."

"But she is. If she runs, I'll track her down."

Lowering her arms slowly, Lisa said, "I'll go somewhere you can't find me."

"I'll find you," Donald swore. "I'll punish you."

"Not while I'm with her," Pearce promised.

"No one can stop me."

*****

Blinking her eyes, Lisa found herself lying in her bed. Pearce bent over her, wiping a cool cloth along her forehead. "Are you all right?"

"All right? Yes. Yes, I suppose so."

"You called out."

"I was dreaming."

He said, "Who is Donald?"

"Donald?"

"When you were sleeping, you said the name. Twice."

Lisa sat up. "I've been asleep?"

"Since yesterday," Pearce said. "I came in this morning when I heard you cry out."

She recognized the pearl gray color of the walls surrounding her and the lined cheesecloth curtains over the window.

She was at home. In her bedroom.

Her hand went to the hair on her head. "My bonnet is gone. My shoes are off."

"I put you to bed."

"To *bed?*"

Awkwardly, Pearce said, "I couldn't leave you outside, could I? I wasn't going to lay you on the floor."

"Lay me?"

"I put you in… in… a safe place. On your bed."

Her fingers found the top of her blouse. "You unbuttoned me."

"Only the top two buttons," he said, trying to sound calm but not quite succeeding. "I wanted you to be comfortable."

"Get out," she said in a low voice.

Pearce escaped into the hallway as the door slammed shut behind him.

Chapter Twenty

By the time Lisa entered the kitchen, she'd cleaned herself and replaced her blouse. She couldn't do anything about the skirt. It was in need of a washing, but that was a chore that would have to wait.

Despite her lengthy rest, she still didn't feel right. When she'd stood up from the bed, she'd fought against a wave of dizziness. The mirror had revealed that her face wasn't flushed, but her skin still felt warm.

She didn't care to share any of this with her houseguest. Walking slowly, she fought to conceal the wobble in her step. "Something smells good."

Pearce stood at the oven. "Chicken and dumplings."

"You found one of the chickens?"

Holding a large wooden spoon, he stirred something inside her biggest metal pot. "I expect the coyotes finished those birds before the storm had passed."

Lisa sat at the kitchen table. "There's meat in the pot. I can smell it. There was nothing fresh in the larder."

"There's very little of anything in your larder. Barely enough corn meal and flour to make the dumplings. Just a touch of apple cider left, too. Enough, though. You'll find it adds a bit of bite to the broth."

"You cook?"

"A man on the trail has to pick up a few tricks here and there. As I said, I enjoy chicken and dumplings – even when I lack a chicken."

The aroma in the air made Lisa's mouth water. "What did you use? Jerky?"

He grunted a vaguely negative noise.

"If you'd gone hunting, I think the gun fire would have awakened me." A new, more worrisome thought occurred to her. "Not King Richard."

"Ted loved to name his critters." Lifting the spoon to his mouth, Pearce sipped at the fluid. "How old was that bird, anyway? There was no white to its meat, anymore."

"You used the rooster."

"I did."

"I'm not going to eat that!"

"You will, even if I feed you by hand. A body can't function without fuel. You've been starving yourself, either through grief or lack of food. You need sustenance."

"King Richard died almost two days ago."

"Fortunate that it's been cool the last few days." The body of the spoon found something red and he lifted it to his mouth. Pearce ate it with obvious pleasure. "Chewy, but the flavor's there."

"The meat will poison you!"

"I wouldn't eat it if I believed so." He filled two bowls with the stew. Carrying them to the table, he left the first in front of Lisa. "It will help you get better."

From inside the bowl, golden yellow dumplings teased her. Despite her fears, Lisa found herself getting hungry.

With the life he's led, the cowboy probably has the disposition to eat whatever he likes, she told herself. *Just look at him.*

His teeth grinding over the meat in his meal, Pearce's strong features gave him an appearance of invincibility. He swallowed with pleasure, confident that a bit of yard kill wouldn't hurt him.

He likely has the constitution of an ox, Lisa thought sourly. The broth smelled delicious, with a hint of pepper and sweet butter playing in the air. *Although the dumplings are probably safe to eat. But what if Pearce used the rooster's broth to bind the dough?*

She already felt less than her best. She didn't want to risk making herself sick.

"This cock lived a good, long life," Pearce said, his spoon dipping into the bowl. "A meal like this is best if the bird is only a few months old, but beggars can't be choosers."

Using the lip of her spoon, Lisa, pulled a small section of biscuit away. Unable to resist it any longer, she slipped it into her mouth and savored its taste.

Ambrosia.

She took another bite of the dumpling before finishing it. A teaspoon of broth followed her last swallow and she realized she had to have more. This simple meal was somehow the most delicious thing she'd ever tasted.

"I didn't realize I was so hungry."

"This part of the world, it's a sin to let food go to waste."

Abandoning all caution, Lisa dipped her spoon into the stew. Stripped of its sinew and silverskin, the rooster's meat required significant chewing but, as promised, its flavor made up for it. Her spoon *tinked* against the bowl, again and again, as she savored each bite.

Her belly was full before the bowl was emptied. Pushing it away, she settled back in the kitchen chair.

"You liked it," Pearce said, pleased.

Lisa smiled.

"Tell me about Donald," he said.

Her good feelings vanished in an instant.

"The second time you called his name, I was at your bedside. You appeared distressed."

Who is Donald? Lisa folded her hands before her. *How is it I have no immediate answer for this simple question?*

Is Donald the honorable officer of the law that I thought I was marrying? The gentleman that shared cigars with the mayor while I sat primly at his side?

Or is he the bully who beat the dressmaker's husband, hurting him so badly that he fled the state?

Given only a piece of my story, Uncle Ted never asked any questions. Knowing almost nothing about me or my life, Pearce Folsom demands to hear more.

He watched her, his calm expression revealing nothing of his feelings.

Do I lie to him? Lisa asked herself. *In one form or another, wasn't that always my plan?*

Should I tell the truth? If I do, he'll be gone by mid-day. He owes me nothing.

It pained her to think of losing Pearce. The feeling ached inside of her, real and unwanted but undeniably present. She had no desire to question exactly why she felt this loss would sting.

Lightly, she brushed a loose hair away from her forehead. Her skin felt warm, reminding her that she still didn't feel right. "Have you ever been frightened?"

"Everyone's been scared."

"Not you."

Pearce wasn't like the other men she'd met. When he was a child, there must have been times when he'd wanted to cry or felt like running away. Fully grown, she didn't believe he'd ever known such weakness. No matter the odds, he wouldn't run from anybody.

Lisa said, "A year ago, I turned twenty-four years of age. I remember wondering if I wanted to bake myself a cake."

"You leave that task to friends and family."

"All I had was my job. I was a clerk at Ferring and Sons. They're a progressive firm, willing to hire females for the position. Most of their competitors refused to even interview a woman. There were three of us at the company, and they paid us nearly as well as the men."

"Did you bake that cake?"

"It felt too sad. I went into work. I didn't have anywhere else to go. I didn't have –" She sighed. "Didn't have much of anything else at all."

"A woman like you, you must have had a hundred beaus."

"Not nearly so many." Focusing on the bowl in front of her, she refused to meet Pearce's eyes. "When I was twenty-two, I was engaged to a man named Martin Hupp. He was a bit older than me and established, qualities which I admired. He was an accountant, with regular hours and a reliable job. I admired that, too."

"You loved him." Never having met Martin, Pearce said the words without irony.

He can believe as he wishes, Lisa thought.

Martin had been a nice man with limited ambitions. Pleasant in appearance, genial in attitude, he was considered a worthwhile catch by the other two women working in the clerical department. His wit was mild, he rarely angered, and he was dependable.

There's value in a dependable man, Lisa admitted to herself. *Ask anyone who's ever had a feckless partner or an unemployed, alcoholic parent. They'll tell you the same.*

It didn't matter that Martin never set my heart afire. We could have made a home, the two of us. We would have had children. We would have built a life.

Pearce, hot-blooded and clearly reckless, affected her differently than the stable accountant. Even the memory of his kiss was better than any intimacy she'd shared with Martin.

Not that she'd share such feelings with the man in front of her.

"Brain congestion took him, well before his time," she said. "At first, I was lost. Unsure of what to do, where to go, I did what I'd been doing. I stayed at my desk."

Day after day passed as she performed some variation of the same monotonous task but she knew she was lucky to have the job. Even in a big city like St. Anders, there were limited employment opportunities for a woman. Lisa didn't have the temperament to be a teacher and wouldn't have enjoyed factory life, where the workers stitched boots or jackets, shirts or dresses, until their fingers bled. If she hadn't been accepted at Ferring and

Sons, she would have had to work as a domestic, cleaning for others.

Better by far to make her living in an office, shuffling sales reports and filing records.

"Twenty months after Martin died, I continued to spend my nights in solitude. My mother passed away six years ago and I lost my father a year later. All of my friends had married or moved on. I had one living relative, a distant uncle in a distant state."

"Ted."

"I'd lost touch with everyone. Only I remained in the same city, at the same address, doing the very same things I'd always done."

She reflected, *I began to fear I'd spend all of my days in that windowless office, performing meaningless tasks. I had no chance at promotion. Ferring and Sons might have been progressive, but they weren't innovators.*

I was desperate for a change.

Blessedly, Pearce couldn't read her thoughts.

Reaching for the soup bowl, she turned it in her hands. "On that day, my birthday, someone left a copy of the Gazette at the office. I'd seen notices for mail-order brides before, I expect everyone has, but this was the first time I took the time to examine the advertisements. There were almost a dozen listings."

"Lonely men."

Was there disdain in his statement? She believed there was; after all, women flocked around a man as handsome as Pearce. Not knowing what it was like to be ordinary, he – like Quincy Fix – looked down on women like her.

"Lonely men seeking lonely women," Lisa snapped at him. "Do you find such efforts shameful?"

"I didn't say as much, did I?"

"The specific words weren't needed, Mr. Folsom, I heard it in your voice." She stood up abruptly, facing him. "I thank you for the meal –"

Dizziness gripped her as the room swirled in front of her eyes. Lisa's legs buckled as she started to fall.

Pearce's strong arms wrapped around her, holding her. As the room behind him faded into whiteness, she heard him say in alarm, "You're burning up."

Chapter Twenty-One

The buggy's smaller front wheels bounced over a pocket in the trail, sending a shudder throughout the carriage. Pearce gave an alarmed look at the resting passenger beside him.

Lisa's eyes were closed and her cheeks were reddened. Shaded by the buggy's folding hood, she didn't stir as the vehicle rocketed along the gravel path.

Is she still breathing? The thought clutched at him when Pearce realized he couldn't tell if her chest was rising. *She has to be. If anything happens to her….*

The carriage jerked sharply, its right rear wheel striking a large stone lining the path. Tugging on the reins, he directed Pearl to return to the center of the pathway. He was still staring at Lisa when her mouth dropped open and she exhaled softly. Taking a breath in, she shifted in her chair.

Relief flooded over him. Snapping the reins, Pearce urged the horse to go faster. Ever obedient, Pearl increased her speed.

Most likely, this was the fastest she'd moved since she was a filly. He was certain that it was the fastest she'd gone while pulling Ted's double buggy.

This is taking too long, Pearce thought. *If I was on Gambit, we'd be flying over this road.*

No one else in Burdick County rode a mustang. Wild horses, broken or not, were considered too unpredictable. The horse and buggy served as the West's preferred mode of transportation.

A carriage was safe. It was dependable. It was –

Too damned slow! Pearce gritted his teeth. They'd already been on the trail for over an hour.

In truth, he knew the two-seater was his only available option. Lisa wasn't fit enough to travel on Gambit's back. If he'd ridden with his arm around her, he'd have had to sacrifice the steed's amazing speed to keep her safe. They wouldn't have reached the Ridge any sooner and there was a strong possibility that the trip would have been delayed even longer.

A helpless feeling clawed at him. He didn't like it. He was used to finding solutions and resolving problems. He was used to fixing things.

Everything except his own life. That was the one challenge Pearce had never successfully conquered.

The buggy swept beneath a strand of trees and – *Thank you, Lord* – the town of Wyatt Ridge became visible in the distance. Shortly thereafter, the trail widened, growing into a street that fed through the center of the business district. The buggy raced past the first series of structures lining both sides of the road. The carriage's spinning wheels turned heads as Pearl thundered along the stretch.

"Easy, girl." Pulling on the leather straps in his hands, Pearce slowed the animal. "There are other buggies here, too many other people. We can't afford an accident now. Not when we're so close."

Without the wind rushing past him, he suddenly became aware of the sounds around him. The noises jumbled together: the clopping of horses' hooves, the creak of tradesmen's wagons, and the indistinct mutterings of surrounding voices. Pounding through it all was the sound of nails being driven through lumber.

Ahead of him, he saw a different Wyatt Ridge than the one he'd last visited. Empty lots had been replaced by new stores. A wooden sidewalk had grown along the right side of the street and its left-sided twin, not yet discolored by age or footprints, was being nailed together as he passed.

Pearl trotted along, unconcerned by the ringing sound of metal against metal. The harsh noise penetrated Lisa's slumber.

Her eyes opened.

"How do you feel?" Pearce asked.

Slowly, she sat up. "Where am I?"

"The Ridge."

"What am I doing here?"

"You're not well."

"I'm fine. A little tired, that's all." She tightened her fingers around the curved bar at the side of her seat, steadying herself. "Take me home."

"You can barely sit upright." In a voice that brooked no nonsense, he added, "I'm going to get you help."

Guided by her driver's hand, Pearl stopped in front of a white-washed two-story home. Leaving his seat, Pearce dropped to the ground.

Lisa remained on the buggy. Fighting against the fog of her fever, she surveyed the house with surprise. "This is Mike McCauley's place."

"Let's hope the doctor is ready for patients."

"I'm not seeing him." She tried to rise from her seat, but her legs refused to hold her. "He's a quack. His ointments and potions don't work."

"Saved more than he's killed," Pearce argued, lifting Lisa from the buggy and throwing her over his shoulder.

"Let go of me!"

"Once we're inside."

"This instant!" His captive's fists padded against the middle of his back.

Keeping one arm pinned against her legs, Pearce carried her up the building's steps. If Lisa had been at full strength, her blows would have carried an impact. As weakened as she was, her fists made little impression.

This realization worried him further.

His leg brushed the porch swing as he went past it and to the house's front entrance. Using his free hand to twist the entry's brass knob, he threw the door open.

"Pearce Folsom!" Lisa cried.

At the end of the front hallway, a round-bellied man toddled into view. His shirt was open and his suspenders dangled from his waist. Irritably, he said, "What is this?"

"You have a patient, Doc."

McCauley frowned. "Not on Wednesdays. I'll make you an appointment."

"An appointment?"

"You can come here tomorrow."

"Lisa is sick," Pearce told him. "You'll examine her now, Wednesday or not. I'm not leaving until you do."

The force behind his voice stirred the man. Pulling his suspenders into place, the doctor buttoned his white shirt. "I don't appreciate your tone."

"I warn you, it won't improve over time."

"I always require an appointment before I see patients." Before his visitor could respond, McCauley said, "I'll make an exception this time. This one time. But I'll charge you an extra fee for the privilege."

"Fair enough."

Still barefoot but otherwise properly attired, the physician pressed his pince-nez spectacles onto the bridge of his nose. Giving Pearce a puzzled look, he asked, "Have we met?"

Kicking the front door closed, Pearce sighted the examination room. He walked toward it.

The physician hurried after him. "Is that Miss Hanlon in your arms?"

"I'm *not* staying – ooph!" Lisa lost her breath when Pearce dropped her to the office settee. By the time she'd sat up, he'd retreated to the office doorway.

Once the doctor had joined them, Pearce blocked the room's only exit.

Lisa said, "This man brought me here against my will."

"Is this true?"

"Absolutely," Pearce agreed.

The doctor's gaze went to the gun belt around his visitor's waist. "If I must, I'll call the sheriff. He's not far from here."

"Lisa's ill. She needs medical attention."

"Return me to the ranch!" she insisted.

McCauley tugged at an ear. "You've been with her, I take it. What are her symptoms?"

"She was soaked in the big storm. Since then, she hasn't been eating. She can barely stand, and she's running a fever. She's red hot." Although he tried to conceal it, an undercurrent of emotion throbbed in Pearce's voice.

"Don't touch me," Lisa said. "Neither of you is to touch me."

Despite her stern words, she didn't react when the older man placed the back of his hand against her forehead. McCauley nodded at some unspoken thought. He ran his fingers along both sides of her neck before nodding again. "It wasn't wet clothing that caused this."

"Can you help her?"

"Relax, my worried friend. This, too, will pass. In a week or so, she'll fully recover."

"Completely?"

"I promise you."

A long, deep sigh escaped from Pearce. He felt as if he'd been given a gift. "What's the matter with her?"

"Saint Vitus Fire. There was an outbreak in this county, oh, three years ago. The Morris family got it as bad as any. They placed the blame on bad well water."

"The Broken H feeds from a clean source," Pearce said.

"You know that for a certainty?" McCauley rolled up a sleeve, bringing a beefy arm to come into view. "Ted wasn't himself of late, he let a few things slip. Unless you tested the water?"

"No." *I should have checked the well*, Pearce thought. *It wouldn't have taken much time.*

He remembered saddling his horse as he prepared to leave the Broken H. He'd been willing to let Lisa's words drive him away even while recognizing that the homestead needed his skills.

But testing the well was only one of the many issues that needed to be addressed at the homestead. If he was going to do a proper job of tending to the property, he'd have to finish repairing the barn, repair the main house, replace the fence line, build a new chicken coop….

The list seemed endless.

McCauley said, "First of this week, Rupert Capehart came to see me. He displayed the same signs as Miss Hanlon here: poor appetite, flushed face and general weakness. His temperature was high and climbing. Saint Vitus Fire, I diagnosed, despite the fact that no one has seen that shyster take a sip of water since he was a lad."

"What are you saying?"

"No one truly knows what sparks the disease. Bad well water, possibly, if the honorable Mr. Capehart used it as a chaser. Maybe something else. Perhaps something in the dirt or something carried in the air. Keith and Deborah Morris recovered. Capehart will, too, now that he's been treated."

Her eyes closed, Lisa let herself sink against the settee. She appeared content to let the conversation carry on around her.

Pearce asked, "What's the treatment?"

"Since constipation is an issue, I'll start with laxatives. Three of them, thirty minutes apart."

Lisa's eyes opened abruptly. "Purges?"

McCauley put his hand on Pearce's arm. "This is nothing you'll want to see."

"You're right."

"You can wait on the porch, if you like. There's a swing there, as well as a sitting table with some chairs. When the weather's nice, it's rather pleasant."

"I think I'll stretch my legs. See a bit of the scenery."

Pearce allowed himself to be directed toward the front entry. McCauley opened the door. "Give us a couple of hours."

At the end of the front walk, Pearl waited beside the hitching post. Pearce said, "Can I leave the horse?"

"My boy can tend to your animal. Have a sandwich, get a drink. The Glory Hole is the big building at the end of the street. You play farobank?"

"I've seen a cat-hop or two."

"Pearce!" Lisa cried from the examination room.

"By the time you return, she'll be ready to go."

The door clicked shut behind him.

Chapter Twenty-Two

"Take me home!" Lisa's voice carried to the landing. Her agitated tone couldn't be fully silenced, even behind the thick walls of the house.

It's for her own good. Pearce watched as the physician's helper freed Pearl from her harness. *Lisa will understand this in time. She'll realize I was looking out for her best interests.*

"Pearce Folsom!" she shouted from inside.

Quickening his step, Pearce left the porch. The sounds of construction continued around him as he followed the sidewalk. With Lisa in the doctor's care, his mood lifted. She might not believe in the physician, but he had faith in the man. He hadn't cured Ted, but there comes a time in a person's life when a cure simply isn't possible.

Hearing that McCauley had stuck around to dig the grave, he'd earned Pearce's respect. Most of the people in his profession would have left the task to the deceased's nearest kin.

Lisa's in good hands, Pearce reflected. *Two hours for her treatment. Enough time to do what's needed.*

He dropped his hand to his front pocket. Ted's "hidden" coffee can had contained less than a sawbuck, not nearly enough to stock Lisa's pantry, but he hadn't expected to find much. Pearce had his own ideas on how to get her the things she needed.

Ahead of him, a single-bucket carriage slowed to allow a man to cross the street. The walker, his skin bronzed by the sun, strode with purpose down the sidewalk. When the sun glinted against the badge on the stranger's chest, Pearce felt a sinking feeling.

The man stopped directly in front of him. Six inches shorter than Pearce, he held himself as if he were a taller man. Not speaking, he let his eyes sweep over the newcomer.

Pearce did his best to appear pleasant and nonthreatening.

The man said, "I'm Sheriff Bishop."

Pearce tipped his head in response. In his previous experiences with the law, he'd learned there was nothing to be gained by opening your mouth and saying the wrong thing at the wrong time.

"I try to meet any visitors who come to the Ridge," Bishop said in way of introduction, the words coming out in a slow drawl. Powerfully-built, his white hair was thinning. It appeared to be the lawman's only physical concession to the aging process. "The interesting ones, anyway. You are just a visitor?"

"I've been here before, Sheriff."

"Must have been a while ago. Otherwise, you'd know the town council doesn't approve of a display of firearms in our community."

He hooked his thumb toward the building at his side. A sign had been fixed to the wall, new enough that its nail heads were bright and without any sign of rust: *All revolvers to be left at the Sheriff's Office.*

"That's new. It wasn't a rule, three years ago."

"It isn't the law yet," Bishop said. "Will be once the calendar year rolls around. The signage is up a tad early, allowing our good citizens to get used to the idea. They bring me their guns to hold, I give them a token. They bring me the token, I return their weapons. Then they leave."

He lifted a shiny brass coin, stamped with a number. He held it in his hand, offering this stranger an opportunity to be among the first to accept this new custom.

If he'd been on this sidewalk carrying an old Army .44, Pearce suspected Bishop would have let him pass without a confrontation. Wearing a pair of silver pistols with ivory handles, he'd sparked the policeman's attention.

Bishop was giving him a choice. Pearce could play the proper citizen and turn over his revolvers or be forever marked as a potential trouble-maker.

With the incident in Tucson fresh on his mind, he didn't want to be considered as a person of interest, but he couldn't afford to be without his guns, either. In a few minutes, he was going to need them.

Pearce asked, "By chance, do you hail from Wilmington?"

"Why do you ask?"

"Just curious."

"I lived in Ashfork, some years ago." The sheriff's arm lowered, the token still pinched between his thumb and forefinger. "It's a bit further up in the mountains. I grew up among a few dozen farmers and miles of empty land."

"I thought I recognized the accent." Taking a deep breath, Pearce said, "My family does a lot of business in North Carolina."

Since the day he'd left the Granville estate, he'd never used his family name to gain favor. This one time, for Lisa, he'd try.

Bishop curled the token inside his hand. "What's your name, friend?"

"Pearce. My father is Randall Folsom."

"Randall Folsom." Bishop's eyes narrowed, accenting the wrinkles on his face. "Folsom Mercantile."

"My family's business."

"Small world." The older man's expression smoothed, locking his feelings from view. "Years back, when Ashfork was new, your father's company kept half of my community alive. He took script when other places wouldn't. I imagine that decision cost him dearly when the rains stopped falling."

Pearce had only been a boy during the years of the drought. Although he vaguely remembered his parents dealing with an army of bankers, they'd hidden their financial problems from him and his brothers.

Bishop continued, "Of course, your father's generosity had its limits. When the crops stopped growing, his policies changed. Script quit being accepted. If a farmer couldn't barter or didn't have gold, he didn't receive the things he ordered. Couldn't get a single bag of seeds from Folsom Merc. A promissory note wasn't enough."

"Everyone was struggling then."

"It was harder or some than others. Folsom Merc is still in business. Bigger than ever, from what I've heard."

"I suppose so."

"Funny how your family's name brings back old memories," he said, not sounding as if it were funny at all.

"I was two states away when I got the letter telling me my uncle had lost his farm. I'd like to say he tried, old Bill Filke, raising tobacco and his sister's son at the same time, but he did a half-assed job of both. Not a surprise he lost it all."

Bishop's comfortable delivery never changed, each word arriving without urgency or emotion. Discussing his uncle's failure, he might as easily have been musing over a change in the weather. His even tone revealed nothing of any personal interest or animus.

"Quite a while ago, though, wasn't it?" Pearce reminded him.

"Family is owed a debt even when it wasn't earned. I still owe Bill Filke."

"What are you saying?"

"Your name carries no value here," Bishop told him. "Knock on my door for a favor, you'll not receive it."

Pearce felt an angry and familiar heat rise inside of him. He couldn't remember any lawman ever favoring him, regardless of the situation. "Anything else you care to share?"

"Wyatt Ridge isn't a moneyed community. Your hand-tooled belt and your expensive toys are going to attract unwanted attention. There aren't any of your kind here."

"My kind? What kind is that?"

"The wrong kind."

Pearce fought to control his anger.

"Want to take a swing at me, son?" Bishop asked. "I'll bet you do. I see it in your face."

As if it had a will of its own, Pearce's hand curled into a fist.

Chapter Twenty-Three

The sounds of the town disappeared in the stillness of the air around them. In that moment, there was only Pearce and the sheriff, standing toe-to-toe.

Bishop's lip curled slightly, unable to fully conceal the smile he was trying to hide.

He wants me to start a fight, Pearce realized. *He's been trying to spark one.*

This realization cooled his anger. Stepping to the edge of the sidewalk, Pearce noticed a thin, pock-faced man partially hidden in the open doorway of Arnold's Dry Goods. The pockmarked observer was watching him, one of his hands resting on the butt of a revolver.

If Pearce hadn't moved to the side, he wouldn't have seen him. Reacting slowly, this second man tried to edge out of sight. Blocked by a customer exiting from the store, he lowered the hat from his head, clumsily trying to cover the badge on his chest.

Caught you, Pearce thought, *and just before you could catch me.*

The sheriff said, "You're tense as a wire, boy, and ready to snap. Something the matter?"

"Not at all," he replied, knowing that Bishop was correct. His entire body remained coiled, ready for action. Fighting against his urge to act, he said, "Last time I hit a man with a badge, he deserved it."

"Or so you believed."

"You're correct about that. Didn't much matter to the judge, though. I still spent three weeks behind bars."

"The experience seems to have taught you a lesson. Maybe you're a mite smarter than I thought." Reaching for the brim on his hat, the law officer adjusted it. "I'm surprised to hear it."

"Surprised about what, sheriff? That I was unfairly imprisoned or that I won't be goaded into a fight I can't win?"

"Surprised your Daddy didn't pull strings to keep his baby boy out of the hoosegow," Bishop responded. "Bring those widow-makers into the Ridge again, Folsom, I'll lock you up. It won't matter if it's before January. I'll find a reason."

His boots striking the wooden planks, the lawman left. When he passed the dry goods shop, the pock-faced man fell in step with him.

How long was your deputy hiding there, Bishop? Pearce wondered. *He didn't follow you as you crossed the street. I'd have seen him.*

Maybe you sent him ahead, the minute you saw my gun belt. By then, you'd already decided I was someone to be watched.

Your personal dislike of the Folsom family was simply a bonus. Guess I should be grateful I'm still free.

Pearce had been arrested without cause before, most notably in Santa Fe, New Mexico. Of course, in Santa Fe, he'd been a younger man, still enamored with risk-taking.

He'd been caught with his trousers down in the mayor's bedroom. The mayor's wife had remained hidden beneath the bed covers while he was being escorted from the house.

"Nothing happened," Pearce muttered, entering the dry goods store. "There wasn't time. Besides, I didn't even know she was married!"

"Pardon?" a heavyset woman said. Maintaining a proprietary air, she remained behind the store's front counter.

Pearce surveyed the inside contents of the room. Shelving lined the walls. Wherever there was an inch of space, it had been filled with product or loaded with boxes. Food items and other consumables were the largest part of the building's first floor inventory. Actual dry goods – clothing and crockery, small farm equipment and ammunition – had been relegated to the back wall.

"What happened to the General Store?" he asked.

"Tal Clifford went bust over a year ago," the heavyset woman told him. "This is as good as you'll find."

"Looks pretty fair."

"Economy's getting better. Upstairs or down, you'll find what you want. I have everything from dime novels to rutabagas. If you should happen to have a taste for turnips, the rutabagas are thirty-seven cents."

"I'd rather buy potatoes," Pearce said.

"I have those, too. My name is Felicia Arnold, I own this place. There's not a Mr. Arnold, so don't ask if there is."

"Can I speak to Mr. Arnold?"

Her laughter boomed after Pearce as he continued inside. Away from the front wall's large single window, the shop was blanketed in gloom. A line of lanterns was positioned on a side shelf, black behind their glass. They wouldn't provide light until purchased.

Pearce examined a canister on the shelf before him. It was a tin of Nobel's Baking Powder, just one of the many items he'd hoped to find. His eyes adjusting to the darkness, he located most of the things he wanted. There was oatmeal and spices, molasses and dried beans, honey and more.

The carriage was going to be filled on its trip back to the Broken H. He began to load his arms.

Felicia said, "When Ted Hanlon's buggy rolled by, I saw you holding the reins."

"I'm helping out at the ranch." The statement was true enough in its way. Stacking his initial selections on top of the front counter, Pearce went to the other end of the room for a second set of purchases.

"You don't look like a handyman."

"What do I look like, Felicia?"

"The best kind of a bad mistake."

This time, Pearce laughed.

"If you're good with your hands, all the better." She let her words linger in the air before adding, "Most of the men around here have signed on with one of the construction crews. There's plenty of work available for someone who knows his tools."

"Nice to hear."

"I noticed Louisa Hanlon sharing the buggy with you. She didn't appear to be well." A brass spyglass rested beside the woman's hand. She rocked it casually with her forefinger, unembarrassed by her curiosity.

"I brought Lisa – Louisa – to the doctor." Normally, Pearce wouldn't have shared his personal matters with a stranger. In this case, it didn't matter. The moment Lisa left the doctor's home, word would spread throughout the community.

McCauley had been quick to share his thoughts about Rupert Capehart and the Morris family. As soon as anyone asked about Lisa's health, he'd share those particulars, too. In a town this size, private information didn't remain private for very long.

Pearce had soon collected a second assortment of goods to join the first. With the pile growing, Felicia Arnold began a tally, jotting down quantities and prices.

He went through the store a last time.

This one is for me, he thought, adding one small bag to the pile. *I haven't had a decent cup of Arbuckles in days. Once we're back at the ranch, I'm brewing a pot of coffee.*

Felicia pushed a sheet of paper toward him. "Here's your total."

The string of numbers had added up quickly. The figure at the bottom of the sheet was larger than Pearce had expected.

"I don't take rock," the storekeeper said. "If you're carrying gold or silver, you'll need to bring it to the assay office first."

Releasing his buckle, Pearce placed his gun belt and pistols on the top of the crate near the doorway. "I can offer something better."

"You can keep it. Tal Clifford took barter; it was one of the reasons he went belly-up. My shop operates on cash on the barrelhead. Greenbacks or coins."

"Even without the belt, these guns are easily worth your total. Put them in your window, you'll sell them tomorrow."

"Andy Bishop wouldn't approve. No, thank you."

"Do you need the sheriff's permission t run your business?" Pearce could tell his words had stung the woman. "If I must, I'll sell the guns to someone else."

"I doubt it." There was a comfortable certainty behind her words. "Who do you know wants them?"

"There's always someone."

"Who would you approach? One of the drunks at the Glory Hole?"

"I wouldn't sell a weapon to a drunk."

"That's because you're an honorable man."

Honorable? Pearce had been called many things but "honorable" had never topped anyone's list. "There are those who would disagree with you."

Felicia made a scoffing noise. "I don't rely on the opinions of others."

"I don't have a choice, Felicia. If I had the money, I'd give it to you."

"I suppose you could talk to Clancy Foster, our newly-arrived scribe. When he got here, the first thing he did was to buy himself a Winchester rifle. Second thing he did was prove he didn't know how to use it. I don't doubt he'd love to own a pair of pretty pistols."

There was disapproval in her voice.

Pearce asked, "Where do I find him?"

"One street over, at Amy Marlatt's place," she said. "There's a big 'Rooms to Let' sign. If Clancy can scrape together your asking price, he'll meet it. Then he'll swagger along Main Street, acting as if owning a fancy rig somehow makes him a bigger man."

"I'll go there, then."

"If you do, chances are Clancy will shoot himself in the foot by the end of the day. Unless the fool shoots someone else first."

"Are you serious?"

"Sadly."

"There has to be others."

"Not anyone decent." The brown eyes in her square, plain face told him she was telling the truth. "Anyone buys those is someone looking for trouble. That's what I thought you were, trouble, 'til you opened your mouth."

Reluctantly, Pearce replaced the belt around his waist. "What did I say to change your mind?"

"It's what you didn't say. Trouble enters a room and wants everyone to know it's there. You didn't talk about yourself at all. You didn't even state your name."

"I'm Pearce. Pearce Folsom."

"You staying here, Pearce?"

"Maybe. Might just be passing through."

She grinned. "Not in any hurry, though, are you? That's a healthy amount of rice and beans you've placed on my counter."

"It's not –"

"Not for you, it's for Louisa Hanlon. Am I right?" When he didn't answer, she lifted the sheet from her counter. "Last time she was here, she paid her uncle's debt and left. She didn't buy anything for her pantry. She can't have had much left in stock. Ted lived month to month and there's nothing growing on that ranch she inherited. So, what's she been eating?"

"Not enough," Pearce admitted.

"You sound strangely concerned for your employer." Her smile grew larger as she considered him. "That's a natural thing when a man's smitten."

"The hell I am!" The words burst from his mouth.

If Felicia was offended by his curse, she didn't show it. "Yet you offer your own belongings in an effort to fill her larder. Oh, darling, you're half in love and don't even know it."

This wasn't a conversation that Pearce wanted to have with a shopkeeper. "Love is a strong word."

"Don't be ashamed of it. It's a fine emotion." Taking her pencil in hand, she ran a line through a few of the items. "You don't need the sugar; honey will suffice. Don't need the coffee beans, either; water is better for you and cheaper, too. You can take most of the rest of this."

Pearce studied the store owner. She was direct, she was honest, and she was blunt. Qualities he admired in any person, male or female.

He could at least try to be as open with her. "I'm carrying nine dollars and change. Less, once I settle with McCauley."

"Let me give you a tip about Doc. When you see him again, he'll demand six dollars for services provided, no matter how little he's done. You pay him half and tell him Felicia said not to waste it at the faro table."

"I will."

She wiggled her pencil at the pile of supplies. "I'll run you a tab, Pearce. A month's supply, essentials only, but enough to get Louisa on her feet again. In thirty days, she starts making payments or you do."

"What if we can't afford to pay you?"

"If such a thing happens, you'll return to build me a set of cabinets for my basement. A full set, too, uppers and lowers." She patted his hand. "Ted Hanlon did me right when I needed it. If I can return a favor to his niece, I'm good for it."

Chapter Twenty-Four

Climbing the stairs in front of the doctor's house, Pearce found Mike McCauley sitting on the top front step. The round-bodied man pulled a pipe from his mouth.

"I was reading my Bible last night," the doctor said. "The Good Book disappointed me."

"How so?" Pearce eased himself downward, joining the smoker.

"It spoke of God's blessings, but failed to provide a listing of our Heavenly Father's favorite things. Wouldn't you like to know?"

"I haven't rightly thought about it."

"If I were to make such a list for myself, there would be only four items: tobacco, cards, whiskey and women. In exactly that order."

"A curious listing, placing women at the bottom."

"Due to your Miss Hanlon, the gentler sex has taken a precipitous drop in the standings."

Pearce asked, "Did she take offense to your treatment?"

"I assumed her generalized weakness would leave her compliant to my ministrations." The doctor viewed his pipe moodily. "There was a period in which she most definitely regained her vigor."

"She's feeling better."

McCauley turned his head. Under one eye, the skin was darkening.

"She *is* better," Pearce said with relief.

"My fee is six dollars. Considering my patient's behavior, I should charge you seven."

Pearce pressed three dollars into his hand. "Felicia says you're not to lose it at the tables."

"Felicia Arnold is going to be the death of me." McCauley tucked the bills into his upper shirt pocket. "There are times when I suffer from an uncertain memory, Mr. Folsom, but I will remember what occurred this afternoon. I'm positive of it."

"Some things are hard to forget."

"I'm surprised it took me this long to remember you," he said. "Although it was more than a while ago when Ted Hanlon came to fetch me in the middle of the night. You had a bullet in your shoulder."

"Shoulder still aches when the temperature drops."

The doctor puffed on his pipe. An aroma of cinnamon and peat filled the air. "Lisa's in the examination room, first door on the right. Unless, of course, she's decided to rise up and break things. She's a hellion, that girl."

"She has a temper."

"I believe I'll take a stroll while you go and fetch her. Lovely weather today." Standing, the physician stretched his arms over his head. Seconds later, he was on the sidewalk and walking away.

Opening the door, Pearce peered inside the house. The hallway in front of him was quiet. He listened for the sounds of life.

Silence, he thought. *If Lisa's sleeping, I'll need to wake her. We can't stay much later. The sun will set soon and the doctor will want his house back.*

"I know you're out there, Pearce," she called from the side room. "The hinges creaked."

Entering the corridor, he followed the direction of her voice.

"Take me home," she demanded, unseen but nearby. "You'd best not laugh at me. Not as much as a single snicker."

When he entered the examination room, Lisa was sitting upright on the settee. Her hair was mussed and her dress was wrinkled.

It took Pearce a moment to realize that her face had been painted purple.

"Oh," he said.

"It's iodine. Part of the standard treatment, according to Dr. McCauley."

Pearce forced his mouth closed. Pinching his lips together, he fought to keep a grin from his face. Despite his best efforts, a choked noise escaped from inside his throat.

"If all of this doesn't cure me, I'm going to kill him," Lisa said. "Then you."

*****

Somewhere in the quiet surrounding her, it felt as if something was wrong. Opening her eyes, Lisa lifted her head from the pillow.

It wasn't an unexpected noise that had disturbed her slumber. No, she'd come awake because of what she hadn't heard.

King Richard wasn't crowing.

"King Richard is dead," she remembered. *The rooster isn't calling because I ate him.*

Feeling both guilty about the bird and hungry at the memory of the stew she'd enjoyed, she rolled onto her side.

The events of the day before felt a hazy to her. She vaguely remembered Pearce sitting at the edge of her bed, tenderly wiping iodine from her face. He'd insisted on feeding her when she'd just wanted to sleep. She seemed to recall him tucking the sheets over her, looking at her with concern as he tugged the blankets up to her shoulders.

Lisa thrust the blanket to the foot of the bed. Sitting up, she said, "He tucked me in?"

It was the fever, she thought. *Saint Vitus Fire, McCauley called it. He said the disease would leave me weak and forgetful.*

She wasn't in the clothing she'd worn into town. Her wool nightgown was covering her body. Beneath the nightgown, she wore no underclothing.

She'd never slept with her lower region exposed. Not even as a child. Did that mean –? Did Pearce –?

No, it can't be, she thought. *I'd remember. I'm positive I'd remember.*

I must have come home, changed, and failed to attire myself properly.

It was the only acceptable explanation. Still, there was no doubt that Pearce had been with her in her room. Driven by circumstances, he'd cleaned her. He'd fed her.

He hadn't undressed her.

I've never been so sick that I'd let a stranger take off my clothes. Not in any circumstances.

Her imagination presented some new possibilities for her to consider. She could almost see Pearce slowly unfastening her blouse, his large fingers fumbling with its tiny buttons. His hands brushing against her fevered skin as he slid her satin chemise over her shoulders….

A tremble ran through her body.

It never happened, she told herself. She refused to consider whether the imagined event had left her shivering in shame and embarrassment – or regret.

Swinging her legs over the mattress, Lisa sat at the side of the bed. Dizziness accompanied the action but the sensation quickly passed. When she stood, she felt the best she had in days.

It was time to leave her bedroom and rejoin life.

Dressing herself, she marveled that Pearce had chosen to remain at the ranch and tend to her. No one had pressed such a responsibility upon him. Why, she'd practically ordered him to leave.

He stayed because of Ted. She pulled the tortoise shell comb through her hair. *Because of the obligation he owed him. All of the times they'd shared together.*

In the mirror, her hazel eyes stared out at her from inside her pale face. Her uncle was dead and Pearce's obligation to his friend had died along with him. The gun hand hadn't stayed at the Broken H because of Ted Hanlon.

"He stayed because of me."

Her words held in the air, invisible but potent. It was a revelation.

His actions toward her revealed a depth of emotion that she hadn't suspected. A quiet hope awakened within her. Pearce might try to hide his feelings, even from himself, but he couldn't deny what he'd done on her behalf.

He cared about her.

As it had so often in the past few months, a thin worm of self-doubt crawled inside her thoughts: *That's only because he doesn't know you.*

She'd had these feelings before. They were all too familiar to her.

If he knew what you'd done, her black thoughts continued, *if he knew the kind of person you are, he'd be rid of you. He'd have ridden through that storm to be away from you.*

You're not fit for a good man.

You belong to Donald.

The tines of her brush stopped, caught in a tangle at the back of her head. She tugged at it fiercely, feeling her hair break as the comb came free.

When she examined the tines, she found a tiny ball of brown strands. "No more," she told herself.

She didn't have enough hair to yank it out in anger every time she thought about Donald Skroch. And, in truth, she thought about him too often.

She'd made a mistake and she'd paid the price. Maybe it was time to forgive herself.

It was also time for her to find Pearce and tell him the truth about Donald. Tell him that he was coming, tell him *everything*. If Pearce decided to leave afterwards, he could go. She wouldn't try to stop him.

Opening the bedroom door, Lisa called, "Pearce!"

Her cry went without response from the outer hallway. She was surprised at how empty the house sounded. Checking the mirror and deciding she could reasonably pass for human, she went to find her houseguest.

The hall was empty. The adjoining rooms were unoccupied, too.

In the kitchen, she saw the first evidence that she wasn't alone on the property. A square of paper had been left in the middle of the kitchen table.

In large, block letters, Pearce had written, STAY INSIDE. *P.*

"Your honeyed words stir my heart," she told the note's absent author. Crumpling the note into a ball, she opened the oven's firebox and threw the paper inside.

Straightening, she looked through the window in hope of seeing Pearce. He wasn't present, but there was laundry on the clothesline. Before she'd gotten sick, she'd stripped the thick white cord of all the cleaning. This was another chore he'd completed.

A line of clothing marched from one pole to the next, but her eyes soon focused on the fabric at the center of cord. White and frilled, the bloomers flapped gently under the clouded skies.

My bloomers. She averted her eyes, aghast. *Not even the new pair. The old ones. The* worn *ones.*

There was one mystery solved. Dressing this morning, she'd wondered why she couldn't find them. She'd supposed she'd left them at the physician's home. She'd hoped she hadn't.

Now she wished she had.

Crossing through the front room, she went out on the porch. Overhead, gray clouds filled the sky, dampening its beauty.

"Pearce, where are you? Pearce!"

Somewhere in the distance, she heard a sawing noise. Placing the sound, she realized it was coming from the direction of the field, where the ruins of the bird hutch used to stand.

She wondered, *Is Pearce rebuilding the old hen house?*

The thought filled her with a happy feeling. In her limited experience, men didn't devote their efforts to a project unless they hoped to reap some reward. A person didn't repair a chicken coop unless he expected to someday enjoy a plate of eggs.

It would be months before Lisa could afford to restock the shelter. Did Pearce intend to stay that long?

The sawing noise stopped.

An irrational fear stabbed at her, as if the lack of sound meant that Pearce was no longer at the Broken H. Seconds later, she heard the rasp of metal teeth biting into new wood.

Even if he was rebuilding the coop, it didn't mean he'd remain at the Broken H. Waiting for Lisa to awaken, he might have grown bored and decided to start a new project. There might have been a different reason, too. There was no way to tell with a man like him.

She didn't feel like worrying over it. It was enough that he was here at this time.

Her stomach growled, reminding her of the hour. The chicken and dumplings were gone. If they were going to eat today, Lisa would have to make hard tack taste palatable.

"I'll try my hardest." Feeling determined, she returned to the house and opened her pantry. She stared at the shelves in shock.

The larder was full. There was honey, beans and molasses, baking powder and some dried herbs. When she moved the bags and tins aside, she saw still more supplies.

She knew Ted's old coffee can hadn't held nearly enough cash to pay for all of these items. Then she remembered Pearce's money, lost on the night of his arrival.

His roll of bills, she decided. *That's it. He found his money, then took what he owed Ted and bought food with it.*

It was the only possible explanation for the bounty in front of her. The two of them could eat for weeks.

"Time to make lunch," she declared. Moving a bag of rice aside, she lifted the container behind it and carried it to the table.

Chapter Twenty-Five

Pearce had his back to her. His shoulders glistened with sweat and, as she watched, a slender bead of water ran along his spine and down his narrow waist. The droplet disappeared beneath his belt line, giving Lisa reason to reflect on its journey.

Suddenly aware of her presence, he turned sharply. "Lisa."

"Yes?"

"You're supposed to be in bed."

"I'm tired of being tired," she said. "Besides, I wanted to see what you were doing."

Grabbing his shirt, he pulled it on. "You need rest."

"What about you?" she asked. "Isn't it time you rested?"

"I enjoy being busy." He rolled the shirt's long sleeves down his muscular arms. "Didn't you see my note?"

"Did you leave one?"

"In the kitchen. I told you to stay inside."

"I'm not very good at following orders," she teased. Moving closer, Lisa stood face-to-face with him. "Did you think I'd listen to your commands?"

Pearce buttoned his shirt. "You've been sick. With the weather changing, it's best you stay inside."

"I've spent enough time inside for today. I promise, I won't break."

Behind him, the chicken coop stood on wooden legs. It looked better than she'd ever seen it. Reborn except for its straw beds, every stick of the structure had been rebuilt. Its frame was straight and true, ready for a flock of new occupants.

"It's beautiful," she said.

"The outer wood needs staining. I'll need to do it shortly or the elements will eat at it. It won't last the year." He cast a cautious glance at the overhead sky.

"Lunch first."

He looked at her with surprise.

"Since you're working so hard, the least I could do was prepare our meal."

He followed her as they returned to the house. Entering the kitchen, Pearce removed his hat before sitting at the table.

Lisa dipped her ladle into the pot on the stove. "I hope you like cornmeal mush."

"A trail hand lives on it."

She placed a dish in front of him. "I don't have any vegetables but I do have syrup. Ted never liked his cornmeal mush with vegetables, anyway."

"Ted showed you how to make this?"

"He called it, 'coosh'." Keeping a second plate for herself, she sat across from him. "Did he ever make it for you?"

The handle of his spoon remained curled in Pearce's hand. "Ted's mush was... different than this."

"I've heard it said that no one can ruin cornmeal mush."

"You wouldn't think so." Straightening manfully, he dipped the bowl of the spoon into the mixture.

"Three ingredients: cornmeal, water and salt," she reminded him. "I felt Ted preferred a touch too much salt. Since I was missing milk and sugar, I've added a few spices to it."

Pearce placed the mush into his mouth. His lips closed and, almost immediately, a despairing expression filled his eyes.

"Well?"

He swallowed. Reaching for his glass of water, he drained it.

Lisa tasted the food in front of her. "It's gritty. Ted said that's how it's supposed to be served."

Pearce forced his spoon into the mixture. Trying to appear grateful, he brought the yellow mound to his mouth. Swallowing quickly, he clutched at his drinking glass. Too late, he remembered it was empty.

Lisa pushed her filled glass toward him. "It's terrible, isn't it?"

Pearce emptied the second glass.

"It's barely edible," Lisa said. "I've always thought it was terrible but Ted enjoyed it so much."

He put the second glass beside the first. "Your uncle used to lick rocks. Did he tell you that?"

"A lot of the ranchers taste stones. It helps them identify an area's mineral composition."

"Maybe I should make supper," Pearce said.

Lisa carried the dishes to the sink. She said, "We need to talk."

*****

Leaving the dishes to be cleaned later, they went into the main room. Lisa took the rocking chair, feeling more nervous than expected. Wetting her dry lips with her tongue, she said, "As I told you, I was a mail-order bride."

Taking the ladder-backed chair, Pearce positioned it near her. He sat down.

"The advertisement I answered was quite short. It stated simply that a man of good reputation was seeking a wife."

Pearce nodded encouragingly.

Lisa said, "I don't know why I opened the Gazette that morning. I almost never read the paper and, even then, only if there's important news. But there I was, ignoring the front page for the section on mail-order brides. If it hadn't been my birthday, I doubt I'd have responded. If I hadn't…."

He waited for her to finish her sentence

You promised yourself there would be no more secrets. "If I hadn't spent my morning, crying, I would never have put pen to paper."

She waited for some curt or dismissive response. Men didn't understand it when a woman cried. Her first fiancé, Martin, was uncomfortable at the sight of tears. Donald had laughed when she wept.

Outside, the darkening sky sent shadows into the room. She couldn't read Pearce's expression, but he hadn't left and he wasn't laughing. She could continue.

"Donald and I exchanged letters," she said. "I was touched by what he wrote, the sentiment behind his words. He wrote that I was the kind of woman that he found appealing. I – we – agreed to marry."

173

"Without having met," Pearce said.

"We'd shared photographs with one another." It was only after her photo arrived that Donald had offered a proposal. "It was a leap of faith, yes, but I saw it as an adventure, too. Do you see? Moving to a Western city, falling in love with the town sheriff."

"A sheriff." Pearce made no effort to conceal his dislike of law officers.

"I acted rashly. I had regrets almost as soon as I stepped from the stagecoach, but I'd made a commitment. I didn't love Donald, but I wondered if my feelings might change. When I realized they never would, it was my wedding day."

"Your wedding day?" He sounded disapproving.

"Have you always been perfect, Mr. Folsom? Have you never made a mistake?"

"I'm not perfect."

"You act it. You're so sure of yourself, so confident. You've never for a moment believed you had reason to doubt yourself."

"You think so?"

"Not everyone is as blessed as you. Most of us struggle to get along and those who haven't will never understand. I don't know why I bother talking to you."

The silence that followed her outburst was so thick, it almost felt like a physical thing.

"Don't stop talking to me," Pearce said. "I'd like to hear what happened." When she didn't respond, he added, "I want to know about you."

Thunder boomed outside, emphasizing his statement. Almost at the same time, a tapping noise danced above the ceiling. The tapping sound grew in volume and ferocity as rain began to spit from the heavens.

"It's raining," Pearce said, rising.

Lisa cried, "The laundry!"

Leaping to her feet, she dashed for the rear door. Following after her, Pearce reached her side as she started snatching garments from the clothesline.

Falling in sheets, water poured upon them as they worked to rescue the pieces of apparel. Their arms filled with clothing, they ran back through the kitchen door and dropped the rescued garments onto the table.

"I'm soaked." Taking a piece of cloth, Pearce wiped the wetness from his eyes.

Lisa brushed the hair from her eyes. "That's my, um…"

Taking a surprised look at what he was holding, he quickly returned her pantaloons to the pile.

Trying not to laugh, Lisa said, "We always seem to get caught in the rain."

Pearce grinned. "We do at that."

"I remember the first time."

His expression changed as he focused on her. "I doubt I'll ever forget it."

Just like the night of the midnight shower, Lisa realized her clothing was clinging to her. In several areas, the pink of her body was evident behind the thin fabric.

"Pearce," she said warningly.

He pulled her into his arms.

"Pearce!" she protested.

His lips touched hers and he kissed her deeply. Feeling as if she should resist but not wanting to, Lisa pressed her palms to his chest. Pearce relinquished his hold as she caught her breath. His eyes alive with passion, he studied her upturned face.

What's the matter with me? Lisa asked herself. *If I'm going to be truly honest, I should at least be honest with myself.*

She threw her arms around his neck, kissing him heatedly. His tongue coaxed her lips apart.

She gave a soft moan of protest when he pulled away. He told her, "There's someone coming up the porch."

Lisa couldn't hear anything except for the sound of the rain slapping against the surface of the house. Seconds later, a fist started hammering against the house's front door.

Chapter Twenty-Six

Removing a wet bonnet from her head, Felicia Arnold said, "Clancy Foster is getting on my last nerve."

"Felicia," Lisa said, remembering her visitor from their encounter at the lawyer's office. Once seen, the owner of Arnold's Dry Goods wasn't easily forgotten.

"Clancy swears he can read the clouds. He swore it wouldn't rain today." She twisted the cotton hairpiece, sending water running onto the wooden slats below. Dressed in a loose cotton dress, with a blue shawl over her shoulders, she said, "Aren't you going to invite me in?"

Felicia entered, smiling when she saw Pearce standing beside the wood stove. "You're still here, handyman. I suspected you would be."

"I have some things to fix."

"Does that include you?" Felicia asked Lisa.

"Thanks to Pearce, I'm getting better." Instinctively, Lisa liked the other woman. At any other time, she'd have welcomed her to stay.

Just not at this moment.

She thought, *I was in Pearce's arms. I wanted him and he wanted me. Without a word shared, we both knew it.*

I realize you've just arrived, Felicia. I know you've ridden in your buggy for miles, lost hours from your day.

But would you please go home?

Felicia said, "I told Mike McCauley, the old sawbones, he could come with me today. Any doctor worth his salt needs to check on his patient. For some reason, he declined."

"He's scared of Lisa," Pearce said.

"From the way he acted, you might be right." Taking off her shawl, Felicia draped it over one of the hat stand's extended arms. On the adjoining hook, she placed the bonnet. "Whatever you did, Louisa, do it twice as much next time."

"Call me Lisa," she said.

"Done."

"If Dr. McCauley had come calling, I wouldn't have seen him," Lisa said. "He's lost this patient. I'll not undergo one of his treatments again."

"He's the only doctor in this county."

"Let's hope we find another. Until then, I have Pearce."

He reached out to touch her hand.

Noting the gesture, Felicia asked, "With all this rain, the only part of me that isn't wet is my throat. Can I get a glass of something to drink?"

Lisa led her into the kitchen.

Sighting the pan of corn meal mush, Felicia said, "If there's extra, I'm famished."

Pearce had followed after them. Lisa saw him shake his head warningly.

"When I left today, I forgot to pack a lunch," Felicia said.

"It's gone cold," Lisa said.

"It's gritty," Pearce said.

"Honey, I've eaten mush since I was a child. There's always a bit of grit in it." Gripping the handle of a wide-mouthed spoon, the older woman scooped the porridge from its holder. "Warm is best, but cold is still good."

She tasted the yellow mixture. A second later, she threw the spoon into the pan. She waved her fingers at an empty water glass and Lisa filled it.

Felicia spilled the contents down her throat in a long, single pour. Slamming the tumbler to the table, she gasped for air. "My stars."

"Let me get you some more water," Pearce said.

"It's dreadful," Lisa admitted.

Felicia accepted the refilled water glass. "I prayed Ted's recipe had died along with him." Studying the remainder of the meal, she announced, "We can save this."

"You can?" Lisa said.

"You can?" Pearce said.

"Not while there's a man in here, standing over us," she said. "This requires a woman's talents. You're a handyman. Go outside and do something handy."

"In the rain?"

"You're waterproof." When he refused to budge, she added, "If you don't leave this instant, I won't share any of my cooking secrets."

Pearce viewed the back window, streaked with sheets of rain. He was clearly reluctant to abandon the warmth of the house for the chill of the outdoors.

Lisa could imagine the thoughts going through his head: *It's wet and getting wetter. Anything I work on can be fixed on another day.*

A sunnier day. A drier day.

But if I insist on staying here, the mush will remain as it is. The cornmeal bag is near full and the time will come when Lisa will serve it again. Poisoned with a new variation of spices, perhaps, but the same *awful mush.*

And I'll have to force myself to eat it....

He peered down at Felicia. As stout as a tree trunk, the shop owner waved her hands, shooing him from the kitchen.

"I'll check on the horses," he said.

Once he'd stomped out of the house, Felicia said, "Let's scrub out the pan. We need to do this over."

"I thought you could save what I'd made."

"No one can save this. That's one of my secrets, Lisa. If you want to impress your man, it never hurts to perform the occasional miracle. Turning Ted's spackle into something edible doesn't exactly qualify as water into wine, but it's near enough."

"I don't want to impose upon you. We can try this another time."

"Tonight."

From the store owner's determined tone, Lisa knew she'd stay until she'd done as she intended. Silently conceding defeat, she asked, "Who said Pearce was my man?"

"I wouldn't be here if I didn't think so." Finding the pantry, Felicia collected what she needed. Setting a pan of water to heat on the Dutch oven, she added a dash of salt.

"Oh, that's not nearly enough," Lisa said.

"Who told you differently?"

"Uncle Ted."

"There you go. Ted Hanlon started chewing tobacco when he was twelve. The nasty habit colored his teeth and ruined his taste buds. A teaspoon is exactly what we want."

She stirred cornmeal and cold water together as the contents of the pan began to boil.

"Uncle –"

"He poured his cornmeal directly into the boiling water," Felicia interrupted her. Slowly, she fed the mixture into the hot pan. "He didn't know any better. He grew up, thinking mush was naturally lumpy. His mother's fault, I suspect."

"He liked the lumps."

"Must have fallen off of Pearl once too often. Do you have any sugar?"

"No."

"That's right, I told your fella he didn't need to get any. My mistake." Felicia dribbled a fine line of honey into the metal container. Adjusting the pan, she reduced the heat beneath it. "Now we let this simmer for a bit, just until it's nice and thick. Tonight, you'll serve this with a bit of molasses."

Taking a wooden spoon, Lisa moved it through the golden pool. "I don't think either of us have an appetite for more cornmeal this evening."

"This isn't anything like what you've recently eaten," Felicia assured her. "Tomorrow, after the leftover has set up, cut it into slices. Dip the pieces into flour and fry them."

"Fried mush?"

"Don't sound so doubtful. It's delicious. Prepare this properly and Pearce will want to stay home for supper. He'll do anything you like."

At this comment, a flood of ideas entered Lisa's mind, none of which had anything to do with ranch chores. *Such wicked thoughts. A proper lady wouldn't think such things.*

She asked, "How long should this simmer?"

"Ten minutes. When the weather's this wet, a touch more."

Once we're done, you'll return to town, Lisa thought. A glance through the kitchen window promised that travel would soon be possible. "The rain is starting to lighten."

"Monsoon season is temperamental at times." Borrowing the spoon, Felicia brought it to her lips. She nodded approvingly. "As soon as this is done, we can talk."

"More talk?"

"I have another secret to share."

Chapter Twenty-Seven

Felicia chatted about inconsequential things until the food was cooked. Lisa transferred the pan from the top of the Dutch oven and onto a cooling board.

Sitting at the kitchen table, the store owner's pleasant face grew solemn. "I was in my store when the stagecoach came in this afternoon. I watch every Saturday, keeping tabs on who's come to town. If my Ethem decides to return, I'd like to know it first."

"To run him off?"

"Heavens no, he's my husband." She cleared her throat. "Ethem is shiftless, I'm the first to say it. He's always chasing rainbows when the sky is clear, determined to find a pot of gold when there's only an empty kettle to be found. 'Gonna make you rich, Fel,' he's said a thousand times, making me a bit poorer with each misadventure. There are days I'm so mad at him, I could spit. My friends all say I should be done with him. But he's mine, isn't he?"

Lisa joined her at the table. "You told him to leave."

"I told him not to come back. It's a different thing altogether." Her jaw was set, as if she believed Lisa might argue with her.

"Do you expect him to return?"

"A woman can tell when a man is in love with her. He knows he belongs to me."

Not all women. Lisa wished she had such a magical gift.

As if she knew her thoughts, Felicia said, "Just as your Pearce is in love with you."

"There's a certain attraction between us."

"Stuff and nonsense, it's more than that. But you're not quite positive about it because he keeps his feelings to himself. Is that it?"

It's part of it, Lisa thought.

The other part was the mystery of love itself. She felt desire for Pearce, as she knew he did for her, but lust was an entirely different emotion than love.

"Words are cheap, but actions are dear," Felicia said. "When you were sick, your handyman raced that buggy into town as if his own life was on the line. He was desperate to save you."

Lisa didn't remember anything of the trip into town. As ill as she'd been, only Dr. McCauley's treatment for Saint Vitus Fire remained to haunt her.

Felicia said, "After he'd left you with Doc, Pearce came to my store, looking for supplies. Supplies for you, not for himself."

"Food to stock the larder."

"That's right."

"It's not what you think. He owed Ted that money."

"There was money?"

It was Lisa's turn to feel confused. "Fifty dollars. Pearce found his roll of bills and used it to pay you. Didn't he?"

"He didn't have enough scratch to fill a quarter of what he wanted. He offered me his personal IOU just so you could poison your guests with Ted's awful mush." She barked a short laugh, her fist thumping the table.

"You took his promise to pay?" Lisa asked.

"He'll be good for it."

"If that's the secret you wanted to share, I'm glad to know it. I'll be responsible for my own debt."

"That's not it. I didn't mean to say a thing."

"Is it more recipes? It won't be a surprise to Pearce to hear that I'm an awful cook."

"Even at its worst, cornmeal mush never broke a person's heart."

"What then?"

It was obvious from the other woman's face that she was reluctant to share her message. She'd traveled a long distance to offer it but, once the time had come, she was having second thoughts.

"Felicia?"

"Are you in love with another man?" she asked abruptly. "Not your father or your brother. Romantic love, I mean."

"I'm not."

"Have you been?"

Lisa thought of Martin Hupp, the first man who had proposed to her. Her boring but dependable fiancé, never to be remembered with passion.

"There was a time when I told others I was," she admitted. "I wished I was."

"What about your handyman? He loves you, but do you love him?"

"I… I…" Lisa searched for her answer. A relative stranger was asking her a question she still couldn't answer.

Do I love Pearce? She said, "I'm not sure."

"City girls." Felicia rolled her eyes. Taking the other woman's hands in her own, she faced Lisa. "When I knocked on your door, there were only the two of you in the house. Were you pleased to see me?"

"Certainly."

"Liar. How were you feeling before I got here, when it was just the two of you? The truth, now."

"Happy."

"What else?"

"Excited." When Felicia raised an eyebrow, Lisa blushed.

"What else?"

"Safe, secure." Lisa remembered another feeling Pearce brought with him: "Contented."

"Those are the feelings I have when Ethem is home with me. Despite the problems that swirl around that worthless man, I'm more pleased to be with him than without. Always happier when I'm in his arms. In this neck of the woods, we call that love."

Releasing Lisa's hands, Felicia gave the kitchen window a brief look. "If I don't go home soon, it'll be dark out. I don't like riding in the dark. Best to say my piece and be done with it."

"Your other secret."

"Such as it is," she said. "I was working the front counter, wondering if the Cook Brothers had decided to skip this Saturday, when their red and blue coach finally rolled past. It was nearly full up, seven men, a woman, and two children."

"Was Ethem there?"

She shook her head. "The children were fussing at each other, tired of being pinned in such a tight space for so long. The woman shushed her boys as the other passengers stepped out. The men paid no attention to any of it, just glad to be on solid ground once again. All except one man."

Stricken by fright, Lisa thought she knew who it was. "Did this man have blond hair?"

"This fellow had no hair at all. It appeared to me as if he'd had no more sense than to shave this head. Such a look catches a person's attention."

"Did he do something? Say something?"

"He spoke to the children's mother. I couldn't hear what was said; something offensive, I'm sure. The children ran to her and the other men stared at him. No one addressed him directly. They were scared."

"I met a man like that once. Shaven head and all."

"Even without my spyglass, I would have known he was a dandy. He wore an expensive black vest, fine trousers. Tied low to his leg was a single holster gun belt."

"Quincy Fix," Lisa said. Dressed exactly as she remembered him, both from life and from her nightmares. If there was one man that frightened her as much as Donald, it was Fix. "He's not a good person."

"He's a very bad one," Felicia agreed. "There's a dime novel in my store that calls him by name. The writer says that Fix is a gun-for-hire. He's a killer, too. No one knows exactly how many men he's buried."

"Why is he in Wyatt Ridge?"

"One minute, there's more. You mentioned a blond man. There was a blond with him."

Donald. Lisa wished Pearce was there to hold her. If she was in his arms, she was certain her heart wouldn't be beating so loudly.

Through the fog of her fear, she realized Felicia was still speaking.

"… expected the two of them to stop at the Glory Hole, wash away the trail dust. Instead, they crossed the street to my shop."

Donald and Quincy Fix, together? Lisa tried to make sense of it. The pieces didn't fit.

There wasn't a price on her head. A bounty hunter wouldn't have an interest in her. Had Donald hired the other man to watch his back? If so, why? He couldn't possibly be scared of her.

She remembered the dark promise she'd made to herself: *Kill Donald.* Did he somehow suspect she'd turn on him when he arrived?

That didn't make any sense, either. Had Donald known, it would have amused him.

Felicia continued, "The blond man, Donald Skroch by name, unbuttoned his long coat when he entered my store. He wanted me to see the badge on his chest."

"He's proud of the tin on his shirt," Lisa said. "He's a lawman."

"Not here, he ain't," Felicia told her. "Be nice if someone reminded him as much. As far from home as he is, he carries more swagger than our own Andy Bishop. And Andy collects a pay check for maintaining the law."

"What did Donald want?"

"He was looking for a stable, not too expensive, just someplace where he could rent a buggy. Then he asked for directions to the Hanlon ranch."

"You didn't tell him."

"I let him know, a store like mine, there are certain expenses. If he wanted information, he needed to buy something. After he'd paid for a handful of dried figs, I told him what he wanted to know."

Lisa's eyes widened.

"Oh, don't look so stricken," Felicia told her. "If I hadn't helped him, he'd have asked someone else. Almost anyone could have guided him here. I gave him the long route, past Big Spider Gulch."

Lisa clasped her hands. "He's coming after me."

"Not today, child, and not tomorrow, either. His partner was road-weary and refused to go anywhere but the hotel." Sounding bemused, she said, "Tomorrow is Sunday. The killer refuses to do any work on the Sabbath."

"On Monday, then."

"I expect so," Felicia said. "As long as he's talking about himself, Skroch enjoys engaging in conversation. I asked him why he was going to the Broken H and he opened right up. It seems that you two have an interesting history."

Lisa looked at the other woman, expecting to see scorn in her eyes. Instead, she noticed wrinkles of worry creasing Felicia's forehead.

"It's not a relationship I cherish," Lisa said.

"You mustn't leave with him. It's clear to me that Skroch doesn't care for you, not by any definition of the word. When he spoke your name, he acted as if you were something he owned."

"You're right about that." At first, Lisa had been flattered by the purchases he'd made on her behalf. It was only later that she realized he viewed every gift, each and every bauble, as another chain tying her to him.

"He's ridden for days to collect you. On the first of the week, they're coming to the Broken H. Looking for you."

"Him and Quincy Fix," Lisa said, despair coloring her words. "It's hopeless."

"No situation is ever hopeless," Felicia said to her. "You want Skroch out of your life? I have an idea about that."

Chapter Twenty-Eight

"Are you all right?" Pearce asked.

Lisa had barely spoken to him after their visitor left. While he welcomed the much-improved mush, he knew he would have enjoyed it more if his dining partner had finished her serving.

"My stomach feels fine, if that's what you're asking," Lisa said. "I haven't much of an appetite, that's all."

"You need to eat."

She gave him a wan smile.

"Don't tell me you'd prefer Ted's concoction."

"Felicia's recipe is so much better." She raised her spoon as if she was forcing ashes into her mouth. "Delicious."

Something's wrong, Pearce knew, but he was at a loss to explain it. Felicia must have said something to disturb her, but Lisa denied it.

After supper was finished, he lingered in the main room, hoping the vibrant woman he'd so recently kissed would return to him. Pale and distracted, she slipped past him to go to her rocking chair.

"Lisa?"

"Good night." Taking a blanket from the seat of the chair, she draped it over her legs. She closed her eyes, as if she was too weary to keep them open.

"If there's something I can do –"

"Good night," she said, dismissing him.

He fought to hold his temper. While Lisa was recuperating, he'd slept every night in the repaired second bedroom, just in case she needed him. Recovered, she'd apparently decided she couldn't be bothered with him.

"I'm going to check on Gambit and Pearl," he told her. "In fact, I think I'll sleep in the barn."

Lisa kept her eyes closed, offering no objection.

When he was younger, Pearce would have slammed the front door as he left the main house. Wiser now, he closed it firmly but gently.

If I break it, I'll only have to fix it, he reminded himself. *I don't need to add something else to my list of chores.*

Pearce had a hundred things to do, but he no longer had a time table for when he'd leave. So much of it was up in the air, mired in his feelings for Lisa.

If she shared similar feelings for him, she'd decided to hide them this night. Although she'd been a warm and willing partner before their visitor had arrived, Lisa's emotions were now masked.

Walking quickly, he crossed the field between house and barn. The sky was clear and the stars more beautiful than diamonds.

Lisa's been ill, so allowances must be made. In the morning, we'll have another discussion. If she keeps her silence then –

He looked to the stars for an answer. They twinkled at him, offering no guidance.

With some of the women in his past, he'd have demanded answers and expected to get them. With one or two them, he might have bent them over his lap and paddled them until they'd responded – but it took a saucy sort to enjoy that kind of game.

Lisa wasn't playing games, he was certain of it. He cared for her, more than he wanted to admit. If he desired answers for her behavior, he'd have to approach her gently.

If he intended to spank her….

"My imagination is a nasty beast," he said to Gambit as he entered the barn. "It aims to keep me stirred when I most need rest."

A bale of hay was going to be a rough replacement for the straw-filled mattress he'd used lately. Confident that the long day would push him into sleep regardless, he laid out a blanket. Using a rolled jacket as his pillow, he made himself comfortable and closed his eyes.

Minutes later, his eyes blinked open.

Somewhere in the barn's darkness, one of the horses snorted. Outside, an owl hooted so loudly and clearly that it sounded as if it had a home in the building's rafters.

Pearce punched at his jacket, trying to reshape its form. "I can't abide it when a woman gives me the silent treatment. Not when I haven't earned it. Not when we were getting along so well."

Behind his sour feelings, he understood why he'd stormed away from the house. Like a heartsick schoolboy, he'd wanted to revisit the afternoon's passionate embrace. When she'd turned away from him, he'd felt hurt.

What if she's feeling sick again? he thought. *Running a fever? She keeps those things to herself.*

"Hell, and damnation," he said out loud.

Moonlight guided his return to the ranch house. Under Pearce's hand, the door knob twisted silently as he entered the house.

Inside the first room, a lantern was still lit, its glow filling the space. Lisa was in her chair, her head turned away from him. Her chest was rising evenly. When he crept closer, he saw she was asleep, her delicate eyelashes resting softly against her skin.

What in Hades is wrong with you? he asked himself. *Since when have you paid attention to a woman's eyelashes?*

He never had, not even when he was a boy and so interested in the other sex that he could have almost burst.

Back then it was the other female bits and pieces that caught my notice. For good reason, too. The other bits and pieces have their uses, don't they?

But... eyelashes?

"I'm hopeless," he muttered to himself. "Why is it this woman scratches at me so?"

No sooner had he finished speaking than Lisa's mouth dropped open slightly. She gave a light snore.

"There you go, Lisa Hanlon," he told her. "You reveal your true self at last, blasting air like a sailor on leave. No sane man could deal with such a racket, night after night. I finally understand why you had to seek a partner through the mails. It only makes sense."

In truth, he didn't think it made sense at all. A woman like Lisa Hanlon? She could have any man she wanted, as long as the man was willing to accept a touch of challenge in his life.

I'd always heard that mail-order brides were sad creatures, desperate for a mate, he thought. *It's what I've heard from my friends, what I used to say to others.*

What I used to believe.

In this private moment, Pearce tried to view Lisa objectively. Her skin was fair and he'd always been drawn to women of a milky hue. Her brown hair was fine and exactly long enough; her mouth was pink and ideal for kissing; and her body was rounded and ripe, leaving him feeling as if he was fifteen again and as randy as a young colt.

"No woman is without flaw," he told her softly. "My father taught me that."

He didn't care to tell the sleeper the rest of what Randall Folsom had said: *There's no such thing as the perfect woman.*

There's only the perfect woman for you.

Despite his feelings for her, he knew Lisa wouldn't appeal to every man. His older brother, Jackson, preferred a top-heavy woman who felt at home in the kitchen. His younger brother, Nicholas, sought tiny creatures who demanded his total obedience everywhere except inside the bedroom. Possibly there, too.

If I ever see Nick again, I may have to ask for details, he thought.

He missed his brothers, but his choices in life had brought him to the Broken H. Because of this, he couldn't regret the steps he'd taken. Even as he plucked strands of hay from his hair, he knew there was nowhere else he'd prefer to be.

Lisa's lashes fluttered gently. His body responded, creating a growing tightness below his belt line.

Get a grip on yourself, he demanded. *Quit acting as if you've never had a woman!*

You've never had this one, his treacherous mind teased him.

Lisa opened her eyes. "Pearce." She spoke his name with warmth. "You've returned."

Her smile vanished as some new, dire thought occurred to her. Covering her face with her hands, her chest started to heave. Small gasps of air escaped from beneath her palms. Tears leaked down her chin.

"Don't cry." Feeling stricken, Pearce lifted her from the chair. Sobbing, she threw her arms around him.

"Whatever it is, we'll deal with it together. You don't need to cry." He kissed her cheeks, her small nose, her red lips. When she tried to speak, he covered her mouth with his own.

Her lips were wet and tasted of her.

"I thought you might leave," she said. "I treated you so harshly. Why did you stay?"

"You were here."

The words spilled from him, honest and unguarded. He hadn't expected to say it but, once he had, he knew what he'd said was true.

Lisa rested the side of her face on his chest. "Felicia told me that Donald has arrived in Wyatt Ridge. He's coming to the ranch. He'll be here on Monday."

"You don't have to be afraid," Pearce said. "He can't have you. I won't let him take you."

"You don't understand," Lisa said. "He's my husband."

Chapter Twenty-Nine

Tate City – Four Months Earlier

Staring through the bedroom window, Lisa said, "It's supposed to be a lady's privilege to plan her wedding day, Mrs. Stuckey. I've not been allowed to make any of the arrangements."

"I'm certain it will be lovely," the boarding house owner replied.

Lisa let the curtain fall before facing her visitor. "Donald doesn't love me."

"You mustn't say such things, Miss."

"Do you have reason to believe differently? You were present when Donald visited me in your parlor. Twice. From the way he spoke, from the way he acted, do you think he cares for me?"

"Some men express themselves poorly. He wouldn't be marrying you if he didn't care."

"I thought I knew him from the letters he'd written," Lisa said, a feeling of sadness building inside of her. "I couldn't have been more wrong."

Nervously, Mrs. Stuckey said, "Every girl feels a few jitters before she steps to the altar. You don't have time to dawdle. The ceremony's about to begin."

"This is more than nerves." Collecting her suitcase from the corner of the room, Lisa placed it atop the simple blue bedspread. Turning to the pine bureau, she opened its top drawer and began removing her belongings.

"Miss Hanlon?"

Lisa sorted through the items, folding them as she placed them inside the case. "There's a stagecoach due today, isn't there?"

"Every day except Sunday. Tate City is a regular stop for the Cook Brothers."

"When will it arrive at the station?"

"It depends on where you're going, doesn't it?" The gray-haired woman squeezed her hands together. "The coach to St. Anders left yesterday. We'll not see it for another week."

"The next one, then. The next one to anywhere."

"Not for another two hours. You'll be married by then."

Two hours, Lisa thought. *So much time.*
Too much time.

She said, "I need your help."

Worried wrinkles pinched at the corners of Mrs. Stuckey's eyes.

"Donald didn't visit me yesterday," Lisa said. "He told me it was bad luck, the groom seeing his bride the day before the wedding. I suspect he wanted to get drunk and loud, and didn't wish for me to see."

"Boys will be boys, especially the night before their wedding. It's not as if you had other plans. You spent the day in your room."

"Seen by no one except you." Lisa snapped closed the catches on the suitcase. "If you were to go to the church and tell Donald you can't find me, he'll believe you. Especially if I leave a note for him, saying I've returned to St. Anders."

Mrs. Stuckey looked at her tenant as if she'd lost her mind. "To what end? He'll only go after you."

"I expect he will. He'll mount his horse and make chase for yesterday's stage."

"He's good at catching people," Mrs. Stuckey warned her. "That's why they know better than to run. When the sheriff catches them, he punishes them."

The undercurrent in her voice warned her: *And it's not good when he punishes you.*

"But I won't be on the stage for him to find, will I? The Cook Brothers keep record by ticket number, not by name. By the time he reaches the stagecoach to St. Anders, it will have made at least one other stop. People getting on, getting off. Even if he discovers I wasn't there, he can't blame you."

"But what if he does?"

"Why would he? You didn't see me go. You only brought him my note."

The boarding house owner appeared unconvinced. "He might telegraph ahead and ask the station master to hold the team at the next stop."

"It's still a day's ride for him."

"I'm sorry. I can't lie to Sheriff Skroch."

You can but you won't, Lisa thought.

In their short time together, she'd learned two things about her landlady. First, that Mrs. Stuckey loved her dog, Yellow Pete, but didn't share the same warm feelings for anyone or anything else. Second, that she offered no favors without receiving something of value in return.

If Lisa wished to have her favor granted, she'd have to pay a price. She asked, "What do you think of my wedding gown, Mrs. Stuckey? It was sewn in the French fashion."

"It's fancy," she responded warily.

"Donald paid fifteen hundred dollars for it. It was a bargain at that price. Normally, it would have cost much more."

Surprised by the sum, Mrs. Stuckey stretched out her hand as if to touch the gown's fabric. Not daring to be so bold, she curled her palm to her chest.

"If I don't get married, I won't need a gown," Lisa said. "Once I'm gone, who's to say whether I took it with me or not?"

"If you run away, you mean."

"I want you to have the dress, Mrs. Stuckey. Hide it in your attic, somewhere away from your boarders. In a few months, you can take the dress to Breytown and sell it. Three hundred dollars would be a bargain to the right buyer."

"Not in Breytown, that's not far enough." The lines in the landlady's face softened, transformed by greed. "Somewhere further south, I think. I know a lady in Coganville who might be interested."

"As one woman to another, I beseech you. Donald doesn't love me. I don't want him, either. A loveless marriage is a terrible trap."

Mrs. Stuckey folded the wedding gown into her arms. "No promises."

"I understand."

"You'll need to go quickly. Stay here and Skroch's deputy will be dispatched to find you," she said. "There's writing paper in the bedside table."

There was so much she could have written but, in the end, Lisa's note was simple: *I'm sorry, Donald, but I'm returning home. Louisa Hanlon.*

He could make of it what he would. No matter what she wrote, he would be unhappy with her.

She replaced the pen in its holder. "Thank you, Mrs. Stuckey."

Clutching the handle of suitcase, Lisa hurried down the stairs of the boarding house. After stopping in the kitchen, she stepped onto Usher street. She knew exactly where to go. Three days after her arrival to Tate City, she'd retraced her steps to the stagecoach station.

Even then, I had my doubts, she remembered.

Positioned in the middle of the town's biggest thoroughfare, her destination was a modest, single-story building, two streets over from the Third Avenue Church. With almost everyone in town at the chapel, she found herself alone as she hurried along the wooden sidewalk.

Mrs. Stuckey is probably boxing the wedding gown at this very minute, she reflected. *She'll put it where no one can find it. She won't risk Donald finding out the truth.*

No one in the county dares to cross him.

It was her fear of her fiancé's cruelty that caused her to enter the stagecoach station with her head bent and her face covered by one gloved hand. Inside the unimpressive building, there was a clerk's booth centered against the back wall. An area had been cordoned off for customers to stand while they waited to purchase their transportation while a second, larger area occupied the remaining space. It held four long benches with chairs, allowing for a dozen passengers to sit while listening for the arrival of the incoming horses.

A solitary passenger sat on the bench closest to the clerk's work area. His upper lip covered by a thick, black mustache, he watched Lisa as she walked past him and to the opening of the booth.

The age-spotted clerk set his newspaper aside as she approached.

"One ticket, please," she said. She kept her voice low, wanting to hide her transaction from the mustached man. "For the next stage."

The clerk reached for a leather-bound ledger. "Going to Breytown?"

"A bit more distant, please."

Making an exasperated noise, the clerk returned the ledger to its original position. "I can't issue a ticket without a specific destination."

I should have checked the schedule, Lisa thought.

In this situation, she sought anonymity, to be dealt with and quickly forgotten. She didn't want the clerk to remember the lost woman standing in front of him.

He said, "Where are you going? Madison or Needleton? Further? Visalia or Wyatt Ridge?"

"Wyatt Ridge." She said the name gratefully, knowing she'd heard it before. "Didn't I say?"

"Hmmm." Selecting the correct ledger book, the clerk took her money before carefully inking in a ticket number.

"Will the stagecoach be arriving soon?"

The clerk consulted the clock mounted near the entrance. "The station master returns in two hours, bringing fresh horses. The stage will be here at the same time."

Holding tightly to her ticket, Lisa circled past the mustached man to sit on the bench furthest from the entrance. Placing the suitcase at her feet, she tried to remember why she knew the name of Wyatt Ridge.

Uncle Ted, she thought.

Her father had frequently spoken about his brother. Ted Hanlon had moved to Wyatt Ridge, decades before. He had practically founded the community.

Lisa didn't know if her uncle was still alive, much less if he'd remained in that distant location. If he was still there, she'd find him. If he wasn't, she'd think of something else to do.

All that mattered now was that the stagecoach was coming and she had a seat reserved on it.

Two hours felt like a very long time to wait.

Chapter Thirty

When Deputy Gann stepped through the doorway, Lisa's heart fell. Of average height and medium build, Gann spent his days in Donald's shadow. Serving as the sheriff's only deputy, he was quiet and nondescript, easily forgotten and far from intimidating. When she'd first met him, she'd wondered why Donald had ever hired him.

On reflection, she felt she understood. Having worked with Donald for two years, Gann did as he was told. Just as importantly, he'd made no mark on his own. No one on the city council ever mentioned Gann by name. There wasn't one of them who would ever suggest that he might someday replace the man he served.

Taking a seat on the bench, the deputy said, "Half of the county is at the church, watching for you to come down the aisle. Some folks are wondering if you have cold feet. Most think it's the big city way, making people wait like this."

"How did you find me?"

"Sally Stuckey."

Lisa wondered if the deputy had gone to the boarding house. Had he threatened the landlady in order to learn the truth?

"She came to the rear of the church, carrying your dress," Gann explained. "She spoke to Sheriff Skroch in private. We were the only ones who saw her."

Setting her suitcase on her lap as if it might shield her from the deputy, she said, "I won't marry Donald."

"You don't have to."

Lisa hadn't expected this response. She was speechless.

"Even in Tate City," Gann said, "a woman doesn't have to stand beside a man she doesn't love. I promised the sheriff I'd find you and bring you to him. We'll go through the side entrance, avoiding the crowd in the front. If you don't want to be with him, you need to tell him to his face. It's the honorable thing."

"Are you honorable, Mr. Gann?"

"I try to be." He squeezed her arm lightly, offering a token of reassurance. "I expect you do, too."

Sympathy transformed his ordinary face. Donald's second-in-command wasn't nearly as handsome as his master, but his eyes were kind and his manner was warm. If he had been the one who'd contacted her, all those weeks ago, Lisa knew he would have written his own letters of love.

"I'm scared of him," she admitted.

"People can be. I used to think, only bad people." He stood up. "It won't be just the two of you. The sheriff has asked Father Jenkins to be there when you talk."

"I don't know Father Jenkins, not personally."

"If you decide to stay here, you'll like him. He's a good man."

"He delivers a memorable sermon."

Lisa opened the suitcase. She placed her stagecoach ticket on top of her folded blouses before latching the case.

Taking the bag from her lap, Gann said, "I'll leave your belongings in the bed of my wagon. After you see the sheriff, if you still want to leave, I'll bring you to the station myself."

*****

His wide face fringed by a strip of thin beard, Father Jenkins opened his arms and drew Lisa inside his embrace. "I'm glad you're here."

Pressed against his impressively wide body, Lisa felt the air rush out of her.

To Deputy Gann, the preacher said, "We could use your assistance at the front, Lester. The Adams' twins are in a mood for mischief. You know their parents won't do anything to stop them."

Gann left, the anteroom door clicking shut behind him. The room around Lisa was sparsely furnished, with a few simple chairs and a two-drawer desk. A large, leather-bound Bible sat on the top of the desk.

Hanging on the wall across from her, she saw her wedding gown. The landlady's unexpected windfall, abandoned in fear of the town's leading lawman.

Freeing herself from the preacher's hold, Lisa realized Donald was in the room, too. Dressed for their wedding, he had never looked more attractive. Wearing a white shirt and black tie, he tugged at the bottom of his dark silver vest. The pearl buttons on the vest matched the pearl color of his gloves.

"I know what I've done wrong," he told her, "and I'm sorry. I'll make things right. Here and now, whatever you want."

It was the first time she'd ever heard Donald sound humble or worried. The first time he didn't sound pleased to hear his own voice.

"Tell me what you did wrong," she said.

"I didn't write the letters I sent to you. It was wrong of me. I… I'm not good with words, Lisa. I struggle to say what's in my heart. When I talked with Clarence Foster, he knew how to phrase things properly. It was his pen to the paper, but he only wrote what I was trying to say."

Mrs. Stuckey told him I'd discovered the truth, Lisa thought.

"I'm in love with you," he said, with emotion.

"That's – that's the first time you've ever said those words."

Father Jenkins beamed at them. "This is what I was hoping to hear. That's what this day is all about." His hand at the room's only door, he opened it. "I need to finish getting ready. The choir will be ready, too, I promise."

Before she could stop him, the preacher was gone.

Donald came to her. Placing his hands on Lisa's upper arms, he drew her close. "Forgive me?"

But I don't love you. Worse, she'd seen enough of his behavior to doubt she ever would. "Did you read the letters that were sent?"

"Every word, I swear."

"Did you sign them yourself?"

"As God is my witness."

He expressed the vow lightly and Lisa knew why: he was lying. The handwriting in the signature was identical in appearance to the words written above it.

He hadn't signed the letters. She doubted he'd glanced at them. "You used the same closing for each of the letters. Do you remember it?"

"My name."

"Above your name. You didn't write, 'I love you'. What did you put?"

His expression of good-natured forbearance melted away. "We haven't time for games, Lisa."

"Give me your ending words, the ones that closed every letter. Tell me and I'll know I can believe you. I'll stand with you in front of the Father Jenkins. I'll take my vows."

"I don't remember."

"Every letter, Donald, and you don't remember?"

"No."

"If he was still in town, Clarence could tell you, couldn't he? He always ended the notes with, 'Forever yours'."

"That's right. 'Forever', I think I did see that one time. It's so preposterous. Nothing is forever."

"You said those were your words." Lisa struggled in his grip.

"You said you'd marry me. You will, too," he said. "Everyone is waiting. You'll not embarrass me like this."

"I should never have come here."

"You think you can leave?" He squeezed her upper arms so painfully that she cried out. "You decide this now, you stupid bitch? Today?"

Abruptly, he shoved her.

Lisa stumbled, falling to the floor. Using the fingers of his left hand, Donald removed his right glove. When she tried to stand, he knotted his fist and punched her in the stomach.

Lisa fell to the ground. When he lifted his hand once more, she raised her arms to protect her face.

He dropped his fist. Calmly, he replaced the glove.

Lowering her hands, Lisa curled her legs toward her chest. Her arms throbbed and her stomach was a ball of heat. It hurt to breathe.

You bastard, she thought. *You bastard.*

"You'll do as you're told," Donald said. "Get yourself together. In fifteen minutes, we're going to walk down the aisle, arm in arm."

Lisa tried to answer but couldn't. Tears streamed down her face.

"If you aren't standing beside me when I enter the chapel, I will be disappointed. If you disappoint me again, I swear to you, no one will ever find your body."

Slowly, Lisa crawled onto her knees. Donald reached for her, catching her under the arm and yanking her upright. An agonizing jolt tore along her side, causing her to gasp.

Lifting a pocket watch from his vest, Donald checked the time. "Our guests have waited long enough. Best hurry, my darling. Or do you require some further encouragement?"

Later, she would remember almost nothing of the ceremony. Vaguely, Lisa recalled seeing Mrs. Stuckey, seated toward the rear of the church and refusing to meet her eyes as she passed. Deputy Gann was present, too, watching the ceremony with a concerned expression.

When Father Jenkins asked her, "Do you, Louisa Hanlon, take this man whose hands you hold, to be your lawful, wedded husband? To love him and comfort him throughout your life?"— to her unending shame, she said, "I will."

Hating Donald as she said it.

Wishing him dead. Wishing she'd had the courage to accept death herself.

When it was over, the choir sang a closing song as dozens of well-wishers surged forward. Shaking hands but unable to force a smile, Lisa went through the motions of greeting those who approached her.

The crowd had finally begun to shrink when Deputy Gann came up to her. Touching her arm lightly, he said, "Congratulations."

Lisa flinched in pain at his touch.

Frowning, the deputy started to speak when Donald appeared at her side. He kissed her on the cheek. "You look beautiful, Mrs. Skroch. The wedding gown was worth it."

This is how he views me, Lisa thought. *I'm his pretty new possession. He believes he owns me, just as he owns this dress.*

With pride, Donald told his guests, "We're moving the wedding party. The mayor wants to host our celebration in his home. At the mansion! The governor himself is staying over. He's there as we speak."

"Probably popping the first bottle of champagne," a thick voice rumbled from behind them. A dark-haired, beetle-browed man leaned in to say, "Can I have a word, Sheriff? The governor requires some special handling."

"Coming, Mister Mayor." Speaking to his deputy, Donald lowered his voice. "This gown isn't to get stained or soiled. Where are the rest of Lisa's belongings?"

Lester Gann scratched at his chin. "I can't say."

"They weren't at the station?"

Lisa said, "I left everything at the boarding house."

"Sheriff," the mayor reminded him.

Donald waved a hand, begging for a moment's time. "Find Sally Stuckey," he told Gann. "No, better yet, take my wife to the Stuckey place. Watch over her while she packs her belongings."

"Might take a little time."

"Make certain she changes for the party. The green dress, the one I had made special." Donald hurried off, throwing his arm across the mayor's back. Together, they found Father Jenkins and began a conversation.

Lisa followed the deputy to his buggy. A stained, brown sheet had been thrown over the rear of the cart, shielding her suitcase from view.

"The Adams' twins, Evelyn and Eunice, get into everything," Gann explained. "I didn't want them to find your suitcase."

"Why are we here, Deputy Gann?"

He gave her the suitcase. "You can change in the waiting room."

He waited outside the door as she entered the anteroom. When they returned to his wagon, Lisa was dressed in the striking green dress that Donald had ordered.

The shawl she carried was gray and unbecoming but she kept it with her, anyway. Inside its thick folds, it held the knife she'd stolen from Mrs. Stuckey's kitchen.

Gann said, "We'll go south to Coganville. There's a long stretch of nothing until we get there. I have a friend

211

who lives in the area. He'd welcome the chance to give Sheriff Skroch a poke in the eye."

Lisa looked at him with fresh hope.

"Drape the shawl over your head," Gann advised as she joined him in the carriage. "In this light, I doubt you'll be recognized."

"Does the stage stop in Coganville?"

"It does."

Unfolding the fabric, Lisa removed the knife and set it at her feet. Seeing the blade, Gann asked, "Was that for me?"

"Not you."

"Good."

"I don't understand why you're doing this." She tied the shawl's ends beneath her chin.

"Mother taught me, a man keeps his word," Lester Gann said. Unpinning his badge, he threw it onto the dirt below.

Snapping the reins, he sent his horse in motion.

Chapter Thirty-One

"Is that all of it?" Pearce asked. "Everything?"

"No." Shame burned hotly through her, coloring Lisa's face. "After you came here, even after I knew you weren't here to hurt me, I tried to deceive you."

In the lantern's flickering light, he waited for her to explain herself.

"I didn't know you," Lisa said. "I could only see that you were strong, someone who could handle himself. I wanted that kind of man to be here when Donald arrived." Lisa tried to steady her voice. "I needed someone with me, someone who might scare him off."

"What makes you think he'd run from me?"

Because you're so much more than he is, Lisa wanted to say.

It was true, but that didn't mean that Donald would have left. He welcomed a fight if he thought he'd win. Not that he wasn't willing to cheat to get his way.

"I only knew that he wouldn't run from me," Lisa admitted.

Now that Pearce has heard the truth, I'm going to lose him, she thought. If he wasn't in the shadows, she was positive she'd see the disillusion on his face. *Knowing of my deceit, he'll mount Gambit and leave the Ridge.*

As he should. He deserves better.

Her body shook as she fought against her tears. The thought of Pearce leaving hurt her deeply. It tore at her heart, aching like a physical pain.

Felicia would say this proved she was in love with him.

Dropping her gaze, she didn't see Pearce's hand until he touched her. His palm stroked along her cheek, wiping at her tears.

"You needed someone with you," he said. "I'm glad I was here."

"But Donald –"

"A man should never treat a woman in such a fashion. Not any woman, but especially not you."

When the light caught his face, Lisa saw a black anger in Pearce's gaze.

He said, "I'm not frightened of Donald Skroch. He'd better be frightened of me."

"Pearce."

"I used to wonder what it would feel like, to be in love." Pearce's anger melted, its absence pronounced by the tenderness of his gaze. "Now I know."

He swept her from the chair, her blanket falling to the floor. Stepping over it, he carried her to the bench seat that faced the wood stove. When he sat down, he kept her firmly on his lap.

"You are bold, sir."

Pearce kissed her.

A new kind of heat suffused Lisa, delicious and exciting. Breaking the kiss, her thoughts jumbled, she said, "There's more I need to say."

"Let it wait."

"Felicia had more to share."

"Was it a recipe for Queen's Pudding?"

"What? No."

"Shame, really," Pearce said with a grin. "I enjoy a good Queen's Pudding." Then his mouth captured hers, his tongue teasing her.

She struggled in his hold. "Will you listen?"

"I'd rather not."

"Felicia said there's a man traveling with Donald. A mercenary named Quincy Fix."

"Why would Skroch bring someone with him?"

"Donald doesn't know anyone in this part of the country. He must have decided he needed another gunman to back his play."

"In case you'd found someone to help you. Someone who knew how to fight."

"Yes."

"Someone like me."

"No!" The word blurted out instinctively. "Donald is good with guns, but Fix is an expert. He kills people for money. That's his job."

"How do you know?"

"They've written books about him, Pearce."

"Book writers exaggerate."

"Fix shot 'Killer Cole' Tunstall, the bank robber. It was in Abilene. It was four against one, and he killed every member of Tunstall's gang."

"That was Fix?" His easy manner was gone. "Why would a lawman choose a traveling companion like that?"

"Donald isn't concerned about the law," Lisa said. "He wears a badge because it allows him to do as he wants. If a paid gun can help him achieve his goals, he'll hire one."

Pearce fell into silence. Lisa remained in his comforting hold but she knew what he must be thinking:

There's still time enough for us to get away.

Anyone who didn't know Donald would think the same.

We'll flee, as far and as fast as possible. It's our only chance.

Lisa no longer believed that escape was possible. Before she'd arrived here, she'd never once mentioned her uncle, or the town where he lived, to anyone she'd met. There had been no reason to do so, not when Ted Hanlon and Wyatt Ridge were only a pair of names in ancient family stories.

Yet, despite its relative obscurity, Donald had managed to track her to this community. No matter where she ran, he'd find her again. Locating the lost was a game to him, and he was a master at it.

Pearce didn't know her husband. If Lisa shared her fears, he would argue with her, convinced they could find a safe haven somewhere. But he'd be wrong, just as she'd been wrong. Some horrible day, weeks or months or years from now, they'd be found.

When that happened, if Pearce fought to keep her, he would die.

She waited for him to make his argument. Instead, he kissed her tenderly. She kissed him in return.

Somberly, he said, "I'll think of something."

Which meant, he didn't know what to do. He might think of an idea later but, for now, he was lost.

Lisa felt lost herself.

He said, "We'll talk in the morning."

"If you'd like."

Gently, he slipped her from his lap and onto the thin pad of the bench seat. "Good night."

"Are you going?"

"To the barn."

"Stay with me." Lisa's heart drummed anxiously. Somehow, telling him about Donald had made the law officer's presence feel more real.

"We need our sleep."

"I won't stay here by myself."

"You'd prefer the barn? There are mice and rats in there. Spiders by the dozens."

"Then you'd best not stay there, either," Lisa said. "You slept in the second bedroom when I was sick."

"Because you *were* sick. You're better now."

"No one will know if you stay in the house. There's no one around here."

"There's the barn owl."

"Pearce!"

"I'll stay. For this one evening, then."

She longed for him to curl his arms around her again but, bending down, he delivered a too-short kiss. "Good night."

Moving like a man burdened with worries, he left for the spare bedroom. Lisa wrapped the fallen blanket over her shoulders. Entering the main bedroom, she dropped the woolen covering onto her mattress before beginning to undress.

"Maybe we should run," she said out loud.

It would give them tomorrow, and the next tomorrow, and the tomorrow after that. It wouldn't be forever, but they'd have more time together than if they stayed here.

Until one day: *FOUND YOU.*

Naked, she dipped a soft cloth into the bedside basin and began to wash. If she'd been alone in the house, she'd have sat in the tin tub resting outside of the kitchen door. She could hardly wash herself at the woodstove while Pearce was here, although part of her, the sinful part, enjoyed the thought of it.

Not just because he's handsome, she thought. *Not simply because it's obvious that he wants me.*

It's because he loves me. He's not scared to say the words even if I am. There isn't much that scares him.

Not Donald. Not his gunman. No one.

He'd risk his life for me. At the same moment, she knew, *I have to protect him, too.*

It isn't fair to have finally found love only to have it snatched away from us.

Donald would never let her go. When she left him at the wedding party, she'd bruised his reputation. He lived for his reputation.

He'd want the townspeople to be watching when she returned to Tate City. Everyone who was anyone in Dunway County had to know that he'd brought her back.

Everyone had to see that she'd lost and he'd won.

"Quincy Fix will make certain of it," she said, throwing the cloth into the basin. Water splashed over the curved edge, dripping down the side of the bowl.

In the short time Lisa had been with Donald, she'd found him to be brutish and manipulative, but not particularly clever. Hiring Fix was a clever move.

The gunman was another wild card in the deck, something else she hadn't anticipated. A move she didn't know how to trump.

Adjusting the mirror on the bed stand, she viewed her body. The strain of the last few months revealed itself in the weight she'd lost. She didn't like this thinner look, but Pearce didn't appear to mind.

A new and wicked idea came to her. Thinking about it, she blushed.

Do I dare?

Chapter Thirty-Two

Lisa didn't have the nerve. She wasn't that type of woman.

"Well, what kind of woman are you?" she asked herself.

Her uncle had viewed her as his strong but emotionally-fragile niece, needing to be sheltered. Riding beside her in a stagecoach, Quincy Fix had pronounced that she was no better than a harlot, the same as all other mail-order brides. Donald had seen her as his property, someone to obey his commands and to be used as he wished.

What did she think? How did she view herself?

I want to live a life of value, she reflected. *I want to spend my days with a partner I hold dear.*

One I cherish. One who cherishes me.

If it were my choice, I'd like to get to know Pearce better. If he's the man I believe him to be, I'd be content to remain with him. I'd grow old with him.

I'd stay in the Ridge.

This last thought came to her unexpectedly. Almost since the day she'd arrived, she'd planned to leave this foreign land. Limiting her interaction with her neighbors, avoiding the townspeople, she'd wrapped herself in isolation.

Felicia's warmth and good nature had reminded her that there were friends to be found, if only she'd open her heart to them. Pearce's arrival had changed how she'd seen the ranch, as well.

The Broken H wasn't 160 acres of endless chores and useless scrubland. It had potential. There was a life to be built here, if she was willing to try.

If Donald had his way, she wouldn't be allowed to see what she could do. He intended to force her to leave with him, taking her from California – and Pearce.

It wouldn't matter that she loathed him. In his own twisted way, he might find enjoyment in her unhappiness.

No situation is ever hopeless, she remembered Felicia telling her. *You want Skroch out of your life? I have an idea about that.*

But did she?

"No matter what happens, you won't get everything you want," she told the unseen Donald. "I still have one gift you feel belongs to you. But this isn't something the preacher was allowed to give. It's only mine to bestow."

Opening the bedroom closet, she found the party dress that Donald had insisted she wear following their wedding. Emerald green in color, the flowing sheath dress lacked the train, frills or ruffles that were currently in fashion. A dressmaking visionary, Abbie May Foster had designed it for dancing.

"You never did see me in this," she told her missing husband. "You never will. When I carry my memories of this dress, they will no longer have anything to do with you."

Dressed only in a thin chemise, Lisa stepped into the outfit. Made to be worn over a series of undergarments, the fabric hung loosely on her, threatening to spill from her shoulders. Pinching the fabric at the waist, she went into the hallway.

Pearce's door was closed. Taking its handle in hand, she opened it.

"Lisa?" Startled, Pearce stood beside the water basin, a towel in one hand. Wearing a pair of white drawers, he was nearly naked.

Faded scars told the story of his battles in the past. They didn't bother her at all. The entirety of his body was as perfect as she could have imagined.

Quickly, he unfolded the towel to cover his waist. "You should have knocked."

"I didn't care to ask permission." Even though the house was empty except for the two of them, she closed the opening behind her. When she approached him, his expression turned from surprised to quizzical.

"Kiss me," Lisa commanded.

He did as she asked, his lips softly brushing hers. She eagerly responded, her tongue seeking entrance and finding it.

Taken aback by her boldness, he asked, "Are you sure?"

"Yes." Distracted by sudden movement beneath the towel at his waist, she knew it was what he wanted, too.

Releasing her hold on the dress, Lisa felt it slip down her shoulders. Only the swell of her breasts kept it from falling off altogether.

"You are a right tease," Pearce pronounced, his voice growing gruff.

"Do you not know me better than that?" Shifting her arms slightly, she encouraged the fabric to drift still lower.

Brushing over her slender chest, the custom-made dress fell to her feet. "When have I teased you?"

Lisa remained in front of him. The blue chemise clung to her, its gossamer cloth revealing her every curve. She'd never before allowed herself to be so exposed to a man. It excited and frightened her.

"You're so beautiful," Pearce said.

Letting go of the towel, he took her in his arms. She felt his sex press against her as he brought her to his bed.

He kissed her, his mouth finding her lips. His head dropped lower, his teeth teasing her neck as the strap of her gown slipped from her arm.

His mouth dropped lower still. Unable to help herself, Lisa moaned.

His head lifted and he kissed her passionately. When the kiss ended, she saw that he'd somehow discarded his covering. Beneath his flat and muscled stomach, he was ready for her.

He was larger than she'd imagined a man to be. She trembled beneath him.

"What is it?"

"You're my first."

His eyes widened.

"Tell me that you love me," Lisa said.

"With all my heart."

"Tell me that you want me."

"There has never been, will never be, a woman I desire more."

Closing her eyes, she said, "Please, Pearce, don't make me wait any longer. Take me."

*****

223

Awakening, Pearce reached out for Lisa. His hand found only the cotton sheet at his side. It was cool to the touch, as if it had been left unoccupied for a while.

"Lisa?"

The bright morning light told him it was well past sunrise. Around him, the bed sheets were wrinkled and the top blanket was heaped at the foot of the bed. On the floor was the white towel that he had so happily discarded, only a few hours ago.

"Lisa!" Again, his cry went without response. Dressing quickly, he opened the door and went into the hallway.

Why are you so worked up? he asked himself. *This isn't the first time you've made love only to wake up to an empty bed.*

It was, however, the first time in a long time that he'd cared. Entering the master bedroom, he saw Lisa's bed was empty. Its bedspread was undisturbed.

Crossing through the main room, he told himself, *She's probably in the kitchen. Cooking breakfast, maybe. Or, spurred by my comments, preparing some hellish version of Queen's Pudding.*

To his disappointment, the kitchen was also vacant. Praying for a response, he shouted, "Lisa!"

All he heard was the echoed alarm in his own voice.

"What next?" The anxiety he felt was something he hadn't experienced since he was a boy. Even when he'd faced the Prescott Kid, knowing he might die, he hadn't felt this way.

"She'll be here somewhere," he reminded himself. "She hasn't disappeared. No one slipped into the house and stole her away. If there'd been trouble, she'd have cried out. I'd have heard it."

Unable to shake the worry he felt, he left the house and ran to the barn. Reaching the building's big double doors, he threw them open.

The doors banged into the walls, the sound spurring a fluttering of wings. Alone in the stall, Gambit turned to look at him.

Pearl had been taken. The carriage she pulled had gone with her. Where the buggy once stood, there was a fist-sized rock.

Beneath the stone, there was a folded sheet of paper. Above the paper's fold, his name was written in a delicate, feminine hand.

Opening the letter, he read: *My dearest Pearce, I am sorry.*

I am so sorry.

I have to go.

A frown creasing his face, he sat on a bale of hay.

Lisa wrote, *Last night was wonderful. I pray we will have another thousand, thousand days to be together. Since such things are never certain, I will treasure the time we've shared.*

I love you.

She underlined the words, three slashes felt so deeply that the last mark had pierced the paper.

As much as I want to stay with you, I have to be strong. I must confront the man I married. I must convince him to leave Wyatt Ridge and never return.

Donald came for me. I'm the only one who can do this. This is not your fight.

225

I need to know that you are safe so that I can be brave. If you care for me, stay at the Broken H.

Please do not follow after me.

Lisa

Pearce read the note a second time. Crumpling the paper into a tight ball, he tossed it to the ground.

Strapping his gun belt in place, he said, "I need you to run like you've never run before, Gambit. It's time we met this Sheriff Skroch."

Chapter Thirty-Three

Feeling excited, guilty, and sinful when she'd entered Pearce's bedroom, Lisa had expected her emotions to keep her awake until morning. Instead, after making love for most of the night, she'd fallen blissfully asleep beside him.

Pearce had been a skilled and generous partner; parts of her still tingled from the memory of his touch. If she could have remained in his bed, she would have done so.

Oh, but only for another fifty or sixty years, she decided.

When she awoke, it was already dawn. Now, with the buggy's wheels spinning as Pearl moved through the early morning light, Lisa was concerned that she'd be arriving in Wyatt Ridge later than she'd intended.

What's done is done, she decided. *I'll never regret a second of the time we had together.*

Rather than count the minutes ahead of her, she decided to reflect on what Felicia Arnold had said to her the day before.

"You want Skroch out of your life?" the store owner had asked.

"Whatever your idea, it won't work, Felicia. You don't know Donald."

"I've met him, remember?"

"He acts differently when he's in public. Behind his smile, he hides who he truly is."

"Then he's doing a poor job of it. I can't stand the man." Felicia rested her arms on the table. "You need to listen to me. With a little help, you can get that man out of your hair permanently."

"Permanently?" She couldn't believe the other woman was suggesting what Lisa herself had only dared fantasize. "I've thought about it, of course. Frequently. I'm sorry, I don't think I can do it."

"Do what?"

"I can't kill Donald."

"*Kill* him?" It was her visitor's turn to be surprised. "How? With a gun?"

"Isn't that what you meant?"

"Hardly. Put a pistol in your hand, you'd probably shoot yourself by mistake. Or am I wrong?"

Lisa knew Felicia was probably right.

"Even if you got lucky, you'd go to jail," the shopkeeper continued. "Kill an officer of the law? Woman or not, they'd hang you."

"I said, I didn't think I could do it."

Amused, Felicia patted Lisa's arm. "But you did consider it. That's one reason I like you, Lisa Hanlon. Backed into a corner, you're smart enough to weigh all of your options. All of the options except for one."

"What then?"

"Divorce the miserable cuss."

Lisa felt disappointment wash over her. "Only a man can initiate a divorce."

"That might be true in St. Anders. True for most cities and states, for that matter. The rules aren't the same in California."

"It must be."

228

"There's a shortage of female folk here, remember? Laws have been changed to make the place a little more welcoming. Here, women can file as long as she can prove cause."

"What counts as 'cause'?"

"There are a dozen reasons, but only about three that Judge Evans recognizes." Felicia held a finger in the air. "Abandonment."

But I abandoned Donald, Lisa thought.

A second finger joined the first. "Adultery."

Because of last night, that sin is mine, too, Lisa thought.

Felicia raised her third finger. "Extreme cruelty."

"Cruelty?" Lisa felt a surge of hope.

"When the lawyer, Capehart, was talking to me, he said this one is a favorite in court. All I needed was someone who'd swear they'd seen Ethem strike me. Then I'd be single and the store would belong to me alone."

"Did Ethem …?"

"I'd have broken his arms if he dared raise a hand to me. What about Skroch? Did he ever hit you?"

"There weren't any witnesses."

"Were there bruises?"

"It was weeks ago, Felicia. I didn't tell anyone. I certainly didn't show anyone. I was too ashamed."

"Your memory is terrible," the storeowner responded determinedly. "How could you have forgotten? You told me."

"I did?"

"The moment you came into the Ridge. You didn't want me to talk about it, but I wouldn't let the subject drop. Your entire face was black and blue!"

Lisa said, "My arms and stomach."

"The bastard." This time, Felicia's fist slapped the tabletop. The pan of cornmeal mush jumped slightly.

"What if Donald refuses to divorce?"

"It doesn't matter what he wants, does it? He struck you. A man who hits a woman is lower than a prairie dog's belly. You'll stand before the judge whether Skroch likes it or not."

Despite her doubts, Lisa could feel a smile growing over her face.

Felicia's brows knitted together in concern. "There is one thing."

"Go ahead."

"In time, I expect the law will change all across this country. They haven't yet. Once you cross state lines, California's rules don't apply. You'll lose all say-so in the matter."

"I wouldn't be allowed to divorce."

"Not without your husband's permission. You'll remain his wife whether you like it or not."

Resolutely, Lisa said, "I'm not leaving the Ridge."

"What if he's insistent?"

"I won't go without a fight."

"Your handyman would stand up for you, too," Felicia said. "That's why Skroch brought Quincy Fix with him. To make certain that no one can prevent him from doing as he wishes."

Pearce isn't scared of anyone, Lisa thought. *He won't let me be taken.*

But if he goes up against Fix, he'll be killed. I would rather die myself.

I'll have to do this on my own.

*****

Arriving in town, she went to the stable yard. The stable owner provided a stall for Pearl and a storage space for the two-person carriage.

"I'll keep them out of view," he assured Lisa. "Nobody will see your things. Can't imagine anyone would care if they did."

"For safety's sake," she said.

Rationally, she knew Donald wouldn't recognize the spotted horse or buggy even if he came across them. At this point, he had no reason to be watching for her, either. As far as he knew, she was still at the Broken H, blissfully unaware of his arrival in Wyatt Ridge.

Rationality be damned, she wasn't taking any chances. She lifted her heavy umbrella from the passenger's seat, pleased to know its hidden derringer rested beneath the crook.

The stable owner gave her a puzzled look. "Looks worse for wear."

"Let's hope I don't have to use this."

Leaving the stable grounds, Lisa wrapped a turquoise shawl around her head, hiding as much of her face as possible. With the umbrella in one hand, she headed toward the steeple that stood over the New Hope Assembly church.

For all of his sins, Rupert Capehart always attended Sunday services. From her own past experience, Lisa knew that the lawyer preferred to sit in a middle pew during the morning sermon.

The church's large mahogany doors featured twin budded crosses mounted inside raised and curved molding. A stained-glass window arched over the entrance.

Placing her hand on one of the door's brass handles, Lisa hesitated before opening it.

If you'd arrived when you'd planned, you could have entered with everyone else, she chastised herself. *Go in now and Reverend Leydecker will make a fuss.*

Horace Leydecker was greatly offended whenever anyone interrupted one of his sermons. If a straggler entered the church after the front doors were closed, the preacher took it as a personal offense.

In Lisa's first visit to the church, Patrick Doering, the school teacher, had tried to slip in unnoticed. Leydecker had stopped speaking at the sight of this lollygagging member of his flock. He'd stared toward the Heavens, pretending to lose his train of thought. Then, to emphasize his unhappiness, he'd punished everyone in the room by repeating much of what he'd already said.

In short, while preaching God's word, he'd acted most ungodly.

Lisa wouldn't be treated any differently if she entered at this hour. While she never enjoyed being the center of attention, she especially didn't care to be noticed today.

She decided it might be better to wait at the side of the church. Once the collection plates were passed and the choir had sung its closing song, she could watch until Capehart emerged into daylight.

She was passing the entrance when the building's doors were thrown open. From inside the room, the reverend's powerful voice faltered. "You can never…

um… find redemption….” With the doors closing, she heard him ask, “Who *is* that?”

Paying no attention to Lisa, the exiting parishioner was dressed in a stylish black suit and matching tie. An expensive hat covered his shaved head, shading his face and crooked nose. Although he wasn’t wearing a holster or gun belt, she recognized him immediately.

Quincy Fix.

Chapter Thirty-Four

Fix crossed the street. Moving quickly, he followed the curve of the sidewalk and went out of view.

Lisa sank against the church wall. The bounty hunter hadn't looked in her direction, she was certain of it. Well, why would he? Her shawl hid her features and her clothing was unremarkable.

Then a new, frightening thought came to mind: *What if Donald is in there, too?*

Clutching the umbrella tightly, Lisa hurried toward the rear of the church. From the end of the street, a dog barked at her. Satisfied that this newcomer didn't pose an immediate threat, the bent-tailed mutt soon decided to ignore her.

Placing her ear to the building's wall, Lisa listened to hear if anyone else was walking toward the exit. The only sound she heard was the minister's deep voice, returning to form. Muffled but vibrant, Leydecker boomed his words at the audience in front of him.

Lambasting the sinners and praising the saints, she recalled. *And, as he reminds everyone each Sunday, there are no saints in Wyatt Ridge.*

The more she thought about it, the less likely it seemed that Donald would be sitting inside. Although he appeared at Tate City's Third Avenue Church frequently, glad-handing the other members of the congregation, he didn't enjoy the experience. Once he was clear of prying eyes, he preferred to use his Sunday hours in a more casual fashion.

He doesn't have to make a show of his faith here, she thought. *If he's true to form, he's at the saloon. Drinking and gambling.*

He'll be at the Glory Hole the entire day.

But why had the man he'd hired gone to church services? Fix's appearance at New Hope Assembly didn't make any sense to her. Had Donald asked him to go? Was there some ulterior motive behind his visit?

Had Fix been sent there in search of Lisa Skroch?

No, Felicia said Fix doesn't work on Sundays. If he was searching for me, wouldn't that count as 'work'?

Lisa thought so, but Fix might have changed his own rules. She assumed he was the type of man who did whatever he wanted, whether others liked it or not. It fit with the image she carried of him: an uncaring monster, willing to kill anyone if his price was met.

Maybe he came to services to mock those who believe in the Bible, she thought. *Then, once the reverend started preaching about Hellfire and brimstone, he didn't like what he was hearing. He got scared.*

If men like Quincy Fix are capable of being scared.

There were some things she'd never know. Lisa stared at the ground, trying to marshal her thoughts.

In a half hour, maybe less, Rupert Capehart would leave the house of worship. She needed to find him as soon as he did. She'd plead with him to return to his office so that she could immediately file for divorce.

Or would it be better to ask the lawyer to accompany her to the jailhouse first? Sheriff Bishop knew Capehart.

Lisa's words would carry more weight with him at her side.

She'd explain her situation. Once Bishop and his deputy understood what was happening, she'd ask for their protection. Then it wouldn't matter if there was a gunman in Donald's employ.

But what if Donald has already visited the jailhouse? Her pessimistic side rose to life. *Reminding the pair how lawmen always watch out for each other, pleading the case for brothers under the badge. Asking them to look the other way if a bit of a fuss is raised. Exaggerating the misconduct of a runaway bride, fresh from the city and disrespectful of country life.*

"It won't be like that," she tried to assure herself. "Not with Andy Bishop. He's an honest man. He's not like Donald."

"Did I hear my name?"

Raising her head, Lisa swallowed in fear.

Donald was in front of her, his silver badge pinned to his stained and wrinkled wedding vest. Unshaven and puffy-eyed, he smelled as if he hadn't bathed since he'd left Tate City.

"Miss me, my darling?" he asked.

Standing several feet behind Donald, Quincy Fix crossed his arms. He watched the two of them, almost as if he were a disinterested bystander.

"You stink of whiskey," Lisa told her husband. "We're outside of a church."

Donald was standing so close to her, she couldn't move past him. Beneath his vest, his white shirt was open at the collar, misbuttoned at the top and sloppily tucked inside his trousers.

At his waistline, he wore his gun belt. Unlike Fix, he was carrying a pistol.

Lisa said, "I have to go inside. Reverend Leydecker is waiting for me."

Stepping aside, Donald mock-curtsied. "Then you'd best go."

Her heart thumping, she started ahead. When she did, his hand flashed out, grabbing her arm and dislodging her umbrella. She watched as it slipped from her hold, falling to the ground.

He pushed her against the building. "Did you miss me?"

Donald forced his mouth onto hers. His beard scratched at her cheeks as his tongue pushed between her teeth. He tasted of alcohol and stale cigars.

When she tried to escape, his hand caught the back of her hair. Yanking on it, he bent her neck back. He kissed her deeper and more roughly.

There wasn't a trace of passion or desire in his actions. Knowing she didn't like it, didn't want it, he was telling her that her wishes didn't matter. This was a statement of ownership.

She slapped him, startling him enough that he released her.

"Stop," she said.

He laughed, deep and guttural, before rubbing his hand over the reddened area.

"Don't touch me again," Lisa said. She edged away from the building. "You don't have any right."

A mirthless smile on his face, Donald advanced toward her. "I have a husband's right."

She stepped back. "You're my husband in name only."

"In the sight of God and man, you swore your allegiance to me."

Lisa's foot slipped on the uneven earth behind her. One leg twisting behind the other, she fell to the ground.

He loomed over her. "Until death do us part."

"You made me. I had no choice!"

"You've as little choice now. Wait until we're in the hotel. I'll do whatever I like to you."

He yanked her upright. When Lisa cried out, Fix uncrossed his arms. "That's enough."

Donald ignored his words. He leaned forward. When she turned away from another harsh, sloppy kiss, he licked along the side of her face.

"Please," she begged.

Fix said, "Let her go."

"Not your business, Quincy."

"This isn't what I signed on for."

"She has to learn her lessons," Donald said.

Distracted by the other man, he loosened his grip. The burning sensation in Lisa's arm lightened, replaced by a throbbing ache.

"We're going to disagree about that," Fix said.

"She's a mail-order bride, Quince. What was it you said about those kinds of women? No better than a whore."

"Those weren't my words."

"As good as. When Lisa ran off, she proved you were right."

"You're hurting me," Lisa said. Leaning into him, she placed her mouth to Donald's ear. "I should never have run away. I'll never do it again."

Focused on Fix, Donald didn't respond.

"Don't hurt me," she whispered. "I'll do what you want. I can do *whatever* you want."

Surprised at her statement, he turned to her. Closing her eyes, wishing she didn't have to touch him, Lisa let her lips stroke over the stubble on the side of his face. "Please let me go."

"Never," he promised, releasing her arm.

When Donald opened his mouth to speak again, she raked her nails across his face. When he jumped away, she turned and ran.

Cursing loudly, he took after her. Within a few steps, she felt his hand grasp the collar of her dress. Donald yanked at it, the fabric squeezing around her throat. She could hear the cloth tear as she pitched backward.

She hit the ground, hard. For a moment, blackness swam above her. When her vision cleared, she saw that Donald was bent over her.

"Look what you've done," he said. He touched his fingers to the side of his face.

"Let her up," Fix said.

"There's blood." Donald slapped her, so hard that tears filled her eyes. "You don't think people are going to see this? You don't think people are going to talk?"

"You said you were coming here to reconcile." The tight control in Fix's voice had vanished. "You said she'd go with you willingly."

"I hate you," Lisa said to Donald.

"You'll have years to get over it." Wiping his red-tinted fingertips over the fabric of his pants, he ground his boot into her chest.

The heel of the shoe sent a bolt of pain between her breasts. Lisa groaned.

"I told you, no more," Fix said. He took a step toward them.

Drawing the pistol from his holster, Donald pointed it at the advancing Fix. "Stay right there, understand?"

Fix stopped.

"Guess you wish you'd worn your guns to church," Donald said. "In hindsight and all."

From the end of the street, the neighborhood dog started barking again. Somewhere nearby, Lisa could hear a horse running at full gallop.

"You want to tell me what happens next, Skroch?" Fix asked.

"You've got your money, Quince. This isn't any interest of yours. You go about your business, leave me to mine."

"What if I'm disinclined to do so?"

"If I have to put a bullet in you, it'll be a kill shot."

Lisa said, "Let me go, Donald."

He pretended she hadn't spoken.

"You can't force me to leave with you," Lisa said. "Someone will stop you. There are other people around."

"Like the good Andy Bishop?" Watching the gunman but speaking to Lisa, Donald said, "The sheriff and his deputy left town last night, some kind of emergency. Anyone here needs the law, I'm all they've got."

Unable to help herself, she said, "Then they don't have much."

Pausing in his scrutiny of the other man, Donald spit on her. Lisa could feel his thick saliva sliding down her neck. When she turned her head, she saw Fix standing in the middle of the street. His eyes were as cold and unblinking as a hawk's.

A horse whinnied, its rider coming toward them. Ignoring the new arrival, Donald remained focused on the glowering Quincy Fix.

Turning her head to the other side, Lisa watched as Gambit pulled to a stop. Pearce dropped down, his boots striking the earth. Almost simultaneously, he reached for the holster beneath his right hand.

Before Donald could react, he pressed the pistol's silver barrel to the lawman's head. Pearce said, "Get away from her. Touch her again and it's the last thing you'll do."

Chapter Thirty-Five

"Get your foot off of her."

Donald's jaw clenched. Lisa could almost feel the heat of his anger. In his expression, there wasn't any indication that he was afraid of this interloper or his threat. His boot stayed where it was, pinning her to the earth. "Do something smart," he told Pearce. "Get on that horse and leave while you're able."

"Ten seconds."

"You're making a mistake, friend."

"I'm not your friend."

"You'd best hope I feel differently. I wear a badge on my chest. If you hadn't snuck up behind me, you'd have seen it."

"He knows who you are," Lisa said.

A flash of awareness filled Donald's eyes. Almost imperceptivity, he rocked his heel downward.

Lisa bit her lower lip, fighting against the pain. If she cried out, the situation would escalate quickly.

If things spiral, she thought, *Donald will die, Pearce will go to jail, and Quincy Fix will be free to….*

She didn't know how to complete her thought. The man with the shaved head felt like a mystery to her.

Fix said, "Stranger, that's a mighty fancy gun you're holding. An impressive gun belt, too. I believe I've seen it before."

"This has nothing to do with you," Pearce told him.

"The Prescott Kid wore a belt like that one," Fix said. "Hand-tooled and special-made, with the image of Tyler's Butte engraved near the left holster. I imagine there's only one like it in the world." He paused, allowing the others to reflect on his words. "Yet you're wearing it."

"He's not the Prescott Kid," Donald said. "I've got Ted Nelson's wanted poster on my wall."

Fix told him, "You can clear a bit of space. When I was down Tucson way, I heard Nelson was dead."

Pearce cocked the hammer of his gun.

Donald removed his foot from Lisa's chest. He lifted his arms reluctantly, his pistol pointed toward the sky.

"Put your weapon down," Pearce said.

Moving slowly, Donald placed his revolver on the ground. "You took out the Kid?"

"He didn't give me a choice."

"Was it a fair draw?"

"Does it matter?"

Donald kept his arms in the air as he stood up. "I don't know what this woman told you but we're married. She's my wife."

"She told me."

"You still put a gun on me?"

"She doesn't like her husband."

"She belongs to me." Donald said this as a statement of fact.

In most of the country, Lisa knew, he was exactly right.

"Under man's law and God's as well," he continued. "Don't you know your scripture? 'For the wife does not have authority over her own body but her husband does.'"

243

Sitting up, Lisa took a deep breath. "Funny how you never remember the rest of the verse."

Even if he had, she knew Donald would have dismissed the line that followed: *For the husband does not have authority over his own body but his wife does.* He enjoyed quoting the parts of the Bible that echoed his own philosophies. The sections that displeased him, he simply ignored.

Getting to her feet, Lisa brushed at the mark on her blouse. His hands above his head, Donald moved aside to let her pass.

Pearce asked, "Did he hurt you?"

"I'm stronger than he thinks." Picking up the sheriff's pistol, Lisa trained its barrel on Quincy Fix. "Stronger than you think, too."

"Ah, you do remember me." For a man who had a firearm pointed at him, Fix remained remarkably calm. "I wondered if you would. The beautiful mail-order bride."

"The reason you came to Wyatt Ridge," Lisa said.

Fix lifted an eyebrow. "Who told you that?"

"That's why Donald brought you with him. You were supposed to help him find me, then force me to return to Tate City. When you saw me outside of the church, you ran to fetch him."

"You're right, I told Skroch I'd seen you," Fix said. "That's the only part you got right. I wouldn't do it again."

The lie rolled smoothly from his lips. If Lisa hadn't known better, she might have believed him.

Fix said, "From time to time, your husband has paid me to do one job or another. Whenever people have disappeared so far down the rabbit hole that even he can't find them. That's what I do, I track people."

Lisa scoffed, "You're certain that's all you do?"

"I haven't taken any of his money in a good while," Fix said. "Haven't held any of his cash for many months. I didn't see him until he joined my stage at Tate City."

"You're the one who told him I was in Wyatt Ridge."

"I did not."

"You say this is all coincidence?"

"They do happen," the gunman said.

Lisa didn't understand what he hoped to gain with this new fabrication. It might have been a coincidence that Donald was traveling on the same coach as Fix; as unlikely as it seemed, it could even be a coincidence that they had both arrived at the same small town.

But there was no reasonable explanation for why they were riding to the Broken H together, as Felicia had said, unless they were working as a team. If she asked Fix about it, he'd quickly make another excuse for his actions. He was a gifted liar.

Unarmed yet unafraid, Fix remained several feet away from them. He was too far away to endanger her or Pearce at the moment.

Lisa lowered her weapon. Instantly, Pearce pulled her close to him. He hadn't shaved, and his clothing smelled of musk and hay. She didn't care. He'd never looked more attractive.

Focused on the woman in front of him, he his kept his gun hand directed toward Donald Skroch.

"You were supposed to stay at the ranch," she said.

"The only place I'm going to be is with you."

One eye opened, he kissed her. Behind him, she heard Donald make an unhappy sound.

"He hit you," Pearce said. His lips brushed over the reddened skin on her cheek.

This action proved more than Donald could accept. Lowering his arms, he said, "Let me remind you, that's my wife."

Staring into Lisa's eyes, Pearce said, "In name only."

"You think that's how it is? Holding a gun on me means you can steal this slut?"

Pearce's head came up abruptly. "Watch your tongue."

"Or what?" Donald challenged him. "You'll kiss the harlot again?"

"Ignore him," Lisa said.

Donald said, "It's easy to think you're something when you have a pistol in your hand, isn't it, cowboy? It helps you forget who you really are."

"And what's that?"

"Someone as worthless as the tramp I married."

Lisa clutched at Pearce's shoulders. "What he says doesn't matter. He's nothing compared to you."

"Look at how she clings to you," Donald said. "What else has she done with you? Sleep with you? Did the strumpet climb naked into your bed?"

Pearce's face colored in anger.

"Don't," Lisa said. "Please don't."

"He's asked for it." Reaching for the buckle on his gun belt, Pearce released it.

"A fight, sodbuster?" Donald asked. "You'd best listen to the slut. Run while you're able. I might let you live."

To Lisa, Pearce said, "He can say what he wants about me, but not you." He placed his gun belt at her feet. "Keep your pistol aimed at Fix. If he moves, shoot him."

Hearing his words, Fix shook his head. "I'm not a threat to you."

"Glad to hear it," Pearce said. To Lisa, he added, "If Fix so much as breathes wrong, don't go for the head. Aim for the gut. Harder to miss and he'll probably bleed out."

Bleed out? Lisa thought. An image came to mind: Fix, lying in the dirt as a circle of scarlet grew beneath him.

Only if my life depends on it, she decided. She didn't trust the black-suited man, but she no longer knew if he was a villain. When Donald had threatened her, he'd tried to come to her aid.

She told him, "You heard what Pearce said."

"Pearce? That's your beau's name?"

"Don't make me pull this trigger. I swear I will."

Fix laughed softly.

Rolling his shoulders, Pearce stepped in front of Donald. A delighted expression filled the other man's face.

"You're not serious," Donald said.

"You and me. Now."

"How many men have you fought? Maybe a dozen? At best?"

"Raise your fists."

"I've beaten a hundred of your kind."

From the way he held himself, Lisa realized Pearce knew how to fight. She still didn't want him to come to blows with Donald.

Donald fought for the pleasure of it. He liked to see people bleed.

"In five minutes, I'll have you on your knees," Donald continued. "You'll weep for mercy."

"You do like to talk. I'm getting tired of it."

"How do I know the bitch won't shoot –?"

Pearce's fist swung forward, hammering the other man's mouth and knocking him down. Donald hit the ground sharply, the back of his vest sending a puff of dust into the air when he fell.

He climbed to his feet, a trickle of blood dripping from his lower lip. "Not bad for a cowboy."

Dipping his right hand into his pants pocket, Donald straightened. Balling his hands into fists, he swung for the other man's head.

Pearce ducked below the blow. His arm snapped out, popping his opponent under the eye.

Donald shook it off. Grabbing Pearce's collar with one hand, he pulled him in and dug a hard hand into the taller man's side. He hit him hard and fast: once, twice, a third time.

Pearce tore free from his hold. Dropping his left elbow, he protected the area where he'd been pummeled.

"You're in over your head, you lowlife pissant," Donald said. A ham-sized fist shot forward, crashing into his opponent's ribs.

Grunting, Pearce stepped out of range. He tried to hide his pain, but he was hurt.

"There's something on his hand," Lisa warned. There were a series of round, wooden rings looping over the fingers on Donald's right hand.

"It's a knuckleduster," Pearce said. "Cowards carry them."

Lisa pointed the revolver at Donald. "Take it off."

With sudden alarm in his voice, Pearce said, "Quincy Fix!"

Lisa whirled around.

In the few seconds since she'd looked away, the man with the shaved head had moved only slightly. At first, she couldn't tell why Pearce had sounded concerned. Then she saw her umbrella, retrieved from where it had dropped and held behind Fix's back.

"Put that down!"

Fix brought it in front of him. Holding the umbrella's shaft, he casually threw it aside.

Taking solid, heavy steps, Donald advanced on Pearce. Even with the gun in her hand, Lisa felt helpless.

I can threaten him all I like, she thought, *and Donald won't care. He knows I'm not experienced with firearms.*

Trying to shoot him, I'm just as likely to hit Pearce.

Chapter Thirty-Six

"You know why I've never lost a fight?" Donald mused out loud. "I find the other man's weakness and exploit it."

Circling around him, Pearce said, "There you go, talking again."

"I find something that matters to my enemy and I threaten him with it. Usually, it's a family member or a friend. Sometimes it's a woman, a whore like the one I –"

His eyes narrowing, Pearce charged him. Wrapping his arms around the blond-haired man, he drove him to the ground. Donald yelled out as both men smashed against the hard, brown surface.

Stunned, Donald lay on his back as Pearce rose over him.

"I hate cheats," Pearce said. He lifted his leg.

Donald threw his left hand over his face as the cowboy's boot crashed down, striking his other hand and shattering the knuckleduster. "Jesus!"

Grabbing his opponent's vest, Pearce pulled the sheriff to his feet. Cocking his arm, he said, "You will never –"

"You broke my hand," Donald said.

Pearce hit him in the face. "– ever –"

"I'll kill you."

Pearce hit him in the face. "– ever –"

Donald sputtered, spitting blood.

"– speak of Lisa again." Pearce hit him a last time, releasing the vest as he did. Donald tumbled, his legs failing him as he collapsed.

Blood stained the corner of Donald's mouth and there were drops of red coloring his chin. One eye was puffed and red, indicating that it would be purple and swollen by morning.

His one clear eye glared up at them both. Refusing to acknowledge defeat, Donald struggled to his knees as a line of pink drool slid from his open mouth. Awkwardly, he shoved his left hand inside of his vest.

Blam! An explosion of sound tore through the air.

Whirling around, Lisa found Quincy Fix with one arm pointed upward. Lowering his hand, he displayed the derringer he'd taken from her umbrella.

"What are you doing?" Lisa demanded.

He slipped the derringer inside a pocket of his tailored suit. Cupping his hands around his mouth, he shouted, "Fight!"

His face wrinkling in confusion, Pearce stared at him. Donald staggered upright, dropping his hand from his vest. Like Pearce, he turned toward Fix.

"Fight!" the gunman shouted. "Fight, fight!"

The back door of the New Hope Assembly building opened. Reverend Leydecker's housekeeper, Alison, ran outside, drawn by Fix's call. Her husband, Kenneth, followed behind her.

From the front of the building, the rest of the congregation soon appeared. Wearing a dark suit with a red tie, his white hair slicked behind each ear, the preacher led a flow of people toward the combatants.

As people pushed past him, Fix offered one more, very loud, call: "Fight!"

The townspeople gathered in a circle around Lisa and the two men. She recognized some familiar faces. Kevin Tennant, the blacksmith, served as the reverend's muscular shadow while Rupert Capehart lingered at the rear of the crowd.

Felicia Arnold shouldered her way forward. "Where is it, then? Is there a fight or isn't there?"

"I don't allow fighting on church grounds," Leydecker reminded his followers.

A short man in a well-fitting suit bumped past Felicia. Staring at Donald, he said, "You. It can't be."

At a glance, Donald dismissed him. He did a second take, surprise creasing his brow. "Clarence Foster. All this time, this is where you went."

"You shouldn't be here," the orange-haired Foster said.

Felicia asked, "What's the matter, Clancy?"

"Donald Skroch shouldn't be here." His voice rising and panicked, Foster repeated, "He shouldn't be here!"

"Bugger off," Donald told him. "I'll deal with you later."

Foster scurried past Lisa, a haunted expression in his eyes. She heard a thin, keening sound from inside his chest before he disappeared into the crowd.

The blacksmith grumbled, "What about the fight?"

"If there was one, it's over now," Felicia said. Studying the men before her, she added, "Looks like we know who won, too."

Leydecker *tsk'ed*. "Violence is never a satisfactory solution."

"Tell that to Jesus and the money changers," Felicia said. "Lisa Hanlon, what are you doing with a gun in your hand?"

Donald told her, "That's mine."

He made a move to reach for it, only to stop short when Pearce stepped in front of him. The lawman faced the party around him.

"I'm Donald Skroch, duly appointed sheriff of Tate City," he told them. "Prevented from doing my job by this woman." He pointed a thick, discolored index finger at Lisa.

"That's not why you're here," Felicia said.

"I'm in Wyatt Ridge to arrest this man –" Refusing to face Pearce, he waved a hand in his direction "– for the murder of Ted Nelson, the Prescott Kid!"

Voices erupted at this revelation. The people closest to Lisa and Pearce started to distance themselves from the pair.

Only Felicia and Reverend Leydecker remained beside them. Leydecker said, "Is this true, Lisa?"

"It doesn't matter what she says," Donald protested. "I've told you what happened."

"She's Ted Hanlon's niece," the preacher said. "I knew Ted and I've met Lisa. I trust her." Left unspoken was the rest of his statement: *But I have no reason to trust you.*

Leydecker's opinion carried weight with the people of the Ridge. Sensing this, Donald scowled in frustration.

Lisa met the Reverend's eyes. "Donald's not telling the truth. Not all of it."

"Hardly any of it," a softly-accented voice interjected. The church members parted as the speaker

253

approached as if they knew better than to slow his progress.

"Quincy Fix." Felicia spat the name, disgust in her voice.

The bounty hunter gave her a look, but his step never faltered. Intent on delivering his message, Fix walked over to the preacher.

Pearce stayed with Lisa. She held his hand, feeling stronger because he was with her.

In a voice so low that it could barely be heard, Donald said, "Stay out of it, Quincy. I thought you were with me on this."

"Today has been a learning experience for both us," Fix said. Facing the congregation, he said, "Am I speaking loud enough? Can you in the back hear me?"

No one responded. The church-goers seemed afraid to answer.

"The Prescott Kid is dead, that much is so," Fix said. "If Pearce Folsom killed him, the people of Arizona owe the man a debt of gratitude."

A chill ran over Lisa.

She thought, *Did Fix say 'Pearce Folsom'? Folsom? When did he learn Pearce's last name?*

I didn't use it. Pearce didn't use it.

How does Fix know it?

"Ted Nelson died in a gunfight," Fix continued. "I heard the Kid drew first. A fair fight. Skroch knows there's no warrant out for Folsom's arrest. In fact, if he ever decides to return to Tucson, I imagine he could run for mayor."

"Is this so, Sheriff Skroch?" Reverend Leydecker asked.

Donald rubbed his tongue over his broken lip, as if this discomfort prevented him from offering an immediate response.

He's trying to think of a new story, Lisa realized.

"Are you here on official business?" Leydecker asked.

Felicia held up her hand, as if asking for permission to speak. "I know!"

"Stupid cow," Donald muttered.

"This fool here, the one with the badge, came into my store yesterday," Felicia said. "Asking for directions to Ted Hanlon's ranch. He'd come to our town, intending to force one of our neighbors to leave with him. He doesn't know when he's not wanted."

"That woman is my wife," Donald said.

Squeezing Pearce's hand for support, Lisa loudly announced, "I want a divorce!"

Again, voices lifted in surprise. From behind the others, Capehart brightened. He said, "Divorce?"

"That's what you want?" Donald managed a single, barking laugh. "I expect you do!"

Capehart started to push his way forward.

To Leydecker, Donald said, "Tell her, bible thumper, I imagine you know this. Women can't ask for divorce."

Having slid past his fellow citizens at a remarkable speed, Capehart clapped his hand on the clergyman's shoulder. "Let me take this one, Horace."

Leydecker appeared relieved.

Capehart said, "Not only does Lisa have such rights, sir, I'll have you know my client has already asked me to draw up the papers."

"Mr. Capehart?" Lisa said.

He gave her a conspiratorial grin. "Come by my office tomorrow, Sheriff, and I'll have everything ready for your perusal. We can get this settled by mid-morning."

Opening his mouth to speak, Donald's words deserted him. His mouth hung loosely before he closed his teeth with an audible *snick*.

"Things will proceed more smoothly if we can have your signature on the agreement," Capehart added.

Donald's unfocused gaze found Lisa. Hatred filled his eyes. "Give me my pistol."

"No." Lisa leaned against Pearce. He put his arm around her.

"That gun belongs to me," Donald said. "I'll have it, by God, or I will see you in jail."

He was covered with dirt, his face was bruised, and his recent beating had left him barely able to stand – and yet Lisa was still so frightened of Donald, she couldn't move.

"You little shit," he hissed to her. "What do you think I'm going to do with all of these people here?"

It's not here that worries me, Lisa thought. *It's what you'll do... later.*

As if he'd read her mind, Pearce told her, "There are always other weapons to be found." Gently, he removed the pistol from her hand.

Donald took the gun. For a brief, terrifying moment, Lisa was certain he was going to shoot them both.

He shoved the revolver into his holster.

"I'll never sign those papers, shyster," he told the lawyer. "My wife isn't going to divorce me. I won't allow it." To the people in front of him, he said, "Get the hell out of my way."

Seconds later, he was gone.

Chapter Thirty-Seven

Standing in the examination room, Pearce let his shirt drop to the floor. Lisa was shocked to see the large bruises marking the left side of his chest. When she approached him, he held out a hand to stop her.

"Touching isn't a good idea," Pearce said. "Not for a while."

Dr. McCauley said, "You should have paid more attention to your scriptures, Mr. Folsom. Sundays are supposed to be a day of rest."

"This wasn't his doing," Lisa protested.

"I heard he gave as good as he got. Margaret Tennant stopped by for a visit, just before your arrival. She gave me a colorful accounting of today's events, both real and imagined."

"Imagined?" Pearce asked.

"Our blacksmith's wife loves an exciting story. She's not beyond creating her own." Seated, McCauley pushed his chair closer to his patient. His stethoscope hung loosely around his neck, ignored, as he lifted his fingers to Pearce's side.

Pearce flinched at the gentle pressure.

"Hurts, I expect," McCauley said. "Hurts on contact, hurts to take a breath. Am I correct?"

Closing his eyes, Pearce took shallow breaths as the doctor completed his examination.

"Cracked ribs. From the discoloration, I feared it might be worse." Leaving his chair, the doctor opened the two arched panel doors of a yellow pine cabinet. He pulled a roll of cloth bindings from the lowest shelf. "I usually charge an extra fee on holidays and Sundays."

Lisa rose in protest. "This wasn't his doing!"

"Be seated."

"I won't."

"If, if, *if*, you remain in your chair and unmoving, *if* you don't speak to me or interrupt me, I will tend to Mr. Folsom without charge," the doctor said. "On the other hand, if you should feel the need to remain standing, or if you decide to threaten or abuse me – if you once again express a desire to paint me from head to buttocks with iodine – then you can both leave, and good day."

Lisa sat down.

McCauley returned to his patient's side. Placing the first strip of binding above the injured rib, he said, "Exhale."

Pursing his lips, Pearce released a slow stream of air.

The physician encircled the chest twice, knotting the binding on the opposite side from the injury. "There are some folks around here who don't approve of divorce, no matter the reason. Not as many as five years ago, but some. It goes a long way when the Reverend stands with you."

"Margaret Tennant needs to tend to her own business," Lisa said.

She stopped talking when McCauley frowned at her. He told Pearce, "Breathe normally. Is the wrap too tight?"

"It's not bad."

259

"Let's do it once more, then." Sliding a finger below the injured rib, he positioned a second strip of binding. "Who was the fellow who came to town with Sheriff Skroch? What's his name?"

"Quincy Fix," Lisa said.

When Pearce exhaled on command, McCauley pulled this new binding around his chest. "If Mr. Fix was here to assist in your retrieval, why did he fire that pistol? He had to know it would alert the people inside the church."

Like McCauley, Lisa was at a loss to explain the gunman's behavior.

"I might know," Pearce said. When he shifted his upper body, the cloth ties mimicked the move. "When Skroch went down, he reached inside his vest. I saw the silver knob of a large knife as his hand closed over it. He was going to pull a blade on me."

McCauley clucked in disapproval. "Leaving you at a disadvantage."

"Extremely so."

"Fix may have seen the knife or he may have simply known of its existence," McCauley said. "For reasons of his own, he decided to draw the congregation outside. If there were people watching you, Lisa's husband couldn't use his blade."

"Please quit calling Donald, 'my husband'," Lisa said.

"Sorry." He handed the fallen shirt to Pearce. "I'd say Quincy Fix did you a favor. Why?"

"One of life's mysteries," Pearce said.

Lisa thought, *I can't agree more.*

At the door, McCauley told Pearce, "You're not to ride today. Not even in the two-seater."

"We have to go home," Pearce insisted.

"No riding today, no lifting for the next month. Ignore my orders and you'll spend the night, coughing up blood. Or you may puncture a lung."

"I'll get us a room at the hotel," Lisa said.

"They'll want cash up front. More cash than we have," Pearce said. "Besides, with both boarding houses filled, Skroch must be staying there. Fix, too. I don't care to see either of them again."

Stopping at the front door, Lisa peered through the crystal oval placed in its center. "You're wrong."

"If you have a different idea, share it. Otherwise, the Broken H is our only choice."

"I meant, you're wrong about the whereabouts of Quincy Fix. He's not at the hotel. He's sitting on the doctor's front porch."

When Lisa went outside, the tall man stood from the swing to greet her, leaving his hat on its wicker seat. Pearce joined her, placing a hand on her waist.

As simple as the gesture was, it struck her as a protective move: *Bother my woman, you'll be fighting me.*

"What do you want, Mr. Fix?" Her question came out sharply but she didn't care. Even if this man had helped them, he'd done so for reasons of his own. His past behavior and previous history painted him as one of life's blackguards.

"I'm here to apologize," the blackguard said. No longer influenced by the stain of his disapproval of her, his deep voice sounded warm. In other circumstances, his

261

accent might have sounded charming. "For my behavior, both recent and bygone."

"As well you should."

He told her, "When we first met, those many months ago, I misjudged you. Once I learned you were a mail-order bride, I purposely ignored you. Wouldn't speak to you, preferred not to eat alongside you."

Lisa remembered the experience all too well. "Is this your apology?"

"I shouldn't have directed my anger at you. Nor at your companion on the stage, another lovely woman. I was mad at someone else. The only other mail-order bride I'd ever had occasion to know." His face grew tense, drawn taut by some private memory. "I failed to consider the quality of the women before me, preferring to judge them by a choice they'd made. It was a mistake I'll not repeat."

Lisa couldn't help but wonder about the mysterious mail-order bride that had angered Fix. Somehow, she knew this was a story she'd never hear.

One of life's mysteries, as Pearce had said.

She asked, "Why are you in Wyatt Ridge?"

"I was looking for Pearce Folsom."

When Fix reached inside his jacket, Pearce's fingers fell from her waist. His hand dropped to the gun at his side.

Pinching a pair of brown envelopes between his fingers, Fix offered them to the man in front of him. "These are yours."

"What are they?"

"Open them and find out," Fix said. "You've sent me on a merry chase, Folsom, through half of the Western

262

states and a few of the territories. Cost your folks a pretty penny. Not that they can't afford it."

A feminine hand had written Pearce's name on both envelopes. He said, "That's Mother's writing."

"The thicker envelope contains cash money, enough for travel and a good deal more. The thinner one holds a letter."

Taking the slimmer paper packet, Pearce held it. He ran his fingertips over his name, as if it would bring him closer to person who wrote it.

"You haven't spoken of your parents," Lisa told him.

Shaking his head, he didn't speak of them now.

Fix reached for Lisa's hand, returning her derringer to her palm. "I had an umbrella like that once. Too heavy when it rains."

Opening her handbag, she placed the weapon inside.

"There's still a pellet in one chamber, but that spit pistol's not good at any range. That's why I fired it into the air."

"Thank you for that."

"If you're in a place where you need to pull its trigger, you'd best be close to your adversary," he added. "Very close."

Pearce carried the envelope to the small table on the porch. Sitting down, he opened it and removed a single sheet of paper. When he was done reading, he folded the letter and returned it to its sleeve.

"My father's ill," he told Lisa. "Mother wants me to come home. My brothers…."

"Are they all right?"

"They miss me. All of them miss me, even Father. They want me to return to Granville."

Granville, Lisa thought. It was so far from the Ridge. If Pearce left, she feared he'd never return.

"I need to go," he said.

Looking at his face and hearing the tone in his voice, she realized how much he'd missed his family.

I don't want you to go, she thought. *Now that we've finally found each other, how can I lose you?*

If she objected, Lisa believed he'd stay with her. She couldn't do it. She loved him too much to force him to make such a choice.

"I'll send your family a telegram, let them know you're coming," Fix said.

"Appreciated."

Replacing the hat on his head, the gunman told them, "Skroch is sitting center table at the Glory Hole. His right hand is wrapped in cotton and his left hand is filled with a shot glass. When he sobers up, he'll come looking for you."

"I beat him once," Pearce said.

"He didn't know what kind of man he was facing then." Tipping his hat to the couple, Fix said, "I wish you luck."

Chapter Thirty-Eight

Pearce had insisted they buy new clothing and then stop at the bathhouse before arriving at their next destination.

"There was five hundred dollars in the second envelope," he told her. "Travel won't cost nearly that much. If we're going to be guests at someone's home, the least we can do is arrive clean."

Once those stops had been made, they went to Arnold's Dry Goods. Welcoming them, Felicia had immediately closed shop before escorting them to the quiet street where she lived.

Her house was a two-story tall box, the biggest house in her neighborhood but nearly devoid of the stylistic touches that characterized the other homes in the area. As if its builder was aware of his creation's shortcomings, he'd distanced it from the other buildings on the land. It sat alone at the end of the street.

Opening the door of a guest bedroom, Felicia said, "When we purchased this plot of land, Ethem promised me copper-coated cupolas and Dutch gables. What I got was white woodwork and plain glass windows."

With Pearce standing behind her, Lisa said, "Because Ethem never took the time to finish the job?"

"Good gracious, that wasn't it. He had glorious plans for our place. I'm not fancy enough for all those frills. I told him we needed space, with a library for his books and a place for my quilting. I asked for four big bedrooms, so that visitors could have a little breathing room when they came to stay."

"Thank you for having us," Pearce said.

But Felicia wasn't finished speaking. "If he'd had his druthers, Ethem would have built me my very own gingerbread palace. My reward for putting up with a man like him, I expect. He never understood that a home isn't the four walls that surround you. That's just a house. When I fell asleep in his arms, I was home."

Tears glistened at the corners of her eyes. Felicia refused to wipe at them. "Seeing the two of you together, seeing you fight for what's important, it did my heart good. It reminded me of the way things used to be with Ethem. You've given me much to think about."

Lisa felt Pearce's arm curl around her shoulders. She clung to him, knowing that their remaining time together was all too brief.

Felicia said, "I'll be opening shop in the morning, so you'll need to find your own breakfast in the pantry. You have a big day ahead so you'd best get some sleep."

Before she shut the door, she gave Lisa a big wink.

"Felicia's husband was an ass," Pearce said.

He was wrong to go, Lisa wanted to agree, but she couldn't say it out loud. Pearce might misunderstand, thinking she was asking him to stay with her.

As Felicia had said, the guest bedroom was spacious. It was almost twice the size of the master bedroom at the Broken H. The walls were decorated with flocked wallpaper striped in silver and gold. Centered in the room was a bed with four low posts, its mattress draped by a beautiful red and green block pattern quilt. Below the side window, a walnut side table held a basin, two washcloths, and a pitcher of fresh water.

Lisa placed her handbag at the bottom of the wooden clothes cabinet. Pulling aside the quilt, Pearce sat on the corner of the bed. His arms dangled wearily at his sides, as if he was too tired to unbutton his own shirt.

She joined him on the mattress. Gently, she began to undo the buttons over his chest.

"Under Ted's care, the Broken H lasted for decades," he told her. "Treated properly, it can thrive for another hundred years."

"It was a different era," Lisa said. "In the time since I've been here, I've already seen one farm fold. Even the big spreads are barely getting by."

"Not farming, not cattle," he told her. "Properly fenced, the ranch would be perfect for horses. You've seen the mustangs filling the hills around here."

"Those stallions are too wild for the Ridge."

"The town's stable master feels differently. When he saw Gambit, he told me he'd take a half-dozen like him if I could break them." With his shirt open, he shrugged it off of his shoulders. "There's no time now."

"The letter," Lisa said.

"That letter, yes. When family calls, I have to answer. When I was younger, I somehow didn't know that."

"I understand." And she did, if only because of the lessons she'd learned from Ted Hanlon.

When she needed him most, he'd been there for her. Then, when his need was greatest, she was blessed to be there for him.

Feeling as if her heart was shattering, Lisa kissed Pearce. It was the saddest kiss she'd ever given, stitched together with loneliness and a desperate desire to do what was right for the man beside her.

"We're agreed then," he said. "Whether it's a few months or as much as a year, we'll return to the Ridge. We'll catch the horses and I'll break them. It won't be the start of an empire, but it will be the start of our lives together."

Lisa caught her breath.

"That is, if you'll have me," he told her.

"What… what are you saying?"

"Will you marry me, Lisa Hanlon?"

At the happiest moment of her life, Lisa began to cry.

*****

A string of gray clouds muddied the morning sky overhead. Leaving Felicia's house, they began the walk to the lawyer's office.

"What if Skroch won't sign the divorce papers?" Pearce asked.

"According to Felicia, I'll still have grounds to leave him," Lisa said. "As long as I can produce a witness to Donald's behavior."

"To his abuse. I'll tell the judge about Skroch's boot on your chest." His voice sounded darker than the impending weather.

"It would be better if the words didn't come from the man I was going to marry. Felicia will stand up in court."

"I don't care if he wears a badge. One day I'll settle this with Sheriff Skroch."

"I'd rather you not."

Although they'd not yet reached the neighboring houses, Lisa thought she heard the sound of a leaf crackling beneath a heavy foot. Unsettled, she was starting to turn around when Donald stepped in behind Pearce.

"Donald!"

"Quiet." Wrapping an arm around Pearce's neck, he pressed the barrel of his gun to the back of his victim's head. "If anyone makes a fuss, I'll pull the trigger."

Donald's hair was matted, and his face was pale and splotchy. His eyes were red, as if he'd spent the night drinking – or hiding outside of Felicia's house, a bottle in hand, while awaiting their departure from the building.

"It doesn't feel so good, does it, cowboy?" Donald asked. "A revolver pressed to your skull. Doesn't offer a fellow a proper chance."

"Face me, then. Prove you're the better man," Pearce said.

"You'd welcome a fight, wouldn't you? Knowing I'd be at a disadvantage, seeing how you've destroyed my right hand." He jabbed the barrel forward, the steel surface causing Pearce to wince.

"Drop your gun belt." Releasing his hold on Pearce's neck, Donald took a long step away from the other man. He trained his weapon on Lisa.

Pearce reached for the belt buckle. Donald's lips twisted in an ugly smile.

He's going to kill him, Lisa thought. "Tell me what you want, Donald. Do you want me to go with you, be your wife?"

"You were never going to be my wife. You were only going to be my whore."

Leaving his belt and guns at his feet, Pearce straightened. Instantly, Donald moved forward, pressing the gun barrel into his back.

Donald said, "Let's ease around to the rear of the house."

"Off of the street and out of view?"

"For a sodbuster, you pick up things quick. Hands overhead."

"I can't. You cracked my ribs."

The information pleased his captor. "Do it, anyway. Do it or Lisa bleeds."

Awkwardly, Pearce raised his arms.

Fright stabbed at Lisa, not for herself but for the man she loved. "I'll go with you, Donald. I'll be… whatever you want."

His misshapen smile returned.

"I'll return to Tate City. I'll behave."

"I expect you will," he agreed, "once I'm finished here."

"Finished?"

He laughed. The ugly sound was followed by a wet cough. He spat a thick glob of yellow onto the dirt.

"You're a man of the law, Donald," Lisa said.

"All to my advantage, don't you think? Fewer questions later." He prodded with his gun. "I'm not good with my left hand, Folsom, but it's all I've got. You keep standing here, my finger might just slip."

Pearce's lean face showed no fear. "Wouldn't want that to happen."

Barely able to breath, Lisa prayed Donald wouldn't notice as she reached for the catch on her handbag. Balanced between Lisa's thumb and forefinger, the clasp slipped open.

"*Sheriff!*" a voice shrieked.

Fifty yards behind them, a short, orange-haired man in white shirt and brown slacks appeared. A rifle's walnut stock was tucked under his arm.

After a glance, Donald spat a second circle of mucus at his feet. "Clarence Foster."

"You shouldn't have come here, Sheriff Skroch," the little man cried. "You should have left me alone!"

Donald shifted his stance, allowing him to focus on Foster. "I'm not here for you, Clarence. Why would I be?"

"You know why."

"You think I'd cross three states to get my half of the telegraph office money? For sixty dollars?"

"You would. You did." Sounding aggrieved, Foster wailed, "I left Abbie May because of you!"

He waved his rifle at the sheriff.

Pearce had spoken about Clancy Foster. Felicia had told him that the little man owned a Winchester rifle but didn't know how to use it. From the way he was holding it now, Lisa believed she'd been correct.

When Donald gave his attention to this new opponent, Pearce dropped his arms slightly, his biceps tightening. Alarmed, Lisa realized he was readying himself to attack.

Donald said, "Abbie May's better off without you, Clarence. Ask anyone."

At this revelation, Foster vibrated in anger. When he dropped the rifle's butt to his shoulder, the sight on the gun danced in a jerky semaphore.

"Your entire married life, you've been a burden to her," Donald said. "She was never going to succeed with you at her side."

Opening the mouth of her purse, Lisa slipped her hand inside.

"You lie!"

"Piss off, Clarence." Suddenly swinging around, Donald thrust his bandaged hand into Lisa's face. The stench of smoke-filled cotton filled her nostrils. Snarling, he shoved her to the ground.

Lisa's purse flew out of her hands, its contents spilling as it fell. Sliding in the dirt, the derringer spun outside of her reach.

"Did you think I wasn't watching you?" Donald asked. "Did you think I'd let you get the drop on me?"

Behind them, Clarence said, "Face me!"

Donald's reddened eyes stared down at Lisa. "Wait until I get you home."

A *crack* of sound echoed down the empty street. Donald's body jerked, his eyes widening. Taking an uncertain step, he dropped his pistol as he tottered sideways.

A confused expression on his face, he fell to his knees. Wheezing, he collapsed onto the dirt beside Lisa. A line of drool spilled from his mouth as his open eyes stared sightlessly at her.

As quickly as she could, she scrambled upright.

Is he dead? Lisa wondered.

He is. He's dead.

Donald's dead.

On the ground, a pool of blood darkened the soil beneath his body.

"I told you, Donald Skroch," Clarence cried from the end of the street. "I told you to face me!"

Pearce gathered Lisa to him. She pressed her face to his chest and they held each other.

At the end of the street, Clarence Foster raised the rifle over his head and whooped with joy.

Chapter Thirty-Nine

Sheriff Bishop said, "Take a seat."

"I'd prefer to stand."

"Suit yourself." Remaining in his chair, the lawman gave a cold stare to his visitor. "While I was away, it appears I missed all of the excitement. Perhaps you can tell me about Donald Skroch."

"I could," Quincy Fix admitted, "but why waste my time?"

No response from Bishop. He wasn't a big man but, Fix could tell, he considered himself as tough as old jerky. Inside this bare bones, strictly functional, two-cell jailhouse, he viewed himself as Lord and Master.

Fortunately, Bishop's deputy was out of the building. If he'd been present, the sheriff might have felt obligated to flex his muscles.

"You mean to test my patience, Mr. Fix?" he asked.

"No more than you test mine, Sheriff. You had me cool my heels while you spoke to Pearce Folsom, then Louisa Hanlon, then that Foster fellow. Unless their stories differed, you know what happened yesterday."

"I have a reliable source who said you came into town with him. You were working for him."

"Not for a second," Fix said. "I was paid by Randall Folsom."

"Folsom Mercantile." For whatever reason, the man's cold stare dropped a few more degrees. In the sheriff's eyes, Fix had selected the wrong employer.

If asked, Bishop wouldn't say why, but Fix didn't need an explanation. Small town people carried small town grudges. Years might pass, but they refused to let bygones be bygones.

Fix was the same way. It was something he didn't like about himself.

Bishop said, "Reverend Leydecker told me the victim, Donald Joseph Skroch, was in a fistfight the day before his death. Coincidentally, the man he fought was the son of Randall Folsom."

"What are the odds."

His flat affect irritated the smaller man. A twitch crossed his face before Bishop could continue. "The day of his death, Donald Skroch approached Pearce Folsom with intent to kill. Fortunately for Folsom, Clancy Foster, one of our newest citizens, happened to be walking nearby at the time. He also happened to be carrying a fully loaded Winchester rifle. When Skroch refused to lower his gun, when he cocked his pistol's trigger and pointed it at Folsom, Foster acted. He had no choice but to shoot Donald Skroch."

"Can't blame him," Fix decided.

"I can and I do," Bishop said. "Clancy Foster admits he never owned a firearm until he came to the Ridge. Despite this, he made the decision to point his rifle at an officer of the law and shoot him dead."

"It appears that way," Fix said. "Folsom and his woman were present. What did they say?"

"Near enough the same."

"There you have it."

Bishop cracked the knuckles of one fist and then the other. "Let me tell you what I think about Clancy Foster. He's good for nothing. In the short time he's been here, I've brought him in twice for stealing. Little things, items he could have purchased on his own if he'd worked for one solid hour in his entire life. Have you met the man?"

"Think so, briefly. Outside of the church."

"Did he ask you for money?"

"It wouldn't have done him any good if he had," Fix said.

"You have some commonsense, then. Foster's a blight on this community. The one time he thought of someone besides himself, he risked his life to be a hero. Does this seem likely to you?"

"Stranger things have happened." On Bishop's scowl, Fix added, "Can you describe a hero to me, Sheriff?"

"In the picture books, he'd look something like you. Wouldn't shave his head, maybe, but tall and strong. Nicely dressed. But you're no one's hero, are you?"

As far as Fix was concerned, this was just another reason to hate small towns. People who'd barely met one another felt they already knew them. He said, "Stage will be here in an hour or so. I'll be meeting it."

"I didn't say you could go."

Fix left, letting the door bang shut behind him. When he passed Arnold's Dry Goods, the store's owner stared out at him as if she was trying to memorize his face.

Take a long look, you black-tempered shrew, he thought, *because it's your last. Come hell or high water, I'll not return here.*

The relay station stood a block from Main Street, with enough land to maintain its own stable and a series of corrals. Passing through the alley that ran alongside the Glory Hole, Fix stopped when he thought he heard something. It wasn't much, a tiny squeal of sound, but it captured his attention.

At the bottom of a busted-up white oak barrel, he spotted a small burlap bag. The bag was knotted at the neck. As he watched, it squealed once more. A moment later, it gave a vigorous wiggle.

Fix removed the bag from the container. Reaching for the hand-stitched leather sheath strapped to his right leg, he freed his Bowie knife. Gripping its Rosewood handle, he squatted onto his heels before resting the tip of its blade beneath the coarse string that kept the sack closed.

With a flick of his wrist, the string would be severed. When the mouth of the bag fell open, the rats inside would scurry to escape.

He'd seen this a few times before. Some weak-hearted man or woman was clever enough to trap and contain the vermin infesting their home, but didn't have the guts to finish the job. Instead, they dropped the bag in an alley, hoping the captured creatures would starve to death.

"People," he said, disgusted.

Left alone, the rats were more likely to chew their way out of the bag, escaping to pillage other houses. If the creatures were old or weak, they might die inside their fabric prison, but he couldn't abide that idea, either. He hated acts of cruelty.

Best get to it.

It was better for all if the rodents had a swift death. The moment the bag fell open, the second he saw the pink of the rodents' eyes, he'd kill them.

He sliced the knife upward and the string fell, its hold undone. The top of the bag slowly folded open.

A kitten stared up at Fix.

"What in blazes are you doing here?"

He'd never owned a cat but, in his view, this was far from a prime example of its species. Barely bigger than a rat itself, the thing was white-furred with patches of skin plainly visible beneath its hair. One of its eyes was blue while the other one was green.

"You're not much," he told the beast. "You still deserve more than this, though. You're free."

The cat remained in a sitting position, watching him.

"Go on, you worthless puss. You want your master to return and bag you again?"

The cat stretched its body forward. Rubbing the crown of its head along the gunman's finger, it began to purr.

"Scat!" Yanking his finger away, Fix stood up. "Something's the matter with you, cat. After what you've gone through, you should hate people. Get going."

The kitten showed no inclination to follow his advice. Since it wouldn't leave, Fix decided he would.

Stupid thing, he ruminated. *Aren't you thirsty? Hungry?*

The moment you were freed, you should have disappeared down the alley, searching for food or water. Hiding from the bigger, meaner beasties that populate this town. Some of which walk on two legs.

It's a cruel world out there. I'd have thought you'd have learned that lesson.

Chapter Forty

It wasn't long before the stagecoach relay station appeared in front of him. When Fix entered the customer's area, he noted the building's simplicity. The interior held several benches, a pair of tables, and the ticket agent's work area, chair and desk. There was a closed, closet-sized space in the far corner, most likely serving as the station master's office.

No attempt had been made to improve the room's surroundings or decorate its walls. Everything about the space spoke to practicality and an effort to maximize profit. When the day came that the stagecoach line started to lose money, the station's owner could quickly convert his holdings into some other enterprise.

Fix admired his foresight. The man had a vision for the future.

The ticket agent was a burly man with a thin line of beard defining his chin. Pushing his lunch aside, he asked querulously, "Is that yours?"

Following his gaze, Fix looked to see what had irritated the agent. When he finally glanced toward his boots, he saw the patchy-furred kitten tilt his head up at him. "I told you to skit."

In response, the cat cocked its head curiously. It appeared interested in joining the conversation, but only if Fix started making sense.

This time, the gunman noticed how thin the animal looked. When it took a breath, its ribs revealed themselves.

He told the agent, "You have any food? Maybe some water?"

"Not for a stray."

"You've got a glass of water in front of you." Digging into his front pocket, Fix found a bill. "Half a sandwich, too. Sell them to me."

The clerk did, taking the cash before pushing the remains of his meal forward. "You riding the next stage?"

"The one going to Green Valley."

"You can't bring a pet with you. The rules forbid it."

"Why would I have a pet?"

"Exactly," the agent agreed. "Especially not a cat. They're nothing but trouble."

Paying for his ticket, Fix carried his purchases to the nearest table. When he tipped the glass toward the kitten, it lapped at the fluid eagerly.

"I knew you were thirsty," Fix said.

The cat's small body rumbled at the sound of his voice.

"Hey," he called to the station agent. "What can I do with this thing?"

"The little pest?" The man shrugged. "Leave it in the alley. Somebody will take it. Or kill it."

"Kill it?" Fix felt a surge of anger. "How? Maybe bag it and leave it to starve?"

Sitting across the room, the agent scooted his chair backward, as if to distance himself from the newcomer. "I didn't mean anything by what was said."

"You ever do something like that?"

"No. No, I swear."

"Maybe I should put you in a bag."

"Mister…."

Fix turned away from him. Lifting the top piece of bread, he pulled the brown, overcooked meat from the center of the sandwich. The kitten watched him with interest as he tore the chunk of beef into shreds.

He placed the first, smallest sliver of meat on the floor. Despite its obvious hunger, the animal sniffed at the offering cautiously. Delicately, it brought the piece into its mouth and chewed on it.

"I knew you were hungry," Fix said with satisfaction.

From somewhere in the distance, a bugle sounded. The stagecoach had entered the outskirts of the Ridge.

The sound stirred new activity and the station's front door squeaked as new customers came inside. Putting a single finger on the kitten's head, Fix stroked it. A second piece of meat in its mouth, the tiny mouser rumbled at him.

"You're Quincy Fix," a woman's voice said.

Looking up, Fix saw the woman who owned Arnold's Dry Goods. Her face was flushed, as if she'd been running. Her oversized cotton dress was dotted with yellow flowers that didn't disguise the beefy frame hidden inside of it. There were sweat stains at her armpits.

Fix would have preferred to ignore her, but he doubted she'd allow it.

She told him, "I want to hire you."

"Not interested."

"Yes, you are. It's how you make your living." She waved a dime novel at him.

He knew the title without even looking: *Quincy Fix, Gun for Hire*. That book was the bane of his existence. Some sweet day, he'd locate its author and go over the tome, line by line and page by page. "What's your name?"

"Felicia Arnold."

"Go home, Felicia Arnold. I don't deal with women."

"You'll deal with me."

Damned, she was irritating. "The story you're holding was made up. Fictional. I don't kill people."

"Never?" she asked, sounding more curious than confrontational.

"Not anymore."

"Good."

She waited expectedly. When he looked down, he saw the feline waiting expectedly, too. Preferring the cat's company, he offered it another sliver of meat.

Her tone softening, Felicia said, "The book said you find people. It says you're the best at it. Was that part fictional, too?"

"A woman like you should have better things to do than read such trash."

"I need someone found, Mr. Fix."

"Not my concern."

"I'll pay double your usual fee."

Fix sighed. "How would you know my usual fee?"

"Whatever it is, I'll pay what you ask, twice over. But I have to come with you."

"Absolutely not." Dropping the rest of the meat, he left it on the ground. The cat ignored the food, following after him as he returned to the station's front window.

Felicia Arnold followed after him, too.

Through the dirty glass, the world appeared unchanged. Even though he couldn't see the stagecoach, he knew it would be arriving soon. In the distance, he heard the drumming of horses' hooves.

"Please, Mr. Fix. Help me find my Ethem. Help me bring him home."

"Why do you want him found?"

"He's my husband. Has been for over eleven years."

"Until he ran off and left you." She might not have liked his assumption, but she didn't object to it. Fix asked, "Where do you think he is?"

"Out Colorado way."

"Spent a few months there, a couple of times."

Fell in love in San Luis de la Culebra, Fix thought. *Fell in hate.*

Been falling ever since.

"I've got something else I have to do," he continued, half-wondering why he felt the need to lie to her. "I can't help you."

He heard a strangled noise. He considered Felicia's solid, strong face and realized she'd choked back a sob. Trying to stifle the noise, she'd failed.

She didn't look like a woman who cried, not without reason. Nodding, she brushed past him on her way to the station's door.

When he touched her arm, the unexpected contact brought her up short. "I can't bring the cat on the stage with me. Would you take it?"

Sadness filled her eyes. "I don't need a pet. I need my man."

"As a favor to me. It needs a home."

The kitten remained beside Fix's boot, leaning into his foot as if his presence comforted it. Felicia reached out to the animal.

It purred at her touch.

It didn't move toward her, however. It remained with Fix.

"What happens if I don't take it?"

"It dies."

"You're certain?" she asked.

"I have reason to believe."

"What's its name?"

"Trouble."

Felicia gave a half-laugh. "Story of my life, searching for Ethem and only finding Trouble. All right, yes. I'll take it."

At that moment, horses trotted past, kicking up dirt as the stagecoach rolled to a stop. Curious faces turned toward the building as the station master emerged from his tiny room. He hurried out of the entrance to greet the new arrivals.

Fix looked down at the kitten. He considered the woman.

"You know how to ride?" he asked. "On a horse, not in a buggy?"

"I do."

"That could be all right, then." Knowing it was a mistake, he added, "I'll want half the cash up front. Maybe I could spend a few weeks, head up to Colorado with you."

Filled with unexpected happiness, her face transformed. Lit by joy, she seemed a different woman.

For the first time, Fix realized why a man might have fallen for her.

"You're serious," Felicia said uncertainly.

"I must be." Lifting the kitten, he cradled it in the crook of his arm. "In the book you carry, the author says I never kid. Page Seventeen: 'Quincy rarely smiles and he never laughs. He's cold, merciless, and lacks all sense of humor'."

"You said the story was made up."

"They got some parts right."

He held the door open and Felicia passed in front of him. Together, they walked into the sunlight.

Felicia said, "You didn't have the cat when you arrived to town."

"The cat's new," Fix told her. "You ready to go? Let's find Ethem."

www.ingramcontent.com/pod-product-compliance
Lightning Source LLC
Chambersburg PA
CBHW051416170626
46809CB00006B/2191

About the Author

A collector of vintage Barbies and younger boyfriends, Anne Glynn currently resides in the American Southwest.

The author's website is at www.AnneGlynn.com